JoJo's SWEET ADVENTURES

THE GREAT CANDY CAPER

JoJo's SWEET ADVENTURES
THE GREAT CANDY CAPER

BY JOJO SIWA
Illustrations by Claudia Giuliani

nickelodeon
Amulet Books
New York

PUBLISHER'S NOTE: This is a work of fiction. Names, characters, places, and incidents are either the product of the author's imagination or used fictitiously, and any resemblance to actual persons, living or dead, business establishments, events, or locales is entirely coincidental.

Library of Congress Control Number 2021930958
Hardcover ISBN 978-1-4197-5338-1
Paperback ISBN 978-1-4197-5337-4

Book design by The Story Division with consultation with Brenda E. Angelilli

Printed and bound in U.S.A.
10 9 8 7 6 5 4 3 2 1

ABRAMS The Art of Books
195 Broadway, New York, NY 10007
abramsbooks.com

CHAPTER ONE

CHOCOLATE MALFUNCTION!

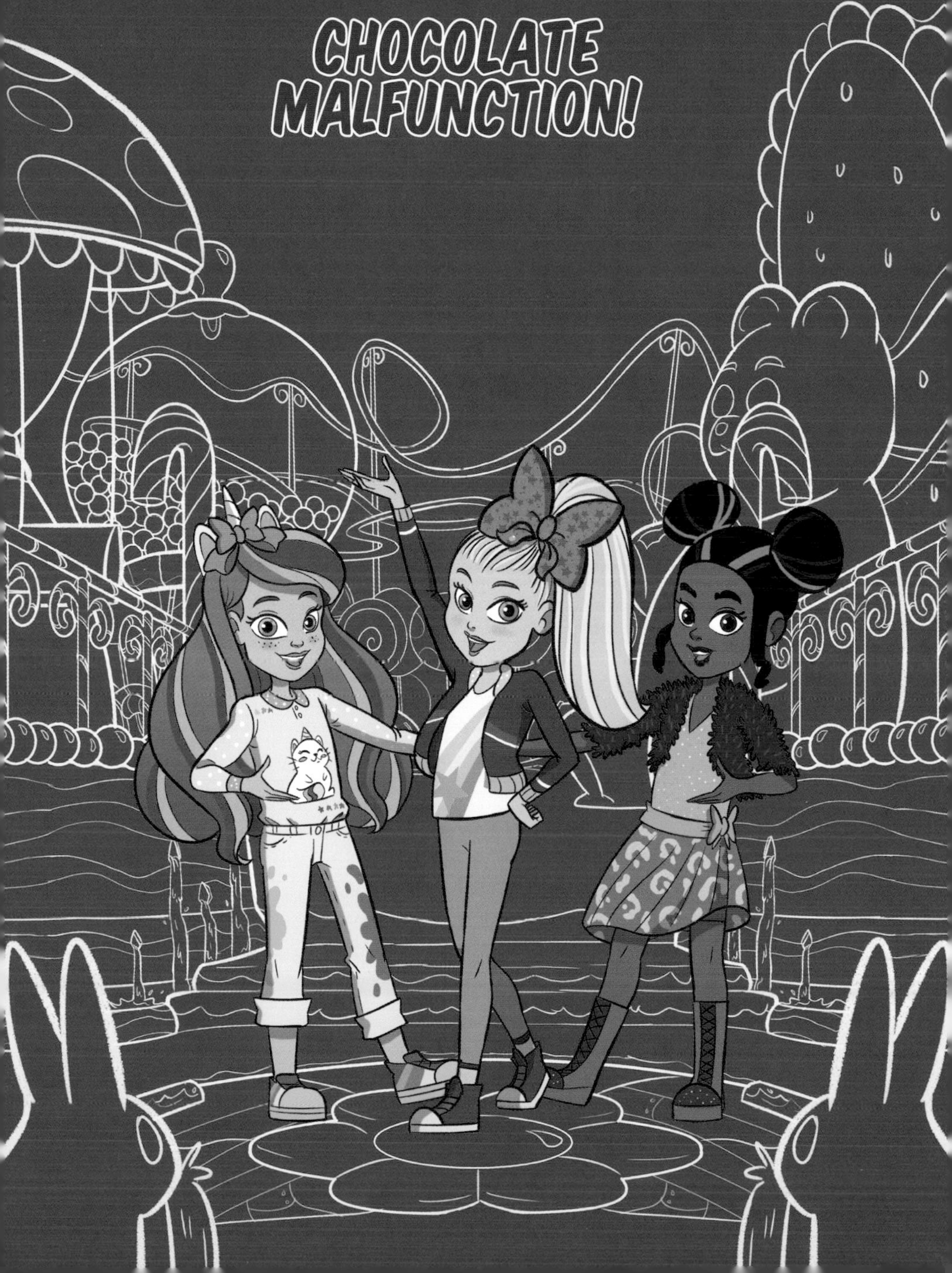

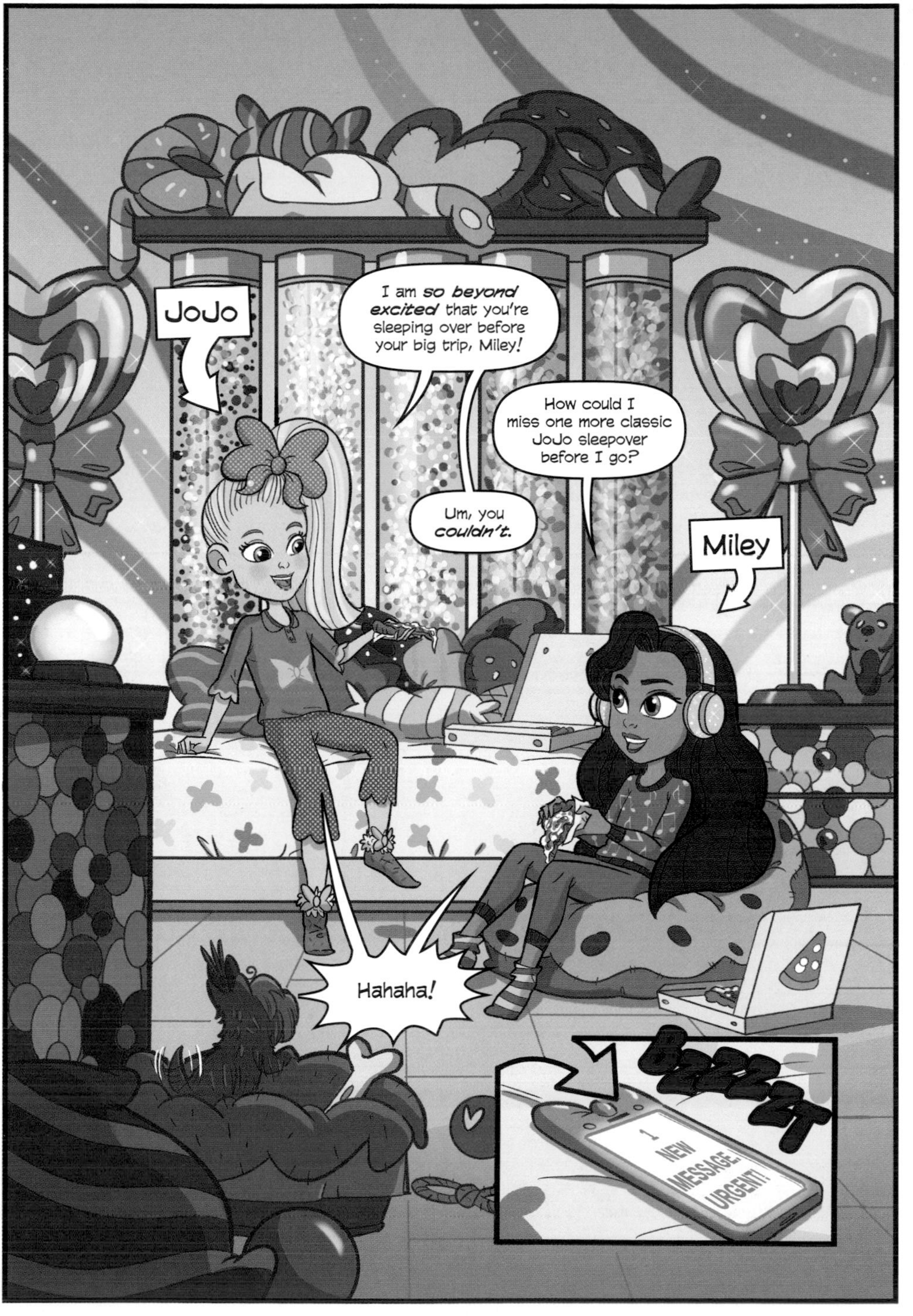
JoJo
I am *so beyond excited* that you're sleeping over before your big trip, Miley!
How could I miss one more classic JoJo sleepover before I go?
Um, you *couldn't.*
Miley
Hahaha!
BZZZZT
1 NEW MESSAGE: URGENT!

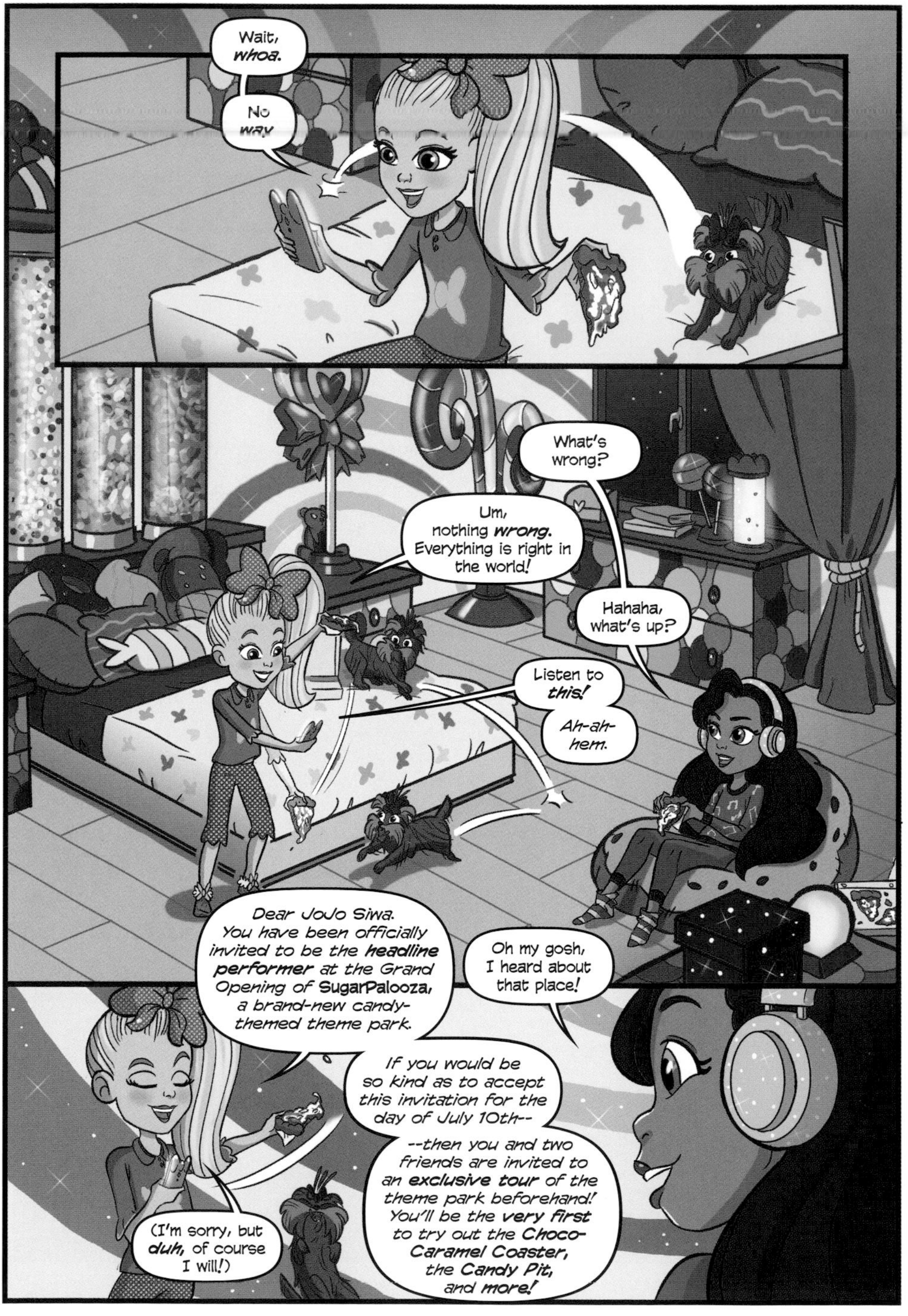
Wait, *whoa.*
No *way.*
What's wrong?
Um, nothing *wrong.* Everything is right in the world!
Hahaha, what's up?
Listen to *this!*
Ah-ah-hem.
*Dear JoJo Siwa. You have been officially invited to be the **headline performer** at the Grand Opening of* **SugarPalooza,** *a brand-new candy-themed theme park.*
Oh my gosh, I heard about that place!
If you would be so kind as to accept this invitation for the day of July 10th--
*--then you and two friends are invited to an **exclusive tour** of the theme park beforehand! You'll be the **very first** to try out the **Choco-Caramel Coaster,** the **Candy Pit,** and **more!***
(I'm sorry, but ***duh,*** of course I will!)

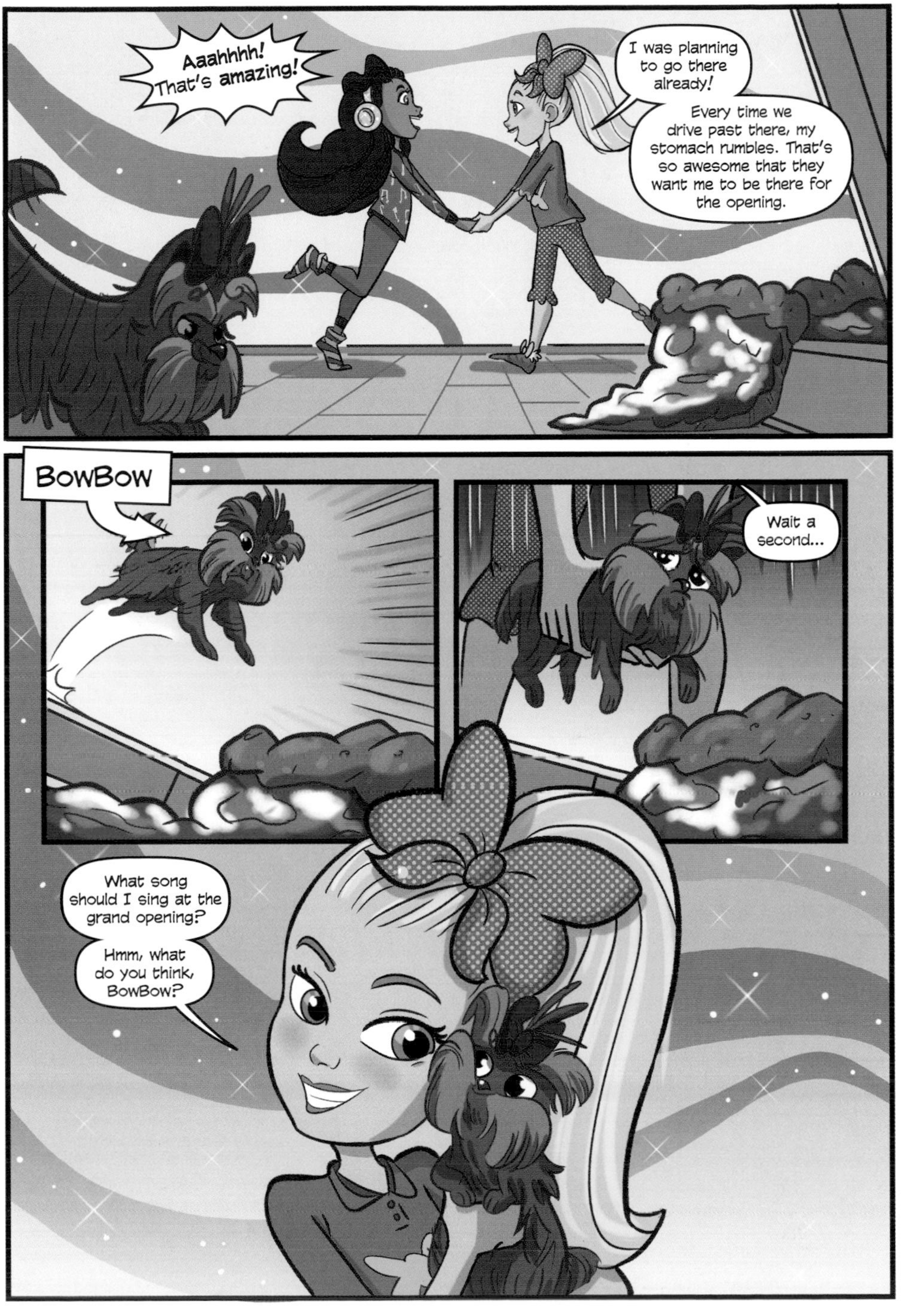
Aaahhhh! That's amazing!
I was planning to go there already!
Every time we drive past there, my stomach rumbles. That's so awesome that they want me to be there for the opening.
BowBow
Wait a second...
What song should I sing at the grand opening?
Hmm, what do you think, BowBow?

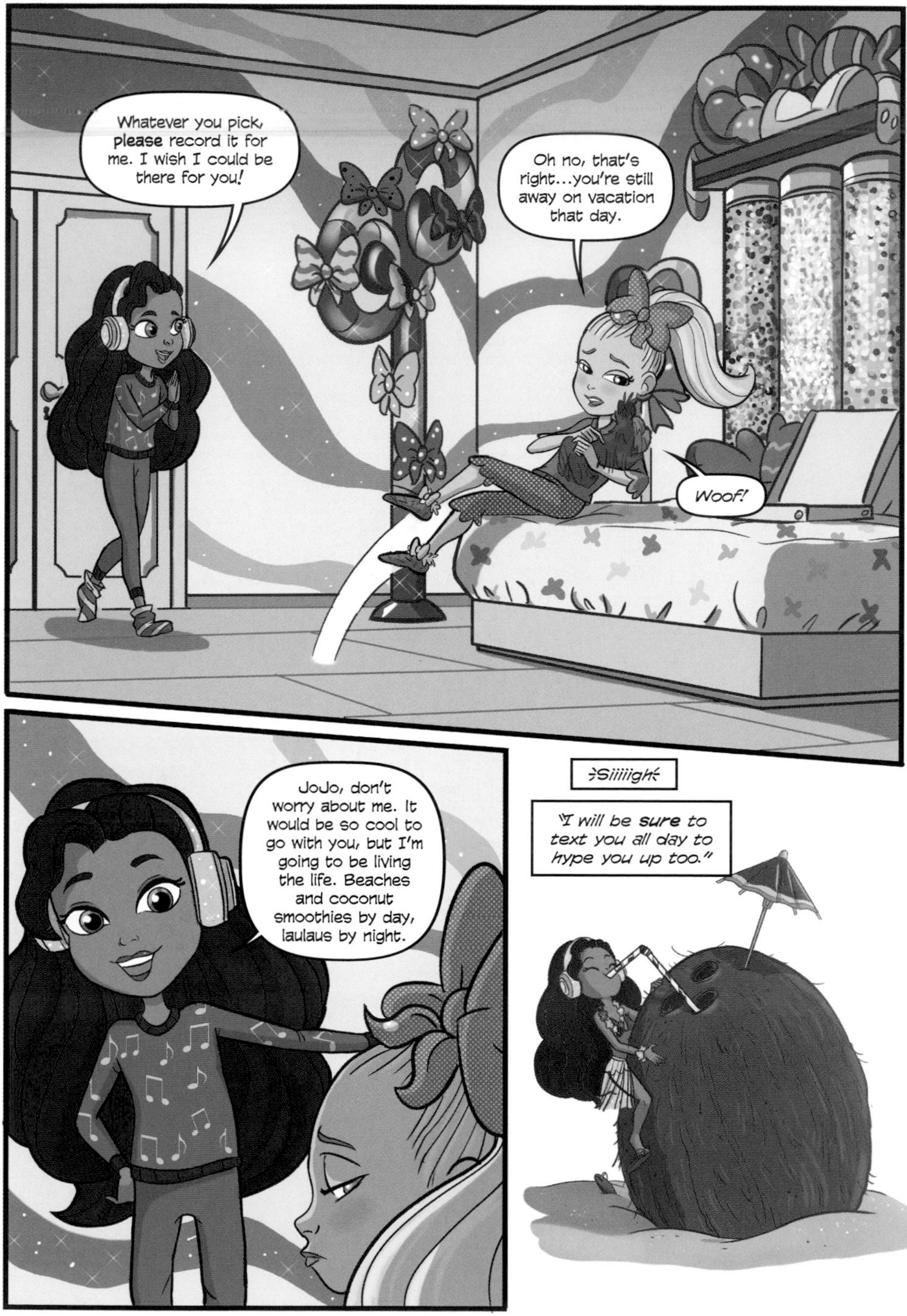
Whatever you pick, **please** record it for me. I wish I could be there for you!
Oh no, that's right...you're still away on vacation that day.
Woof!
JoJo, don't worry about me. It would be so cool to go with you, but I'm going to be living the life. Beaches and coconut smoothies by day, laulaus by night.
Siiiiigh
"I will be **sure** to text you all day to hype you up too."

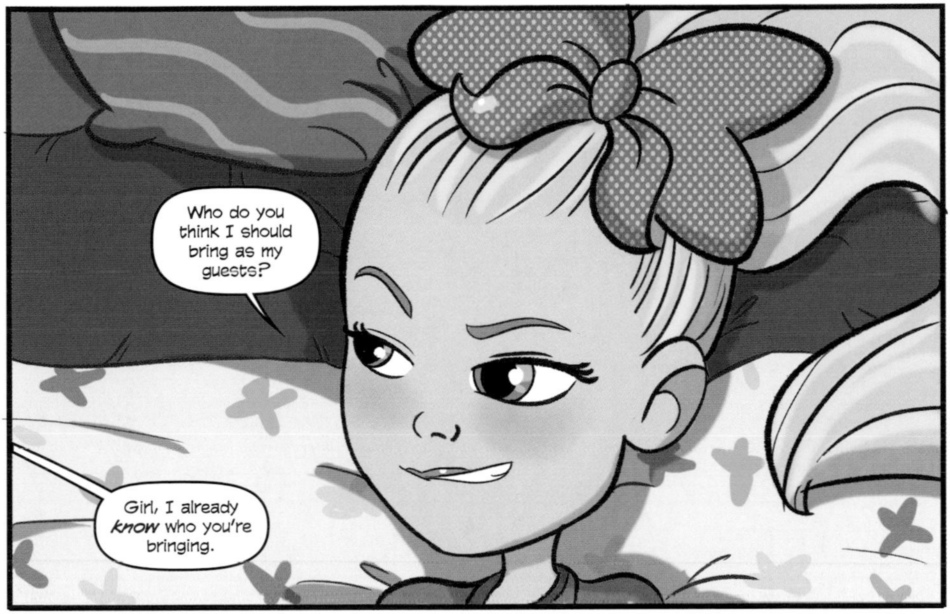
Who do you think I should bring as my guests?
Girl, I already ***know*** who you're bringing.

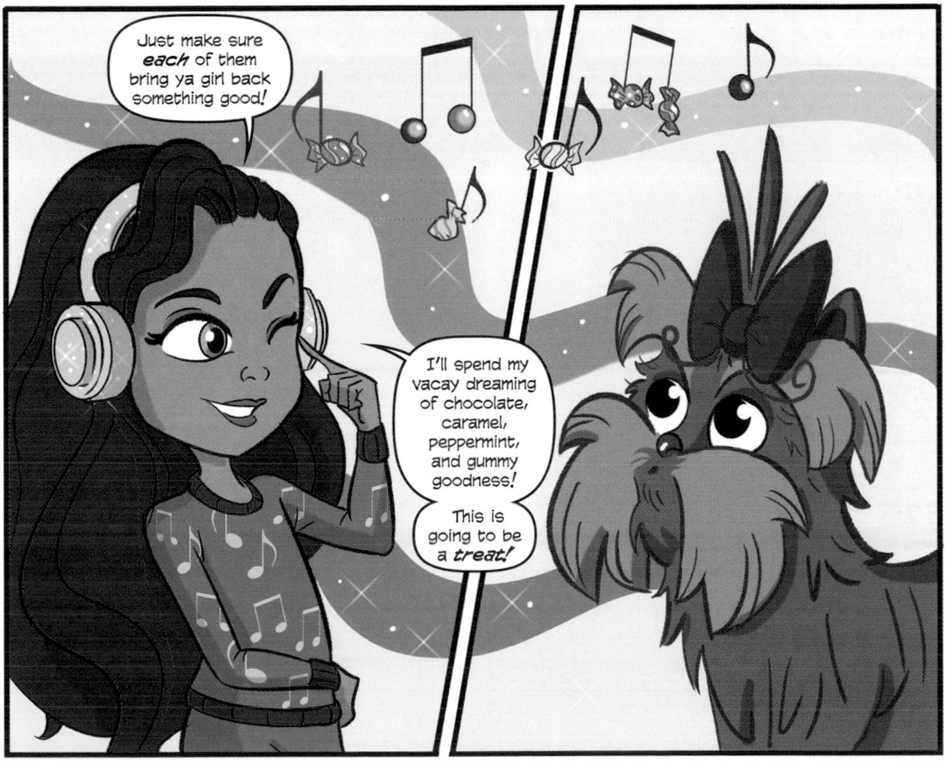
Just make sure ***each*** of them bring ya girl back something good!
I'll spend my vacay dreaming of chocolate, caramel, peppermint, and gummy goodness!
This is going to be a ***treat!***

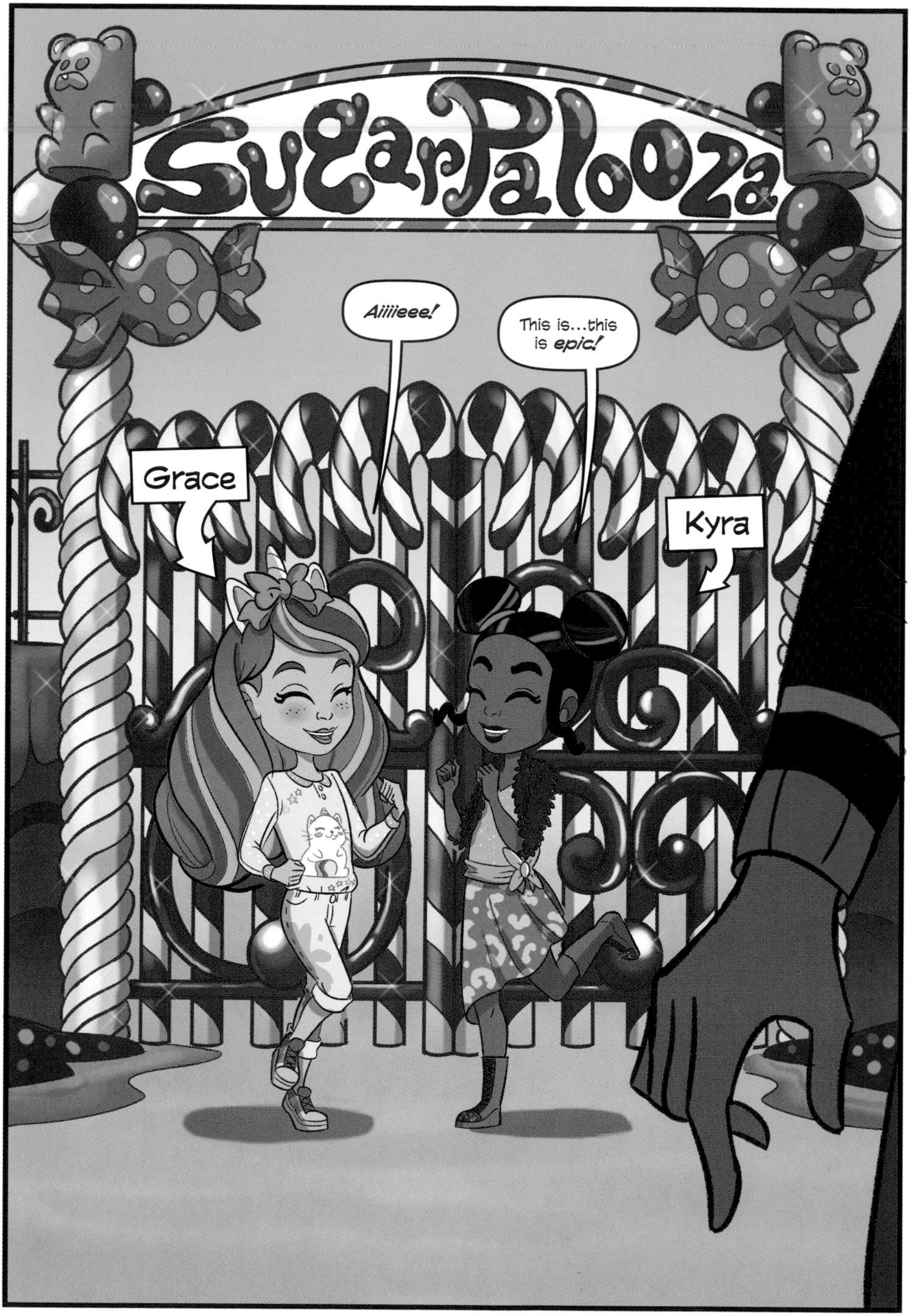
SugarPalooza
Aiiiieee!
This is...this is *epic!*
Grace
Kyra

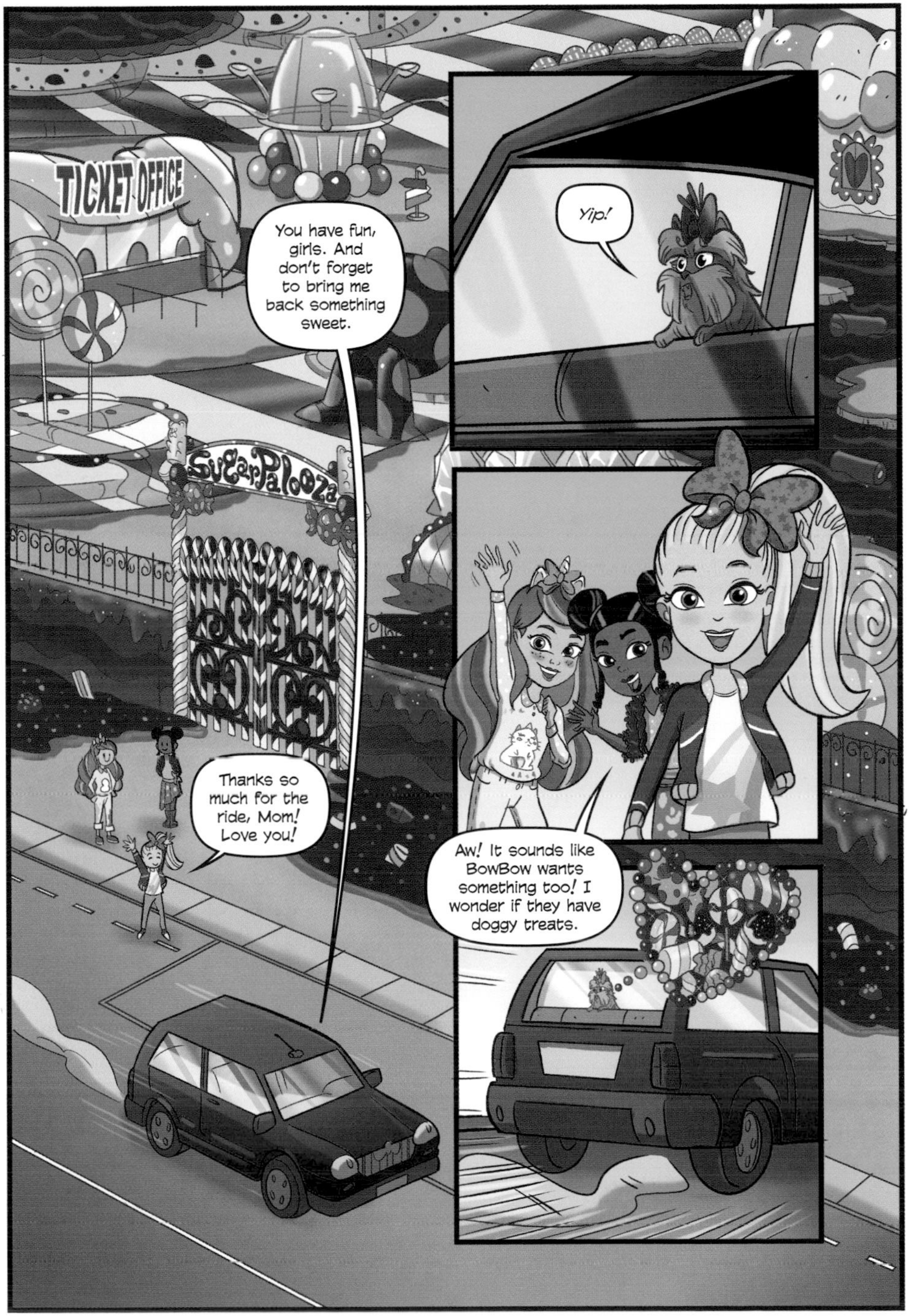
TICKET OFFICE
SugarPalooza
You have fun, girls. And don't forget to bring me back something sweet.
Thanks so much for the ride, Mom! Love you!
Yip!
Aw! It sounds like BowBow wants something too! I wonder if they have doggy treats.

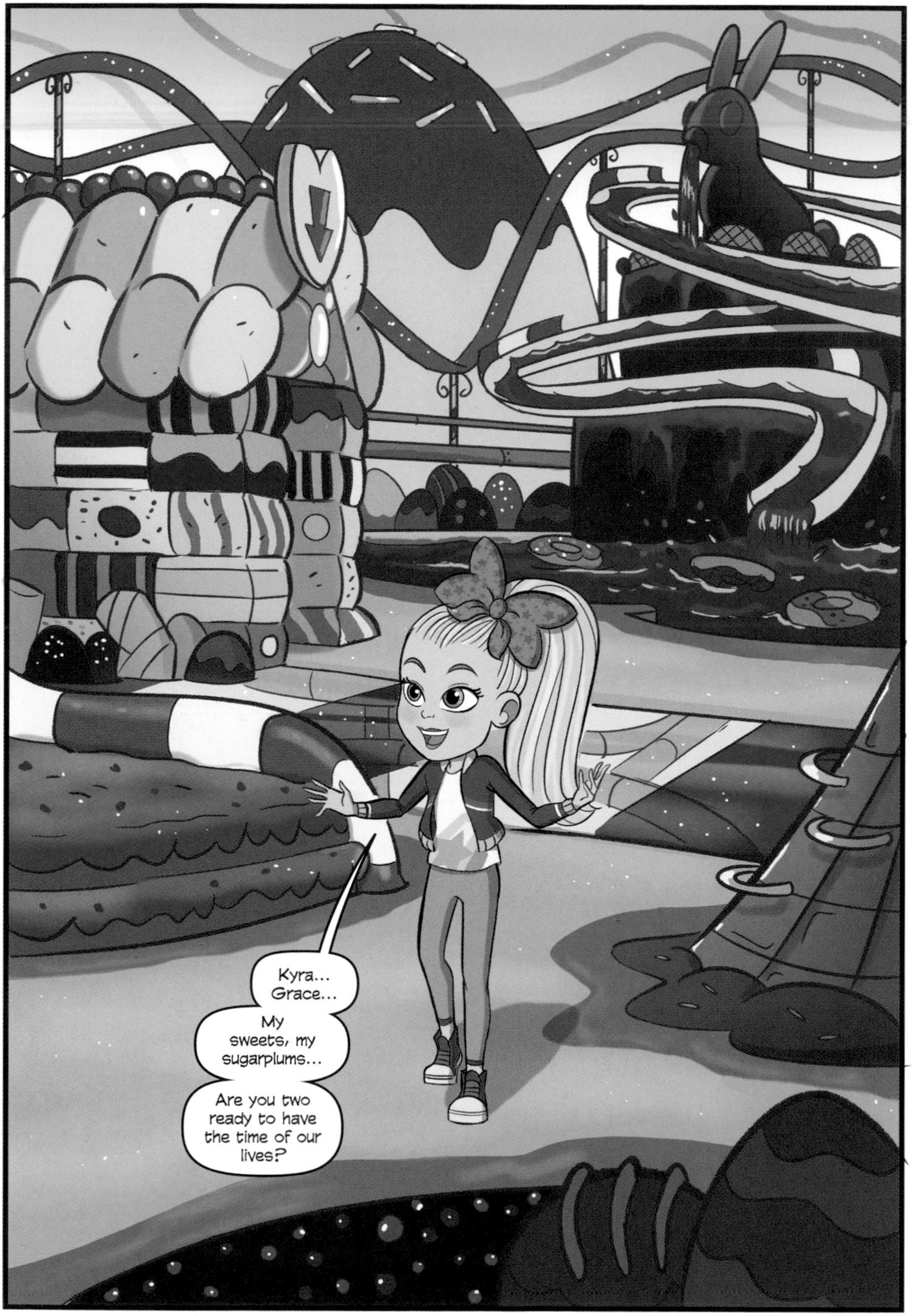
Kyra... Grace...
My sweets, my sugarplums...
Are you two ready to have the time of our lives?

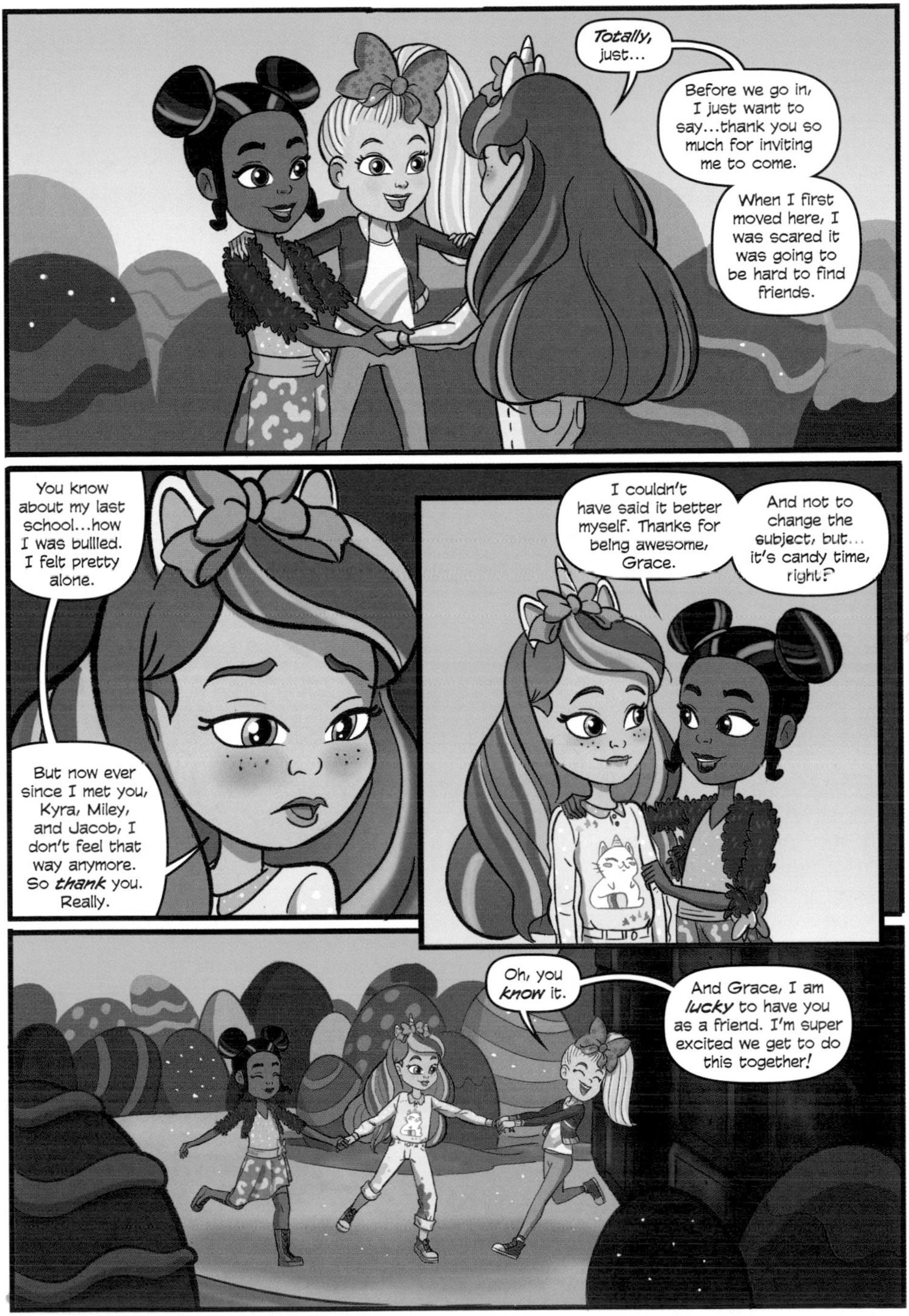
Totally, just...
Before we go in, I just want to say...thank you so much for inviting me to come.
When I first moved here, I was scared it was going to be hard to find friends.
You know about my last school...how I was bullied. I felt pretty alone.
But now ever since I met you, Kyra, Miley, and Jacob, I don't feel that way anymore. So ***thank*** you. Really.
I couldn't have said it better myself. Thanks for being awesome, Grace.
And not to change the subject, but... it's candy time, right?
Oh, you ***know*** it.
And Grace, I am ***lucky*** to have you as a friend. I'm super excited we get to do this together!

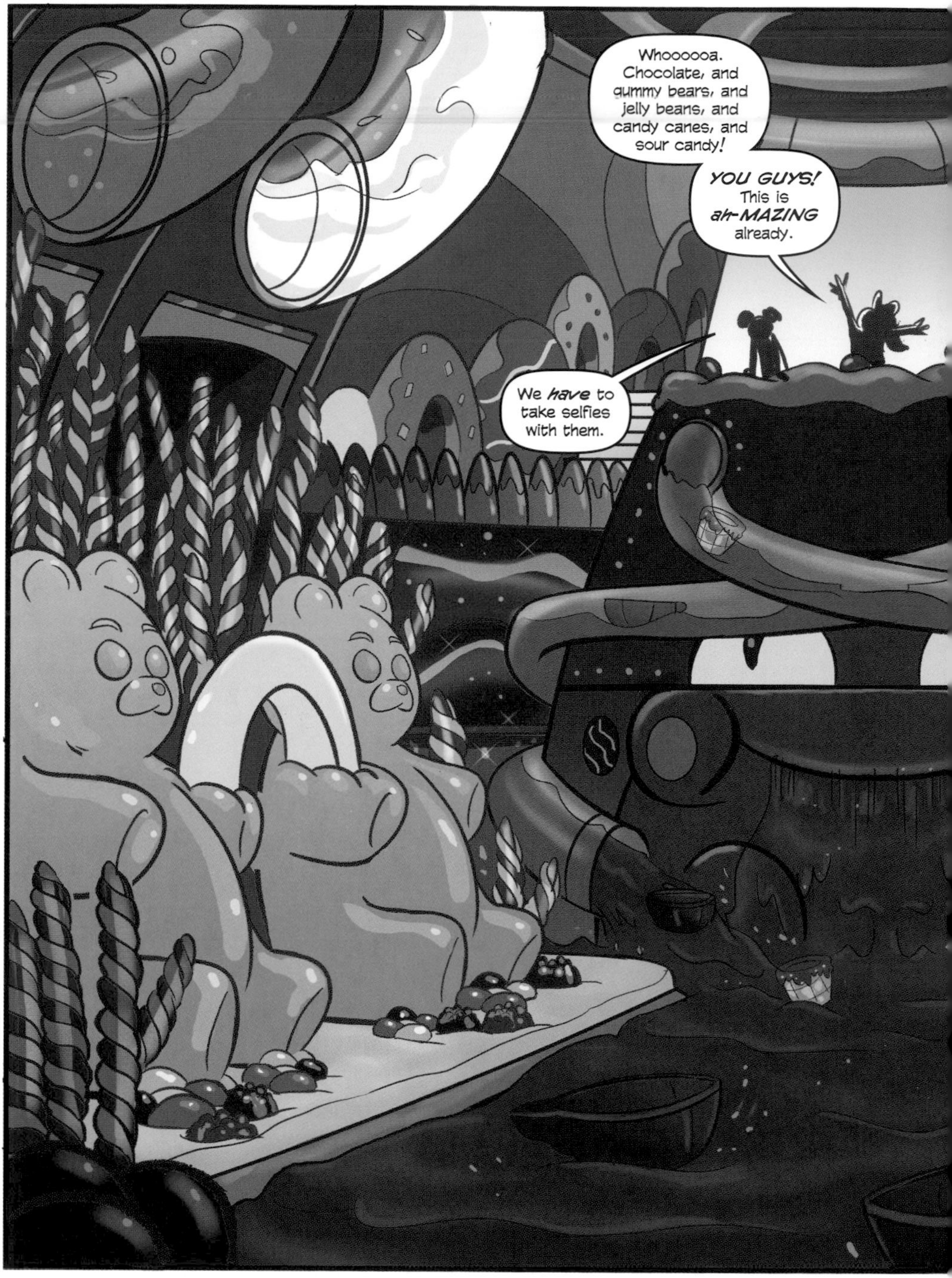
Whoooooa. Chocolate, and gummy bears, and jelly beans, and candy canes, and sour candy!
YOU GUYS! This is ah-MAZING already.
We *have* to take selfies with them.

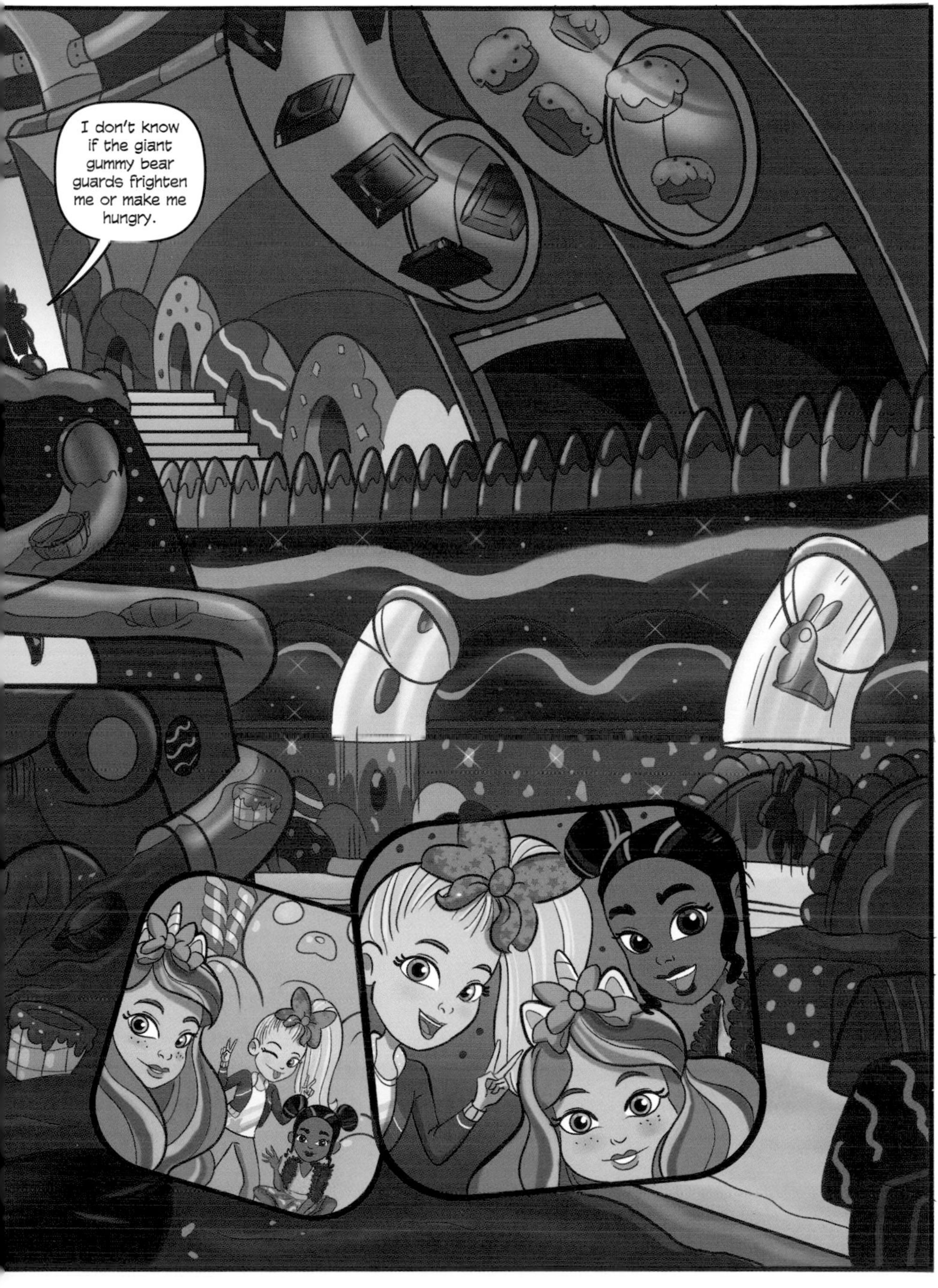
I don't know if the giant gummy bear guards frighten me or make me hungry.

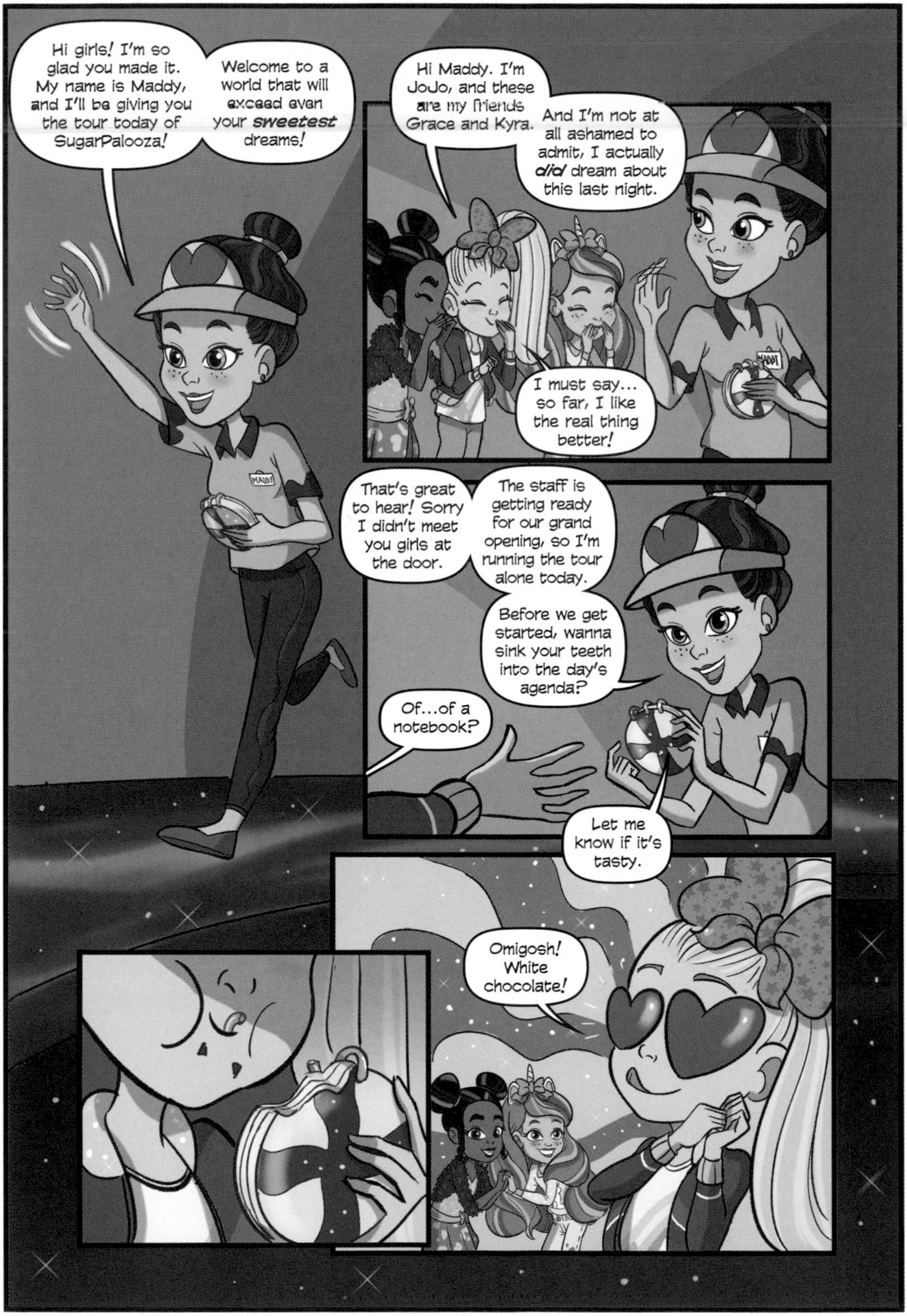

Hi girls! I'm so glad you made it. My name is Maddy, and I'll be giving you the tour today of SugarPalooza!
Welcome to a world that will exceed even your sweetest dreams!
Hi Maddy. I'm JoJo, and these are my friends Grace and Kyra.
And I'm not at all ashamed to admit, I actually did dream about this last night.
I must say... so far, I like the real thing better!
That's great to hear! Sorry I didn't meet you girls at the door.
The staff is getting ready for our grand opening, so I'm running the tour alone today.
Before we get started, wanna sink your teeth into the day's agenda?
Of...of a notebook?
Let me know if it's tasty.
Omigosh! White chocolate!

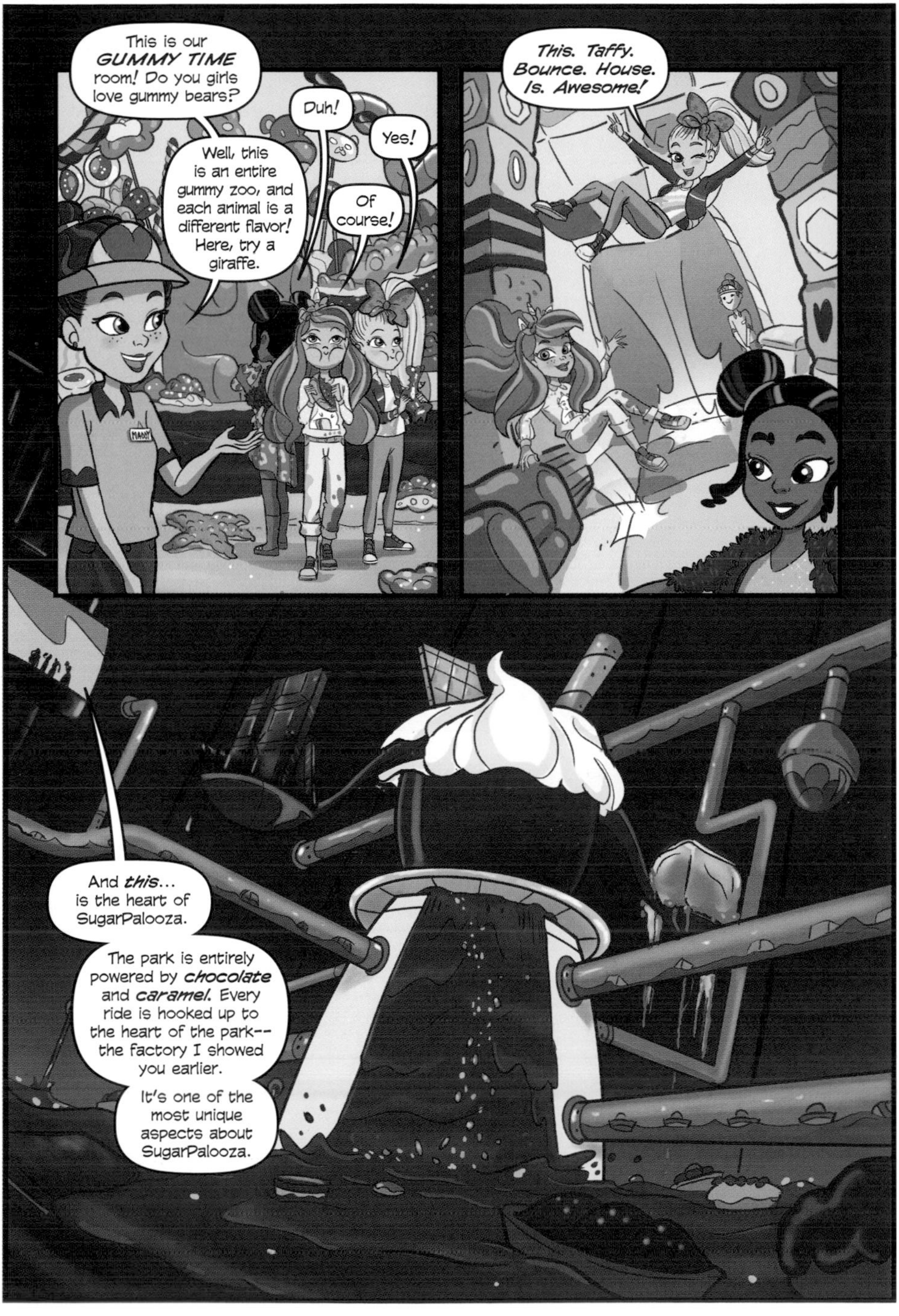

This is our **GUMMY TIME** room! Do you girls love gummy bears?
Duh!
Yes!
Well, this is an entire gummy zoo, and each animal is a different flavor! Here, try a giraffe.
Of course!
MANDY
This. Taffy. Bounce. House. Is. Awesome!
And ***this***... is the heart of SugarPalooza.
The park is entirely powered by ***chocolate*** and ***caramel.*** Every ride is hooked up to the heart of the park-- the factory I showed you earlier.
It's one of the most unique aspects about SugarPalooza.

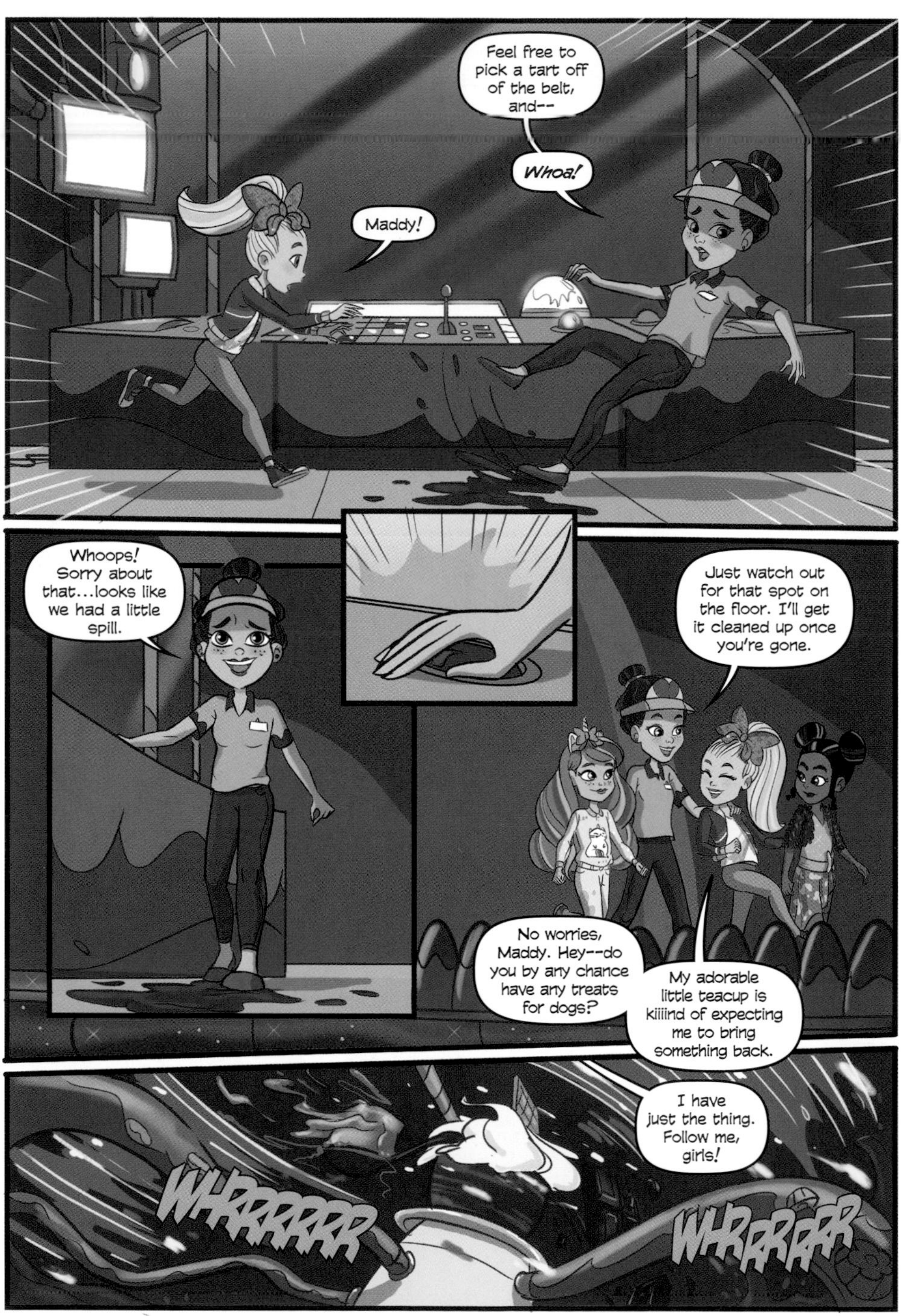

Feel free to pick a tart off of the belt, and--
Whoa!
Maddy!
Whoops! Sorry about that...looks like we had a little spill.
Just watch out for that spot on the floor. I'll get it cleaned up once you're gone.
No worries, Maddy. Hey--do you by any chance have any treats for dogs?
My adorable little teacup is kiiiind of expecting me to bring something back.
I have just the thing. Follow me, girls!
WHRRRRRRR
WHRRRRRR

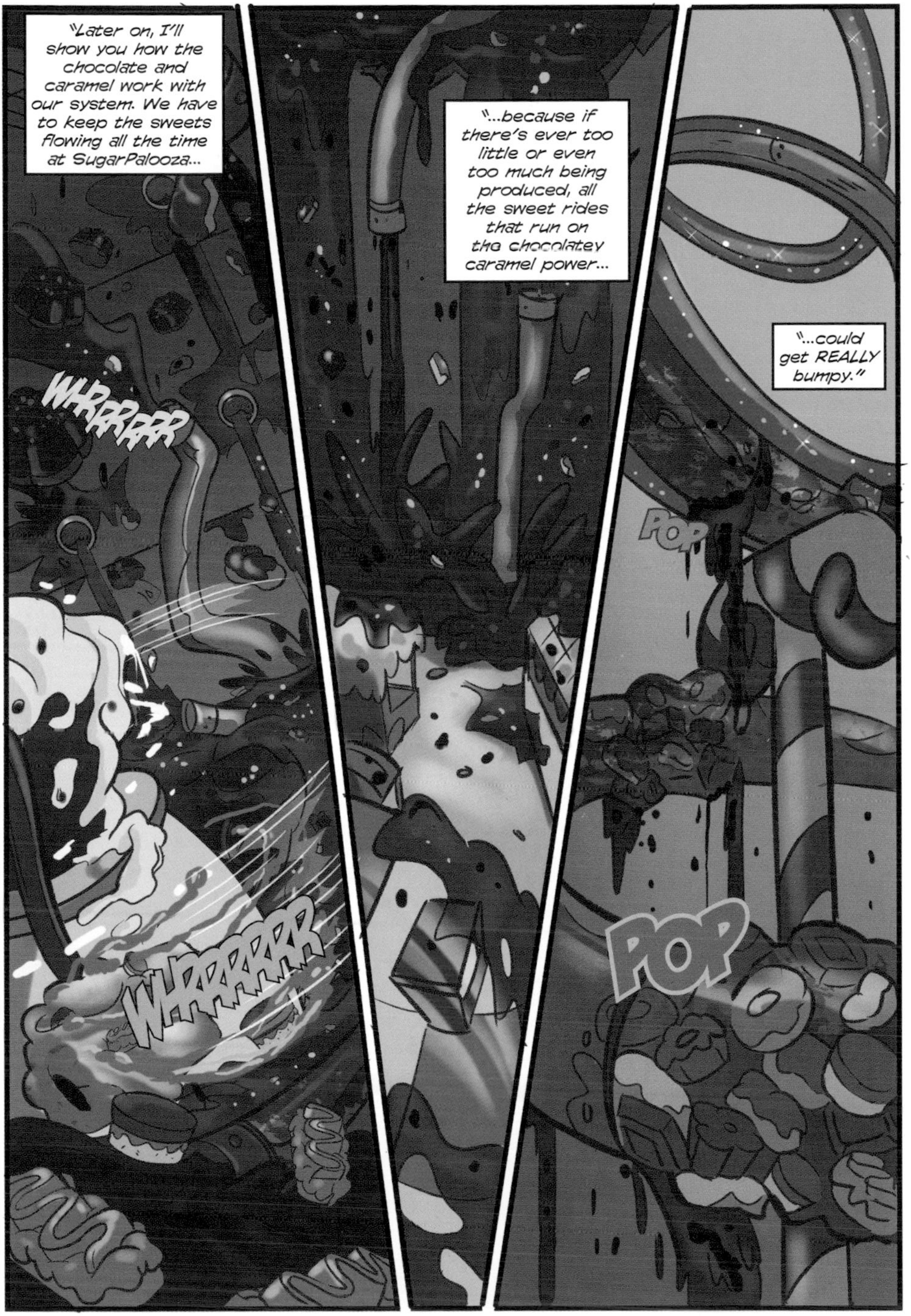
"Later on, I'll show you how the chocolate and caramel work with our system. We have to keep the sweets flowing all the time at SugarPalooza...
WHRRRRRR
WHRRRRRR
"...because if there's ever too little or even too much being produced, all the sweet rides that run on the chocolatey caramel power...
"...could get REALLY bumpy."
POP
POP

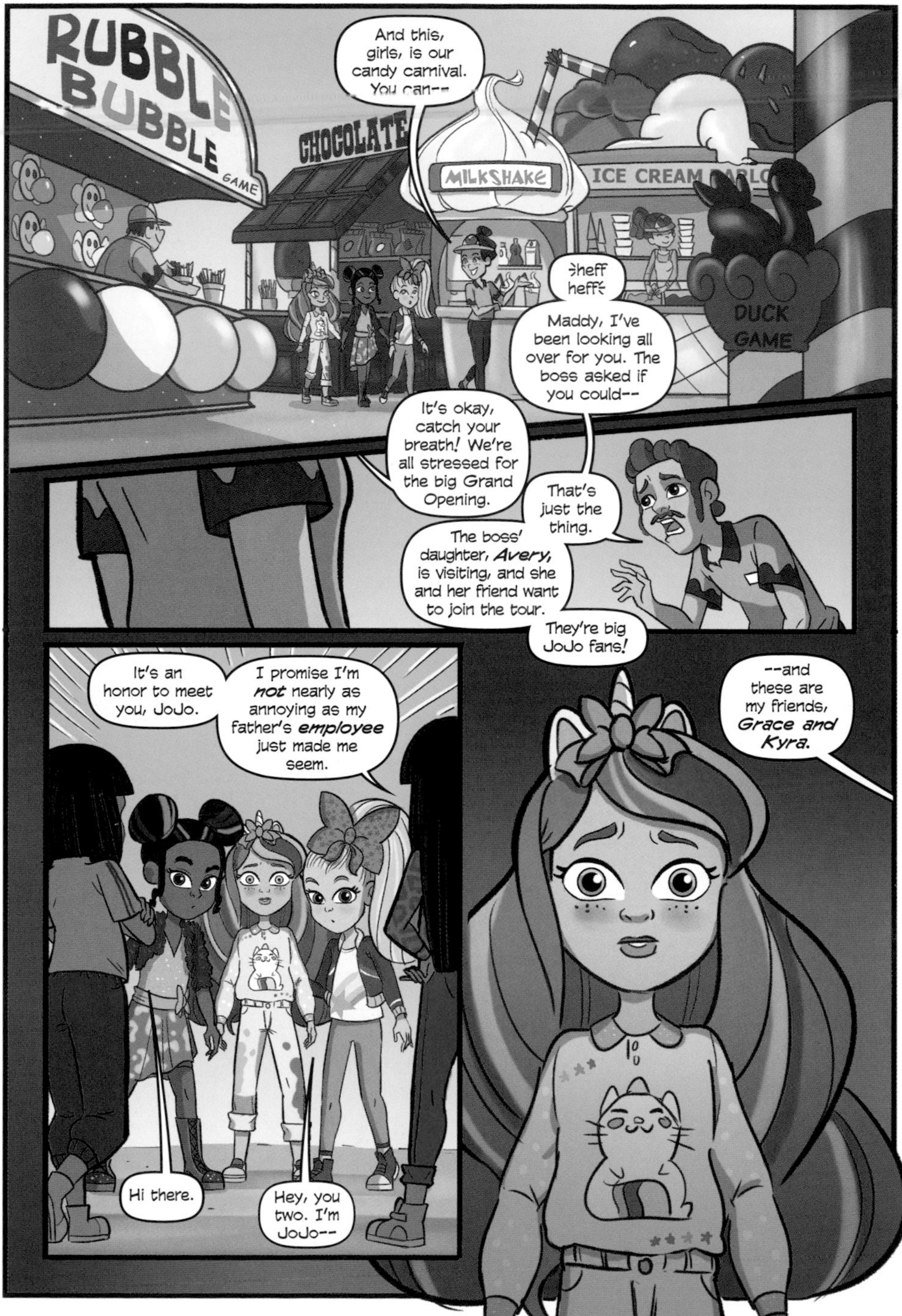
RUBBLE BUBBLE GAME
CHOCOLATE
MILKSHAKE
ICE CREAM PARLO
DUCK GAME
And this, girls, is our candy carnival. You can--
≈heff heff≈
Maddy, I've been looking all over for you. The boss asked if you could--
It's okay, catch your breath! We're all stressed for the big Grand Opening.
That's just the thing.
The boss' daughter, *Avery,* is visiting, and she and her friend want to join the tour.
They're big JoJo fans!
It's an honor to meet you, JoJo.
I promise I'm *not* nearly as annoying as my father's *employee* just made me seem.
Hi there.
Hey, you two. I'm JoJo--
--and these are my friends, *Grace and Kyra.*

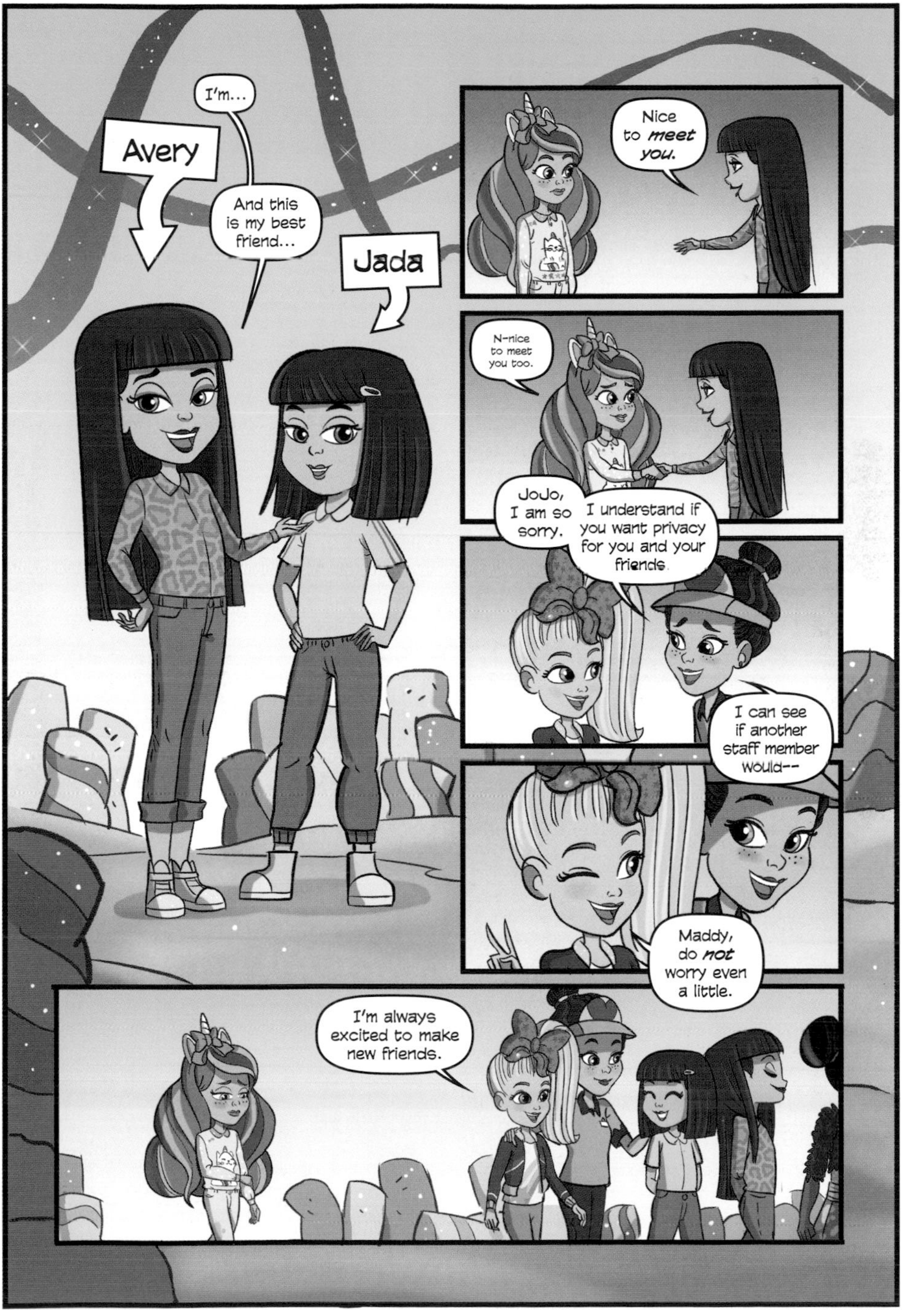

Avery
I'm...
And this is my best friend...
Jada
Nice to *meet you.*
N-nice to meet you too.
JoJo, I am so sorry.
I understand if you want privacy for you and your friends.
I can see if another staff member would--
Maddy, do *not* worry even a little.
I'm always excited to make new friends.

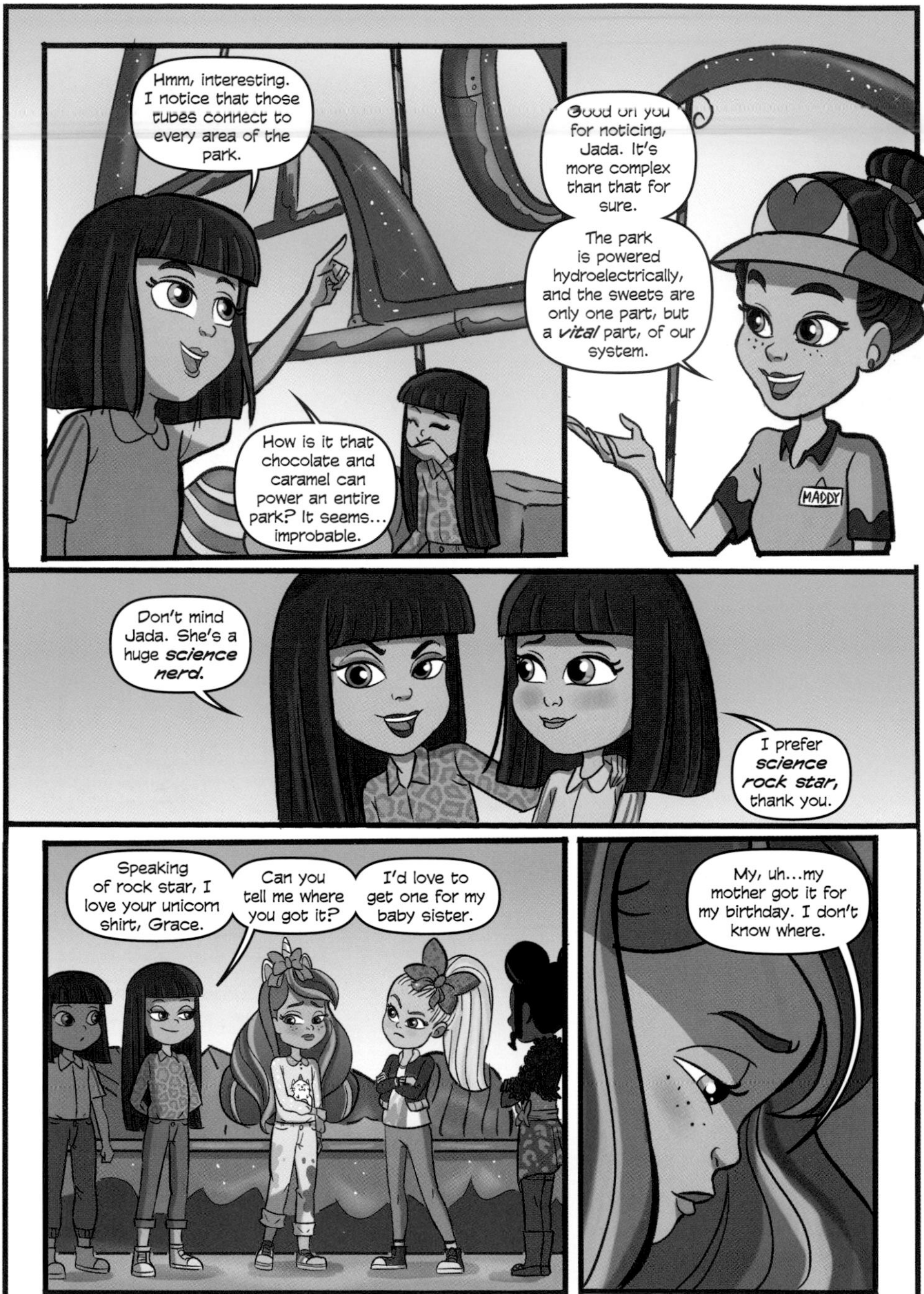
Hmm, interesting. I notice that those tubes connect to every area of the park.
How is it that chocolate and caramel can power an entire park? It seems... improbable.
Good on you for noticing, Jada. It's more complex than that for sure.
The park is powered hydroelectrically, and the sweets are only one part, but a *vital* part, of our system.
MADDY
Don't mind Jada. She's a huge ***science nerd.***
I prefer ***science rock star,*** thank you.
Speaking of rock star, I love your unicorn shirt, Grace.
Can you tell me where you got it?
I'd love to get one for my baby sister.
My, uh...my mother got it for my birthday. I don't know where.

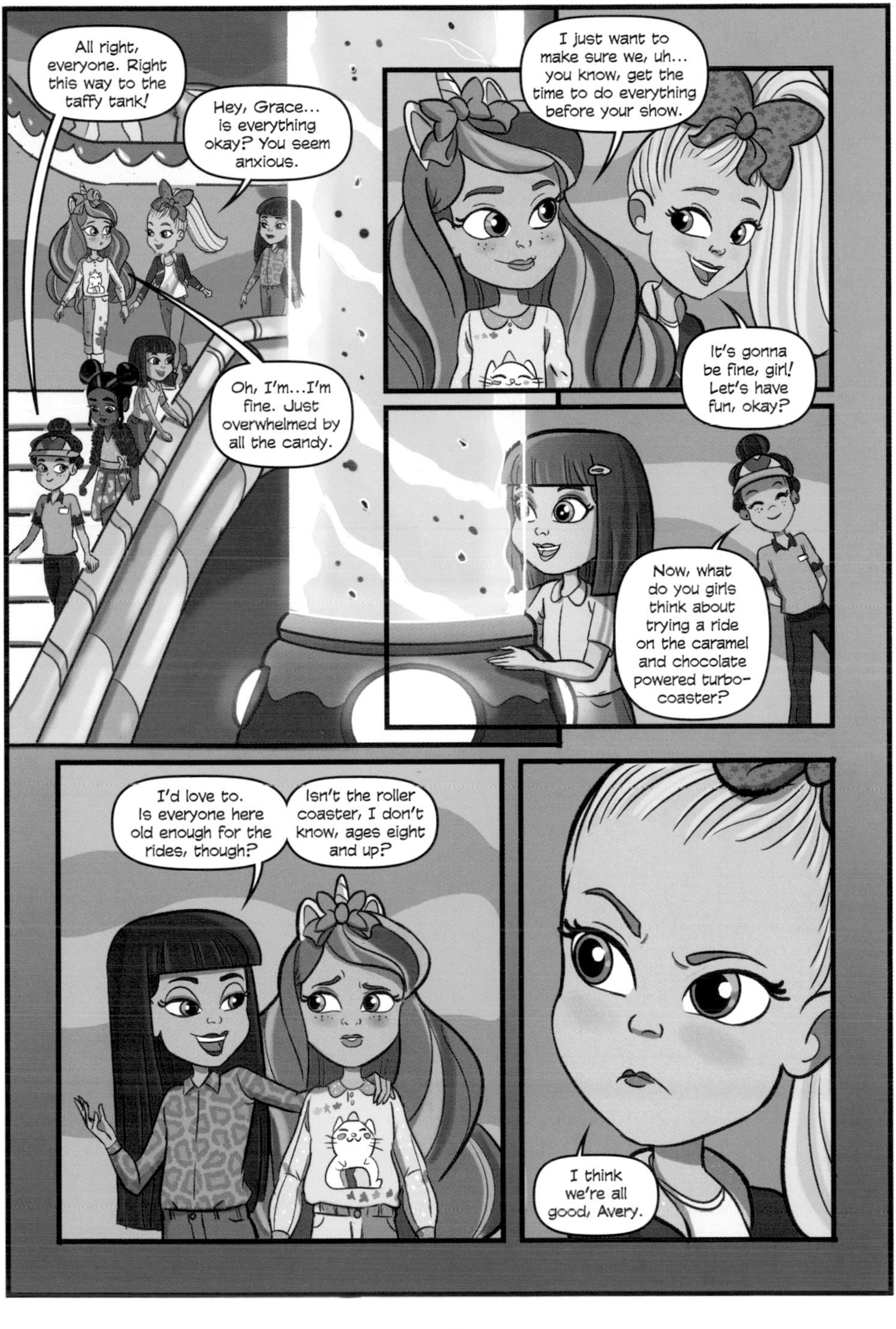
All right, everyone. Right this way to the taffy tank!
Hey, Grace... is everything okay? You seem anxious.
Oh, I'm...I'm fine. Just overwhelmed by all the candy.
I just want to make sure we, uh... you know, get the time to do everything before your show.
It's gonna be fine, girl! Let's have fun, okay?
Now, what do you girls think about trying a ride on the caramel and chocolate powered turbo-coaster?
I'd love to. Is everyone here old enough for the rides, though?
Isn't the roller coaster, I don't know, ages eight and up?
I think we're all good, Avery.

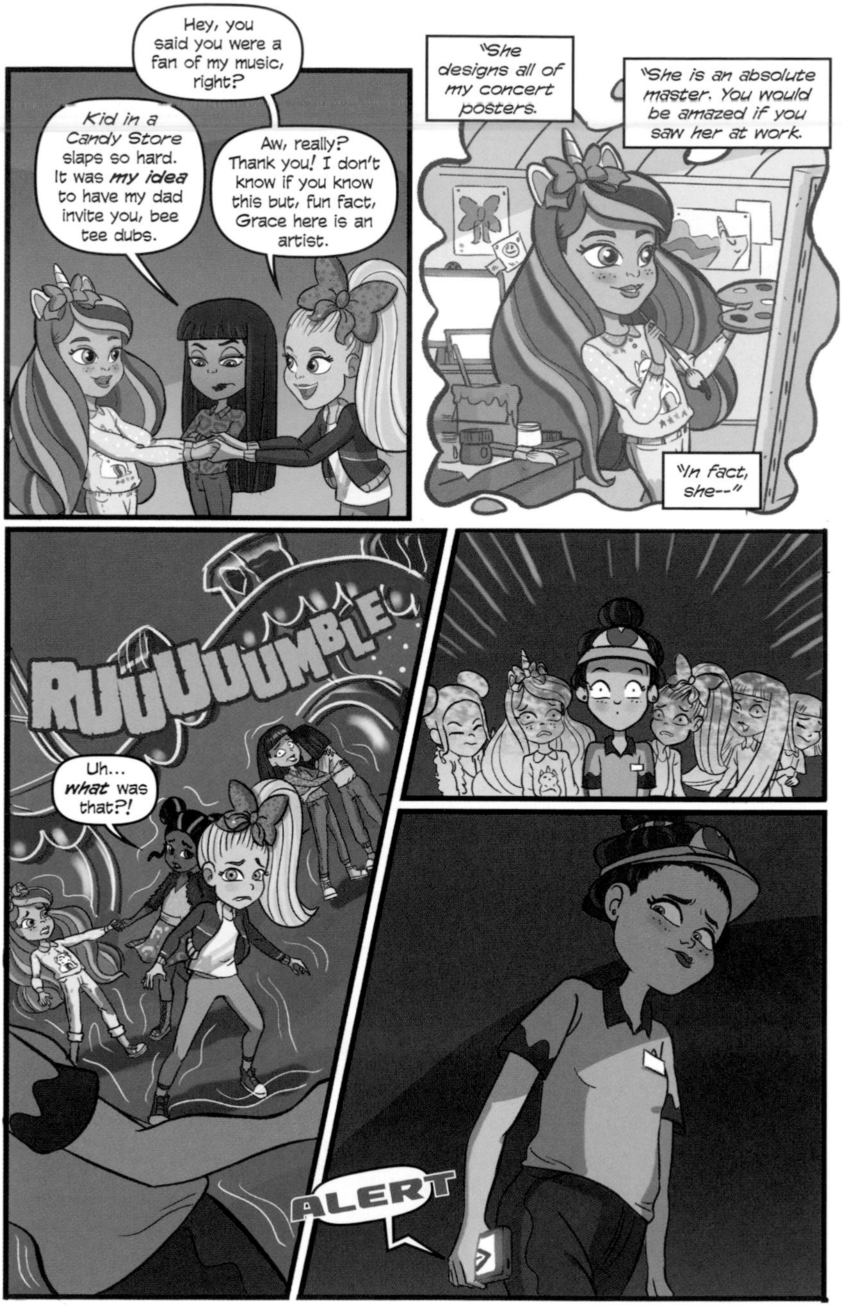

Hey, you said you were a fan of my music, right?
Kid in a Candy Store slaps so hard. It was ***my idea*** to have my dad invite you, bee tee dubs.
Aw, really? Thank you! I don't know if you know this but, fun fact, Grace here is an artist.
"She designs all of my concert posters.
"She is an absolute master. You would be amazed if you saw her at work.
"In fact, she--"
RUUUUUMBLE
Uh... ***what*** was that?!
ALERT

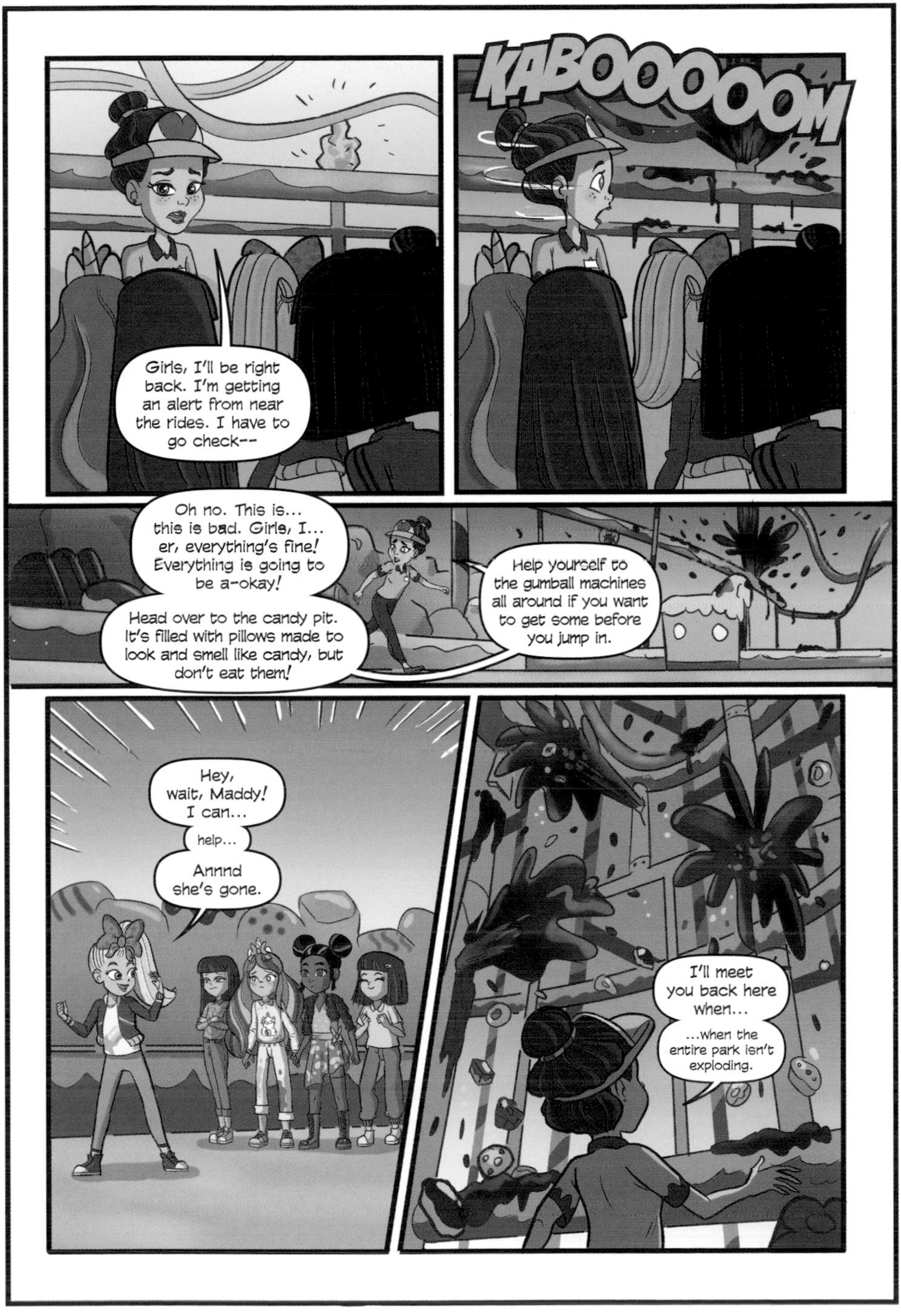

Girls, I'll be right back. I'm getting an alert from near the rides. I have to go check--
KABOOOOOOM
Oh no. This is... this is bad. Girls, I... er, everything's fine! Everything is going to be a-okay!
Head over to the candy pit. It's filled with pillows made to look and smell like candy, but don't eat them!
Help yourself to the gumball machines all around if you want to get some before you jump in.
Hey, wait, Maddy! I can...
help...
Annnd she's gone.
I'll meet you back here when...
...when the entire park isn't exploding.

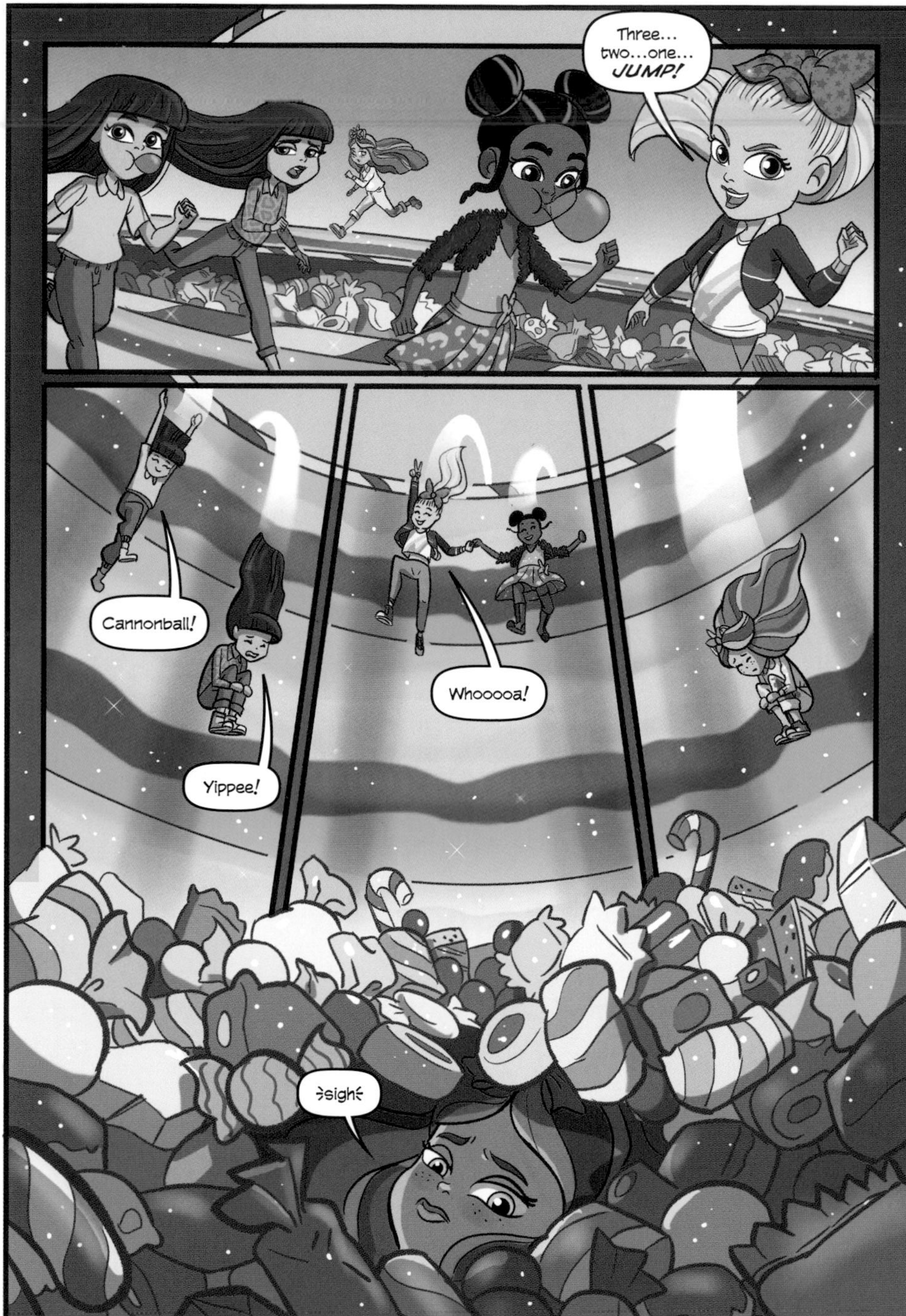
Three... two...one... JUMP!
Cannonball!
Yippee!
Whooooa!
≥sigh≤

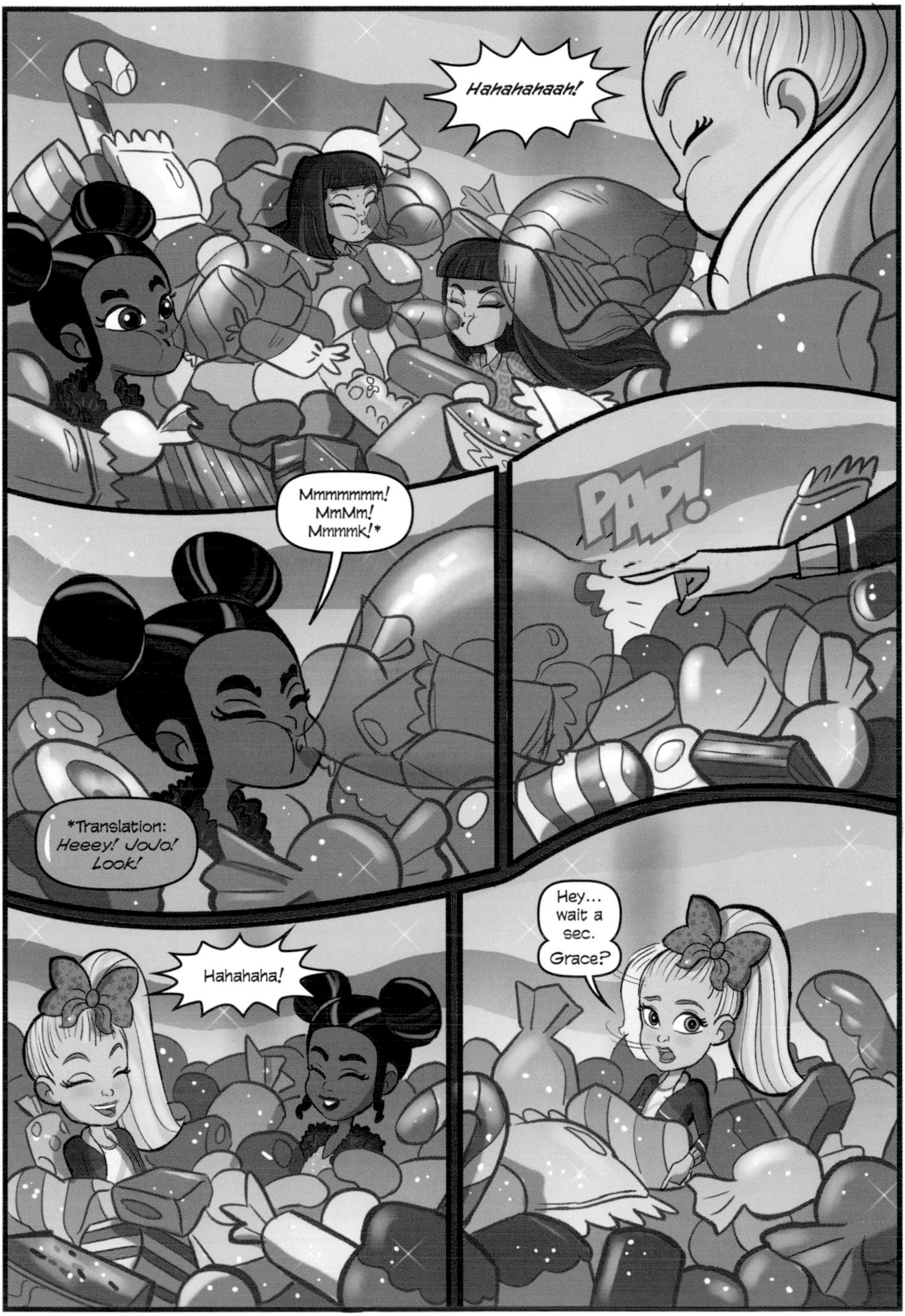

Hahahahaah!
Mmmmmmm! MmMm! Mmmmk!*
*Translation: Heeey! JoJo! Look!
PAP!
Hahahaha!
Hey... wait a sec. Grace?

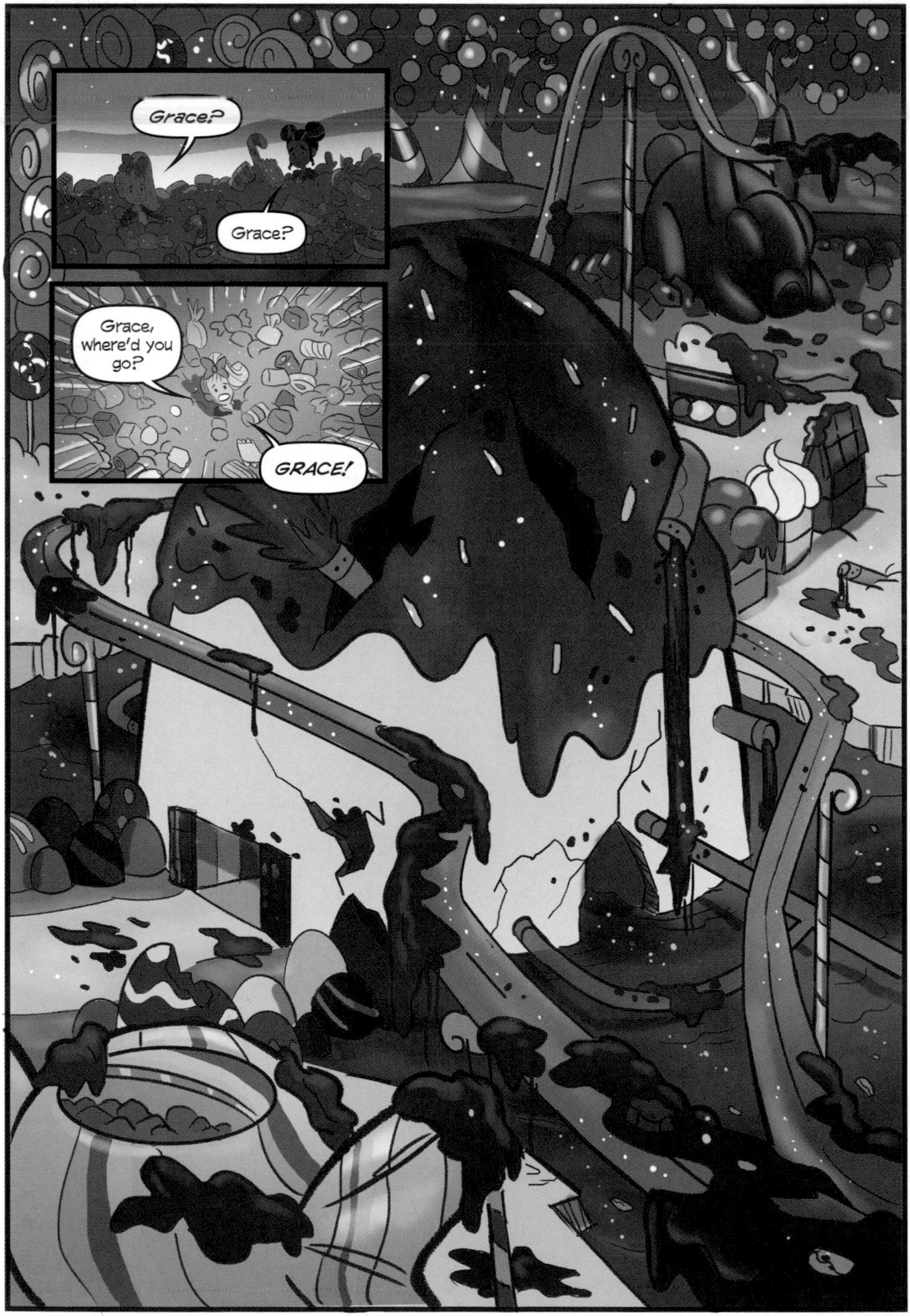
Grace?
Grace?
Grace, where'd you go?
GRACE!

CHAPTER TWO

THE CASE OF THE DISAPPEARING GRACE

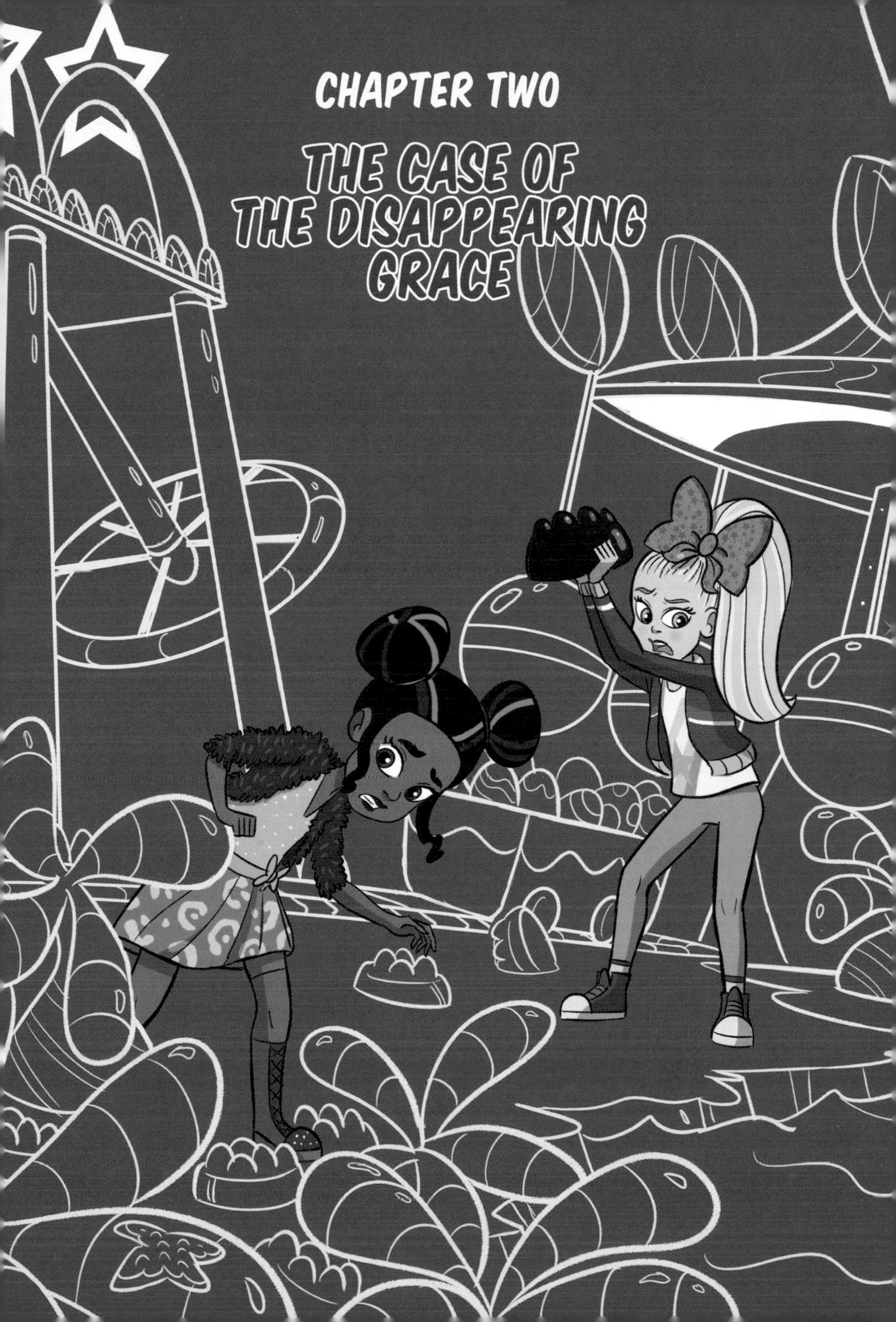

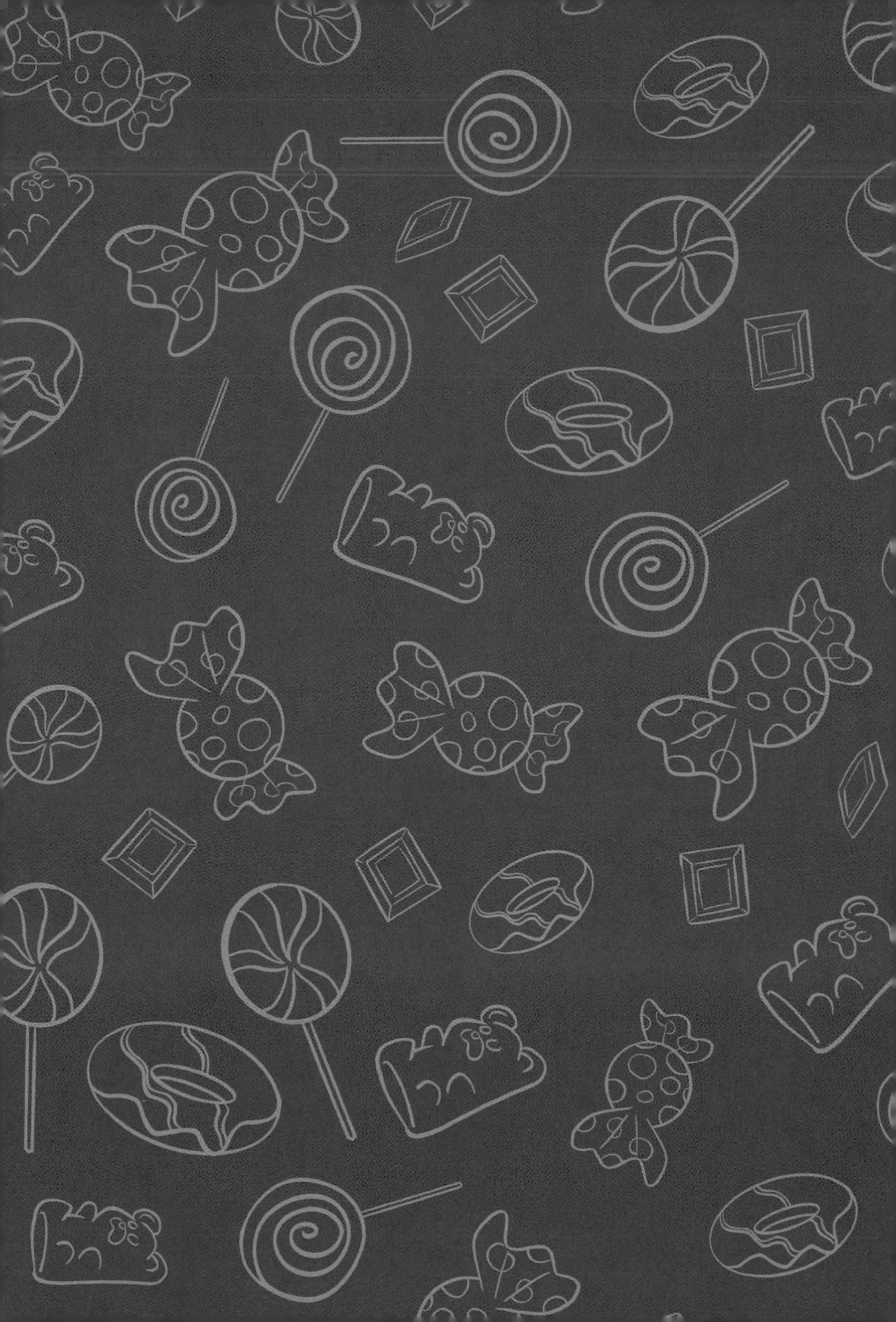

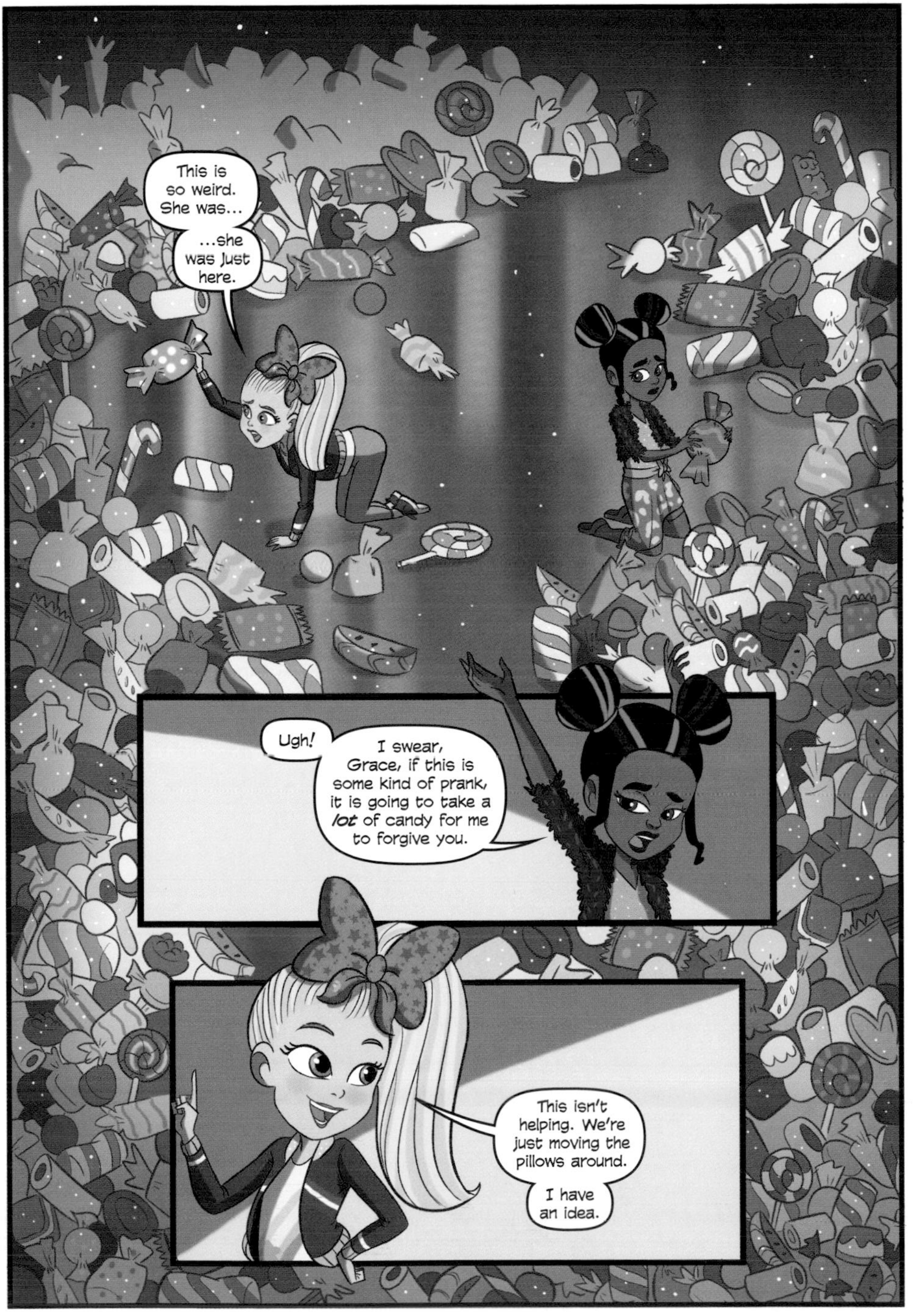
This is so weird. She was...
...she was just here.
Ugh!
I swear, Grace, if this is some kind of prank, it is going to take a *lot* of candy for me to forgive you.
This isn't helping. We're just moving the pillows around.
I have an idea.

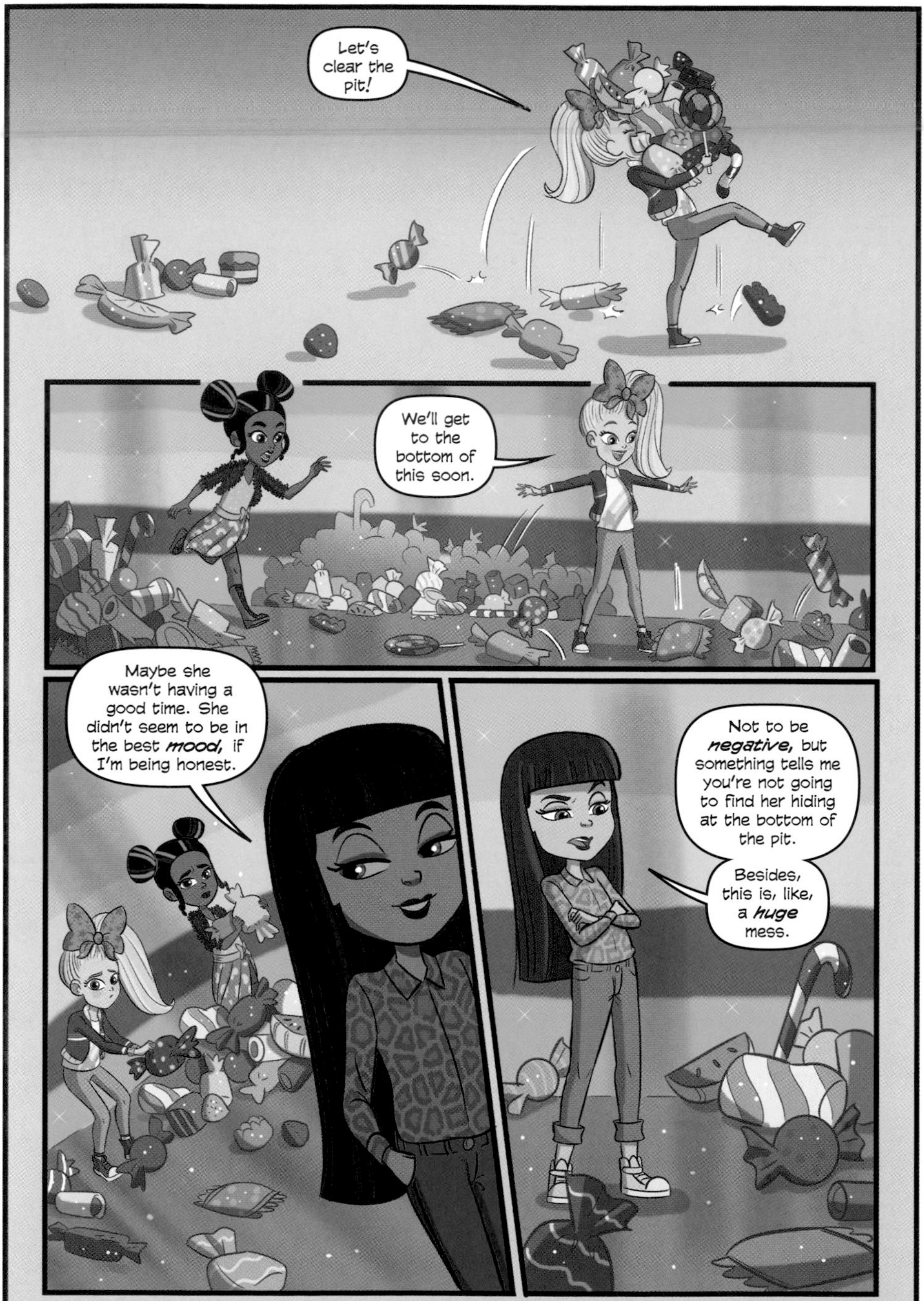
Let's clear the pit!
We'll get to the bottom of this soon.
Maybe she wasn't having a good time. She didn't seem to be in the best *mood,* if I'm being honest.
Not to be *negative,* but something tells me you're not going to find her hiding at the bottom of the pit.
Besides, this is, like, a *huge* mess.

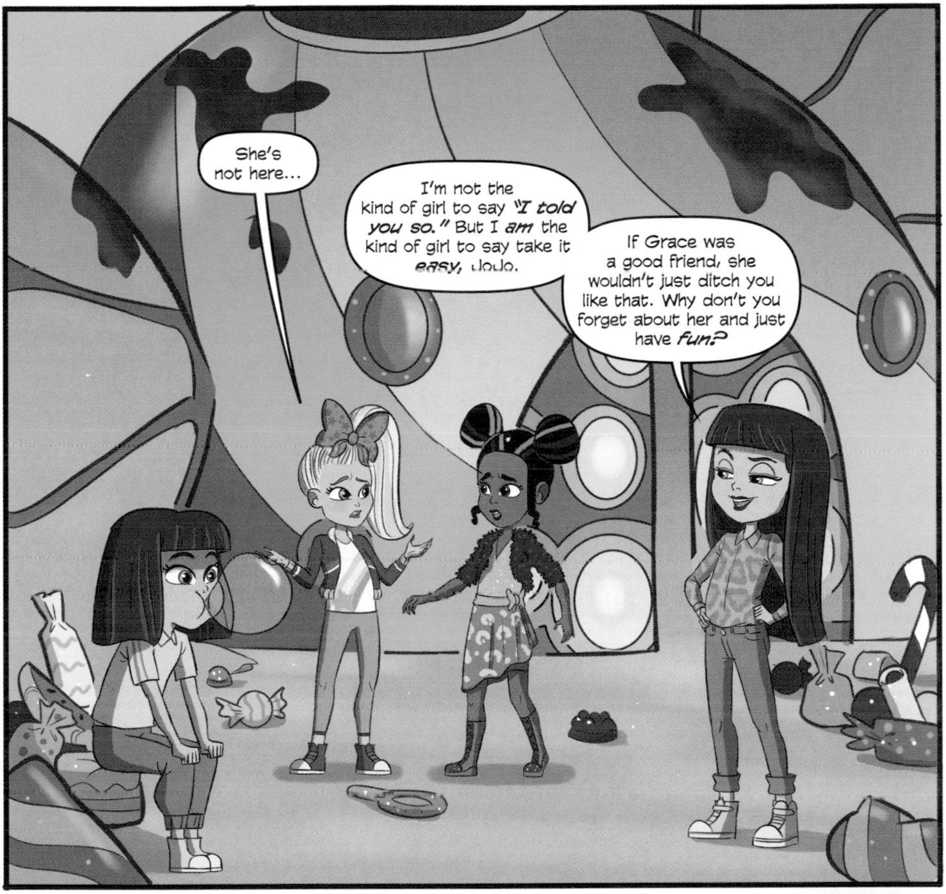
She's not here...
I'm not the kind of girl to say *"I told you so."* But I *am* the kind of girl to say take it *easy,* JoJo.
If Grace was a good friend, she wouldn't just ditch you like that. Why don't you forget about her and just have *fun?*

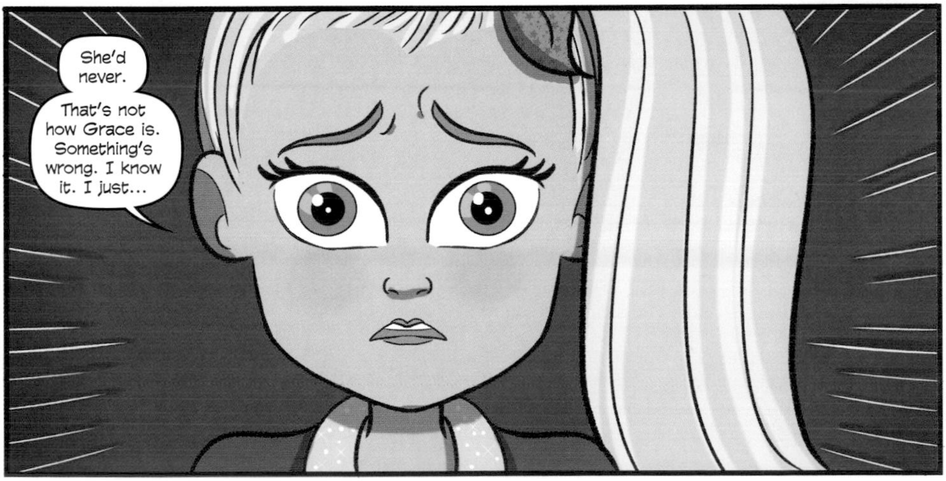
She'd never.
That's not how Grace is. Something's wrong. I know it. I just...

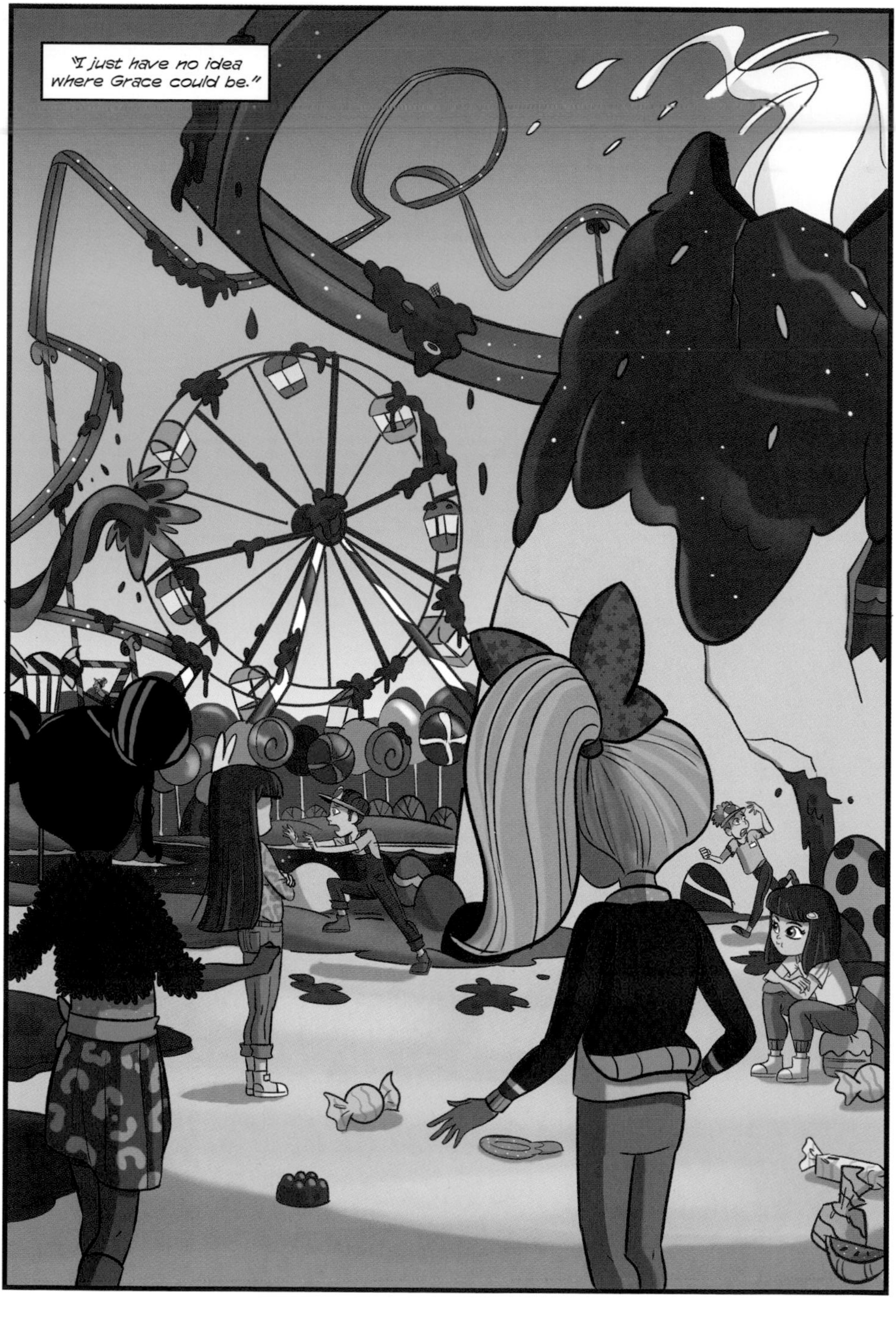
"I just have no idea where Grace could be."

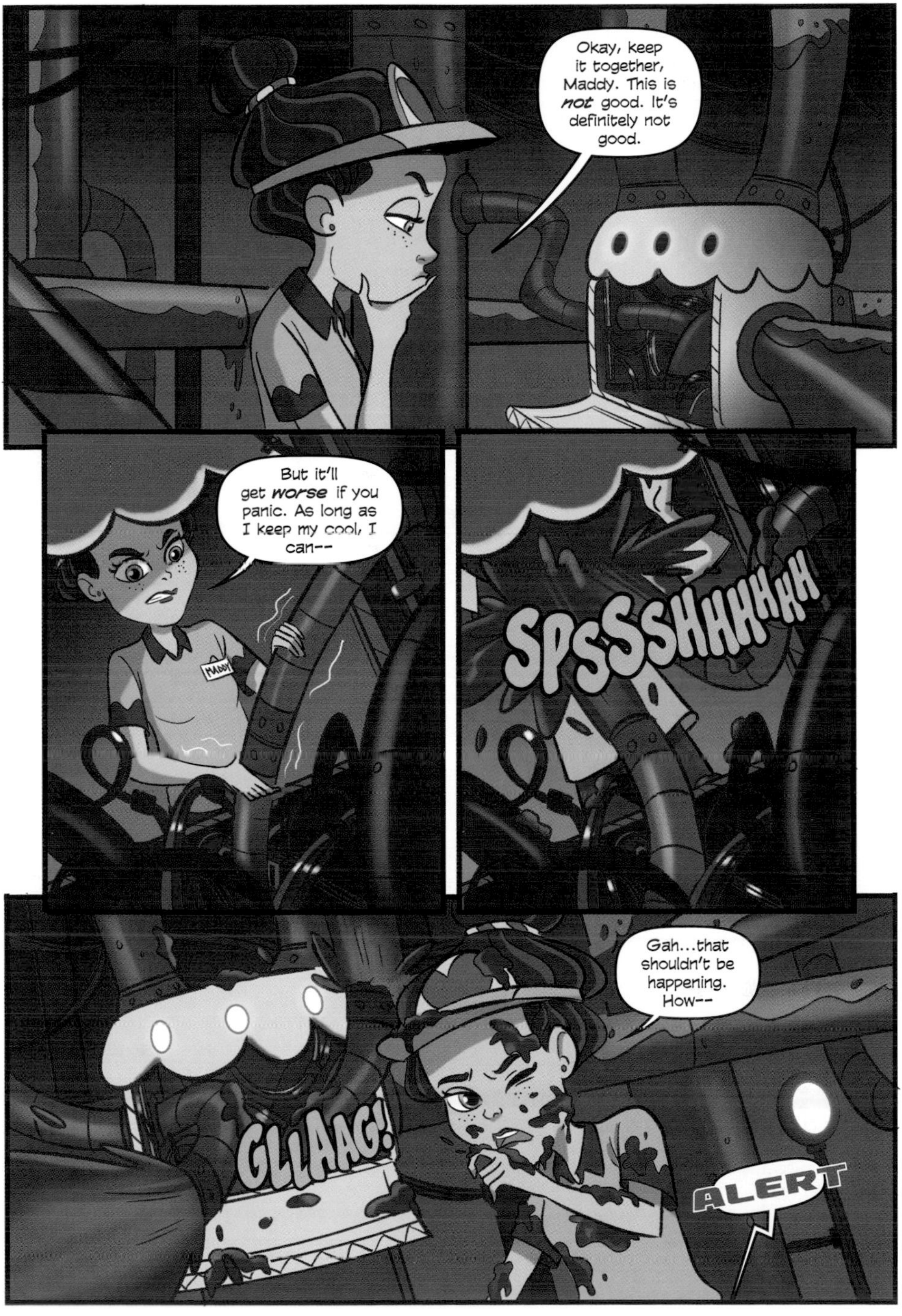
Okay, keep it together, Maddy. This is *not* good. It's definitely not good.
But it'll get *worse* if you panic. As long as I keep my cool, I can--
MADDY
SPSSSHHHHHH
Gah...that shouldn't be happening. How--
GLLAAG!
ALERT

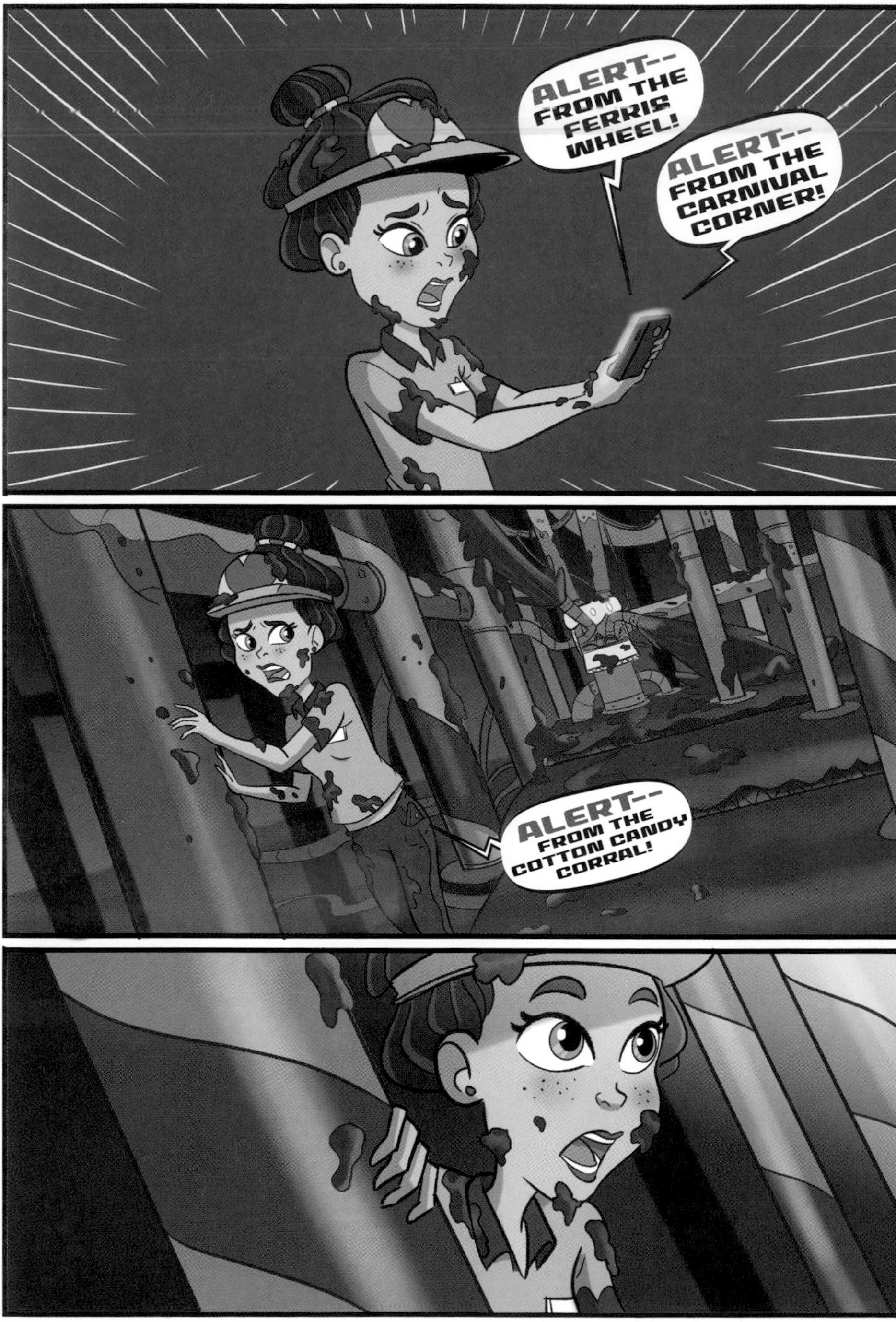
ALERT-- FROM THE FERRIS WHEEL!
ALERT-- FROM THE CARNIVAL CORNER!
ALERT-- FROM THE COTTON CANDY CORRAL!

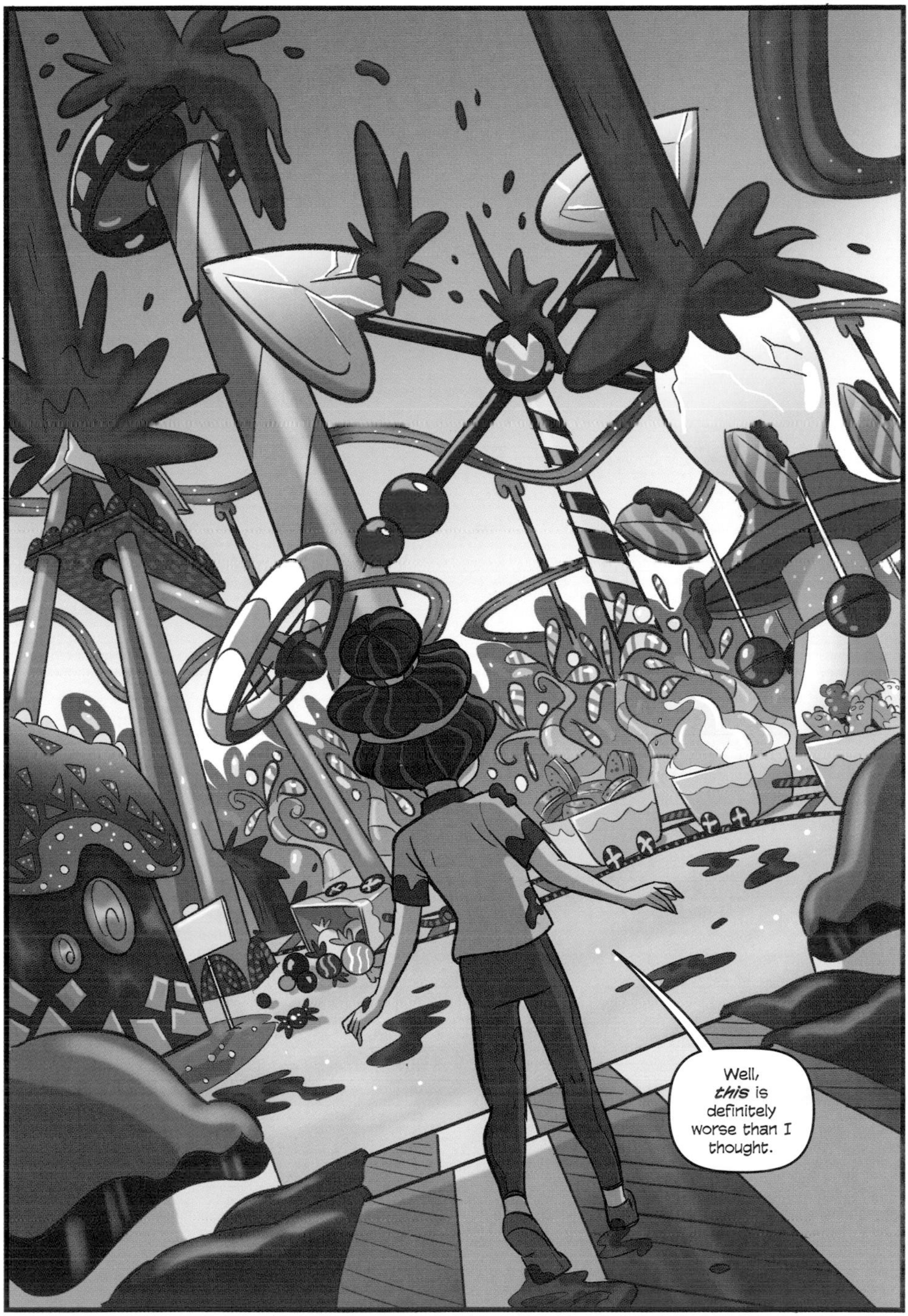
Well, *this* is definitely worse than I thought.

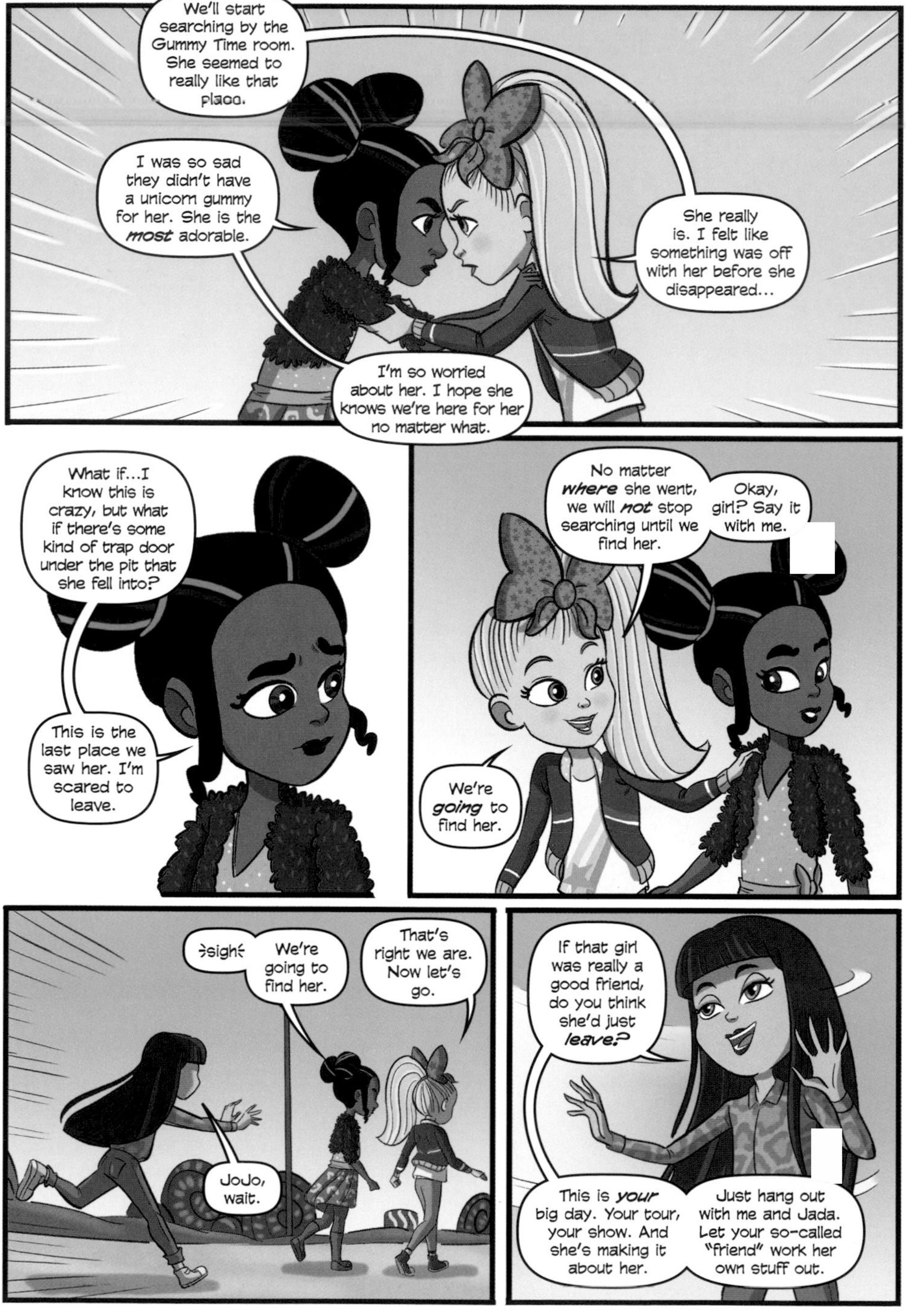
We'll start searching by the Gummy Time room. She seemed to really like that place.
I was so sad they didn't have a unicorn gummy for her. She is the *most* adorable.
She really is. I felt like something was off with her before she disappeared...
I'm so worried about her. I hope she knows we're here for her no matter what.
What if...I know this is crazy, but what if there's some kind of trap door under the pit that she fell into?
This is the last place we saw her. I'm scared to leave.
No matter *where* she went, we will *not* stop searching until we find her.
Okay, girl? Say it with me.
We're *going* to find her.
sigh We're going to find her.
That's right we are. Now let's go.
JoJo, wait.
If that girl was really a good friend, do you think she'd just *leave?*
This is *your* big day. Your tour, your show. And she's making it about her.
Just hang out with me and Jada. Let your so-called "friend" work her own stuff out.

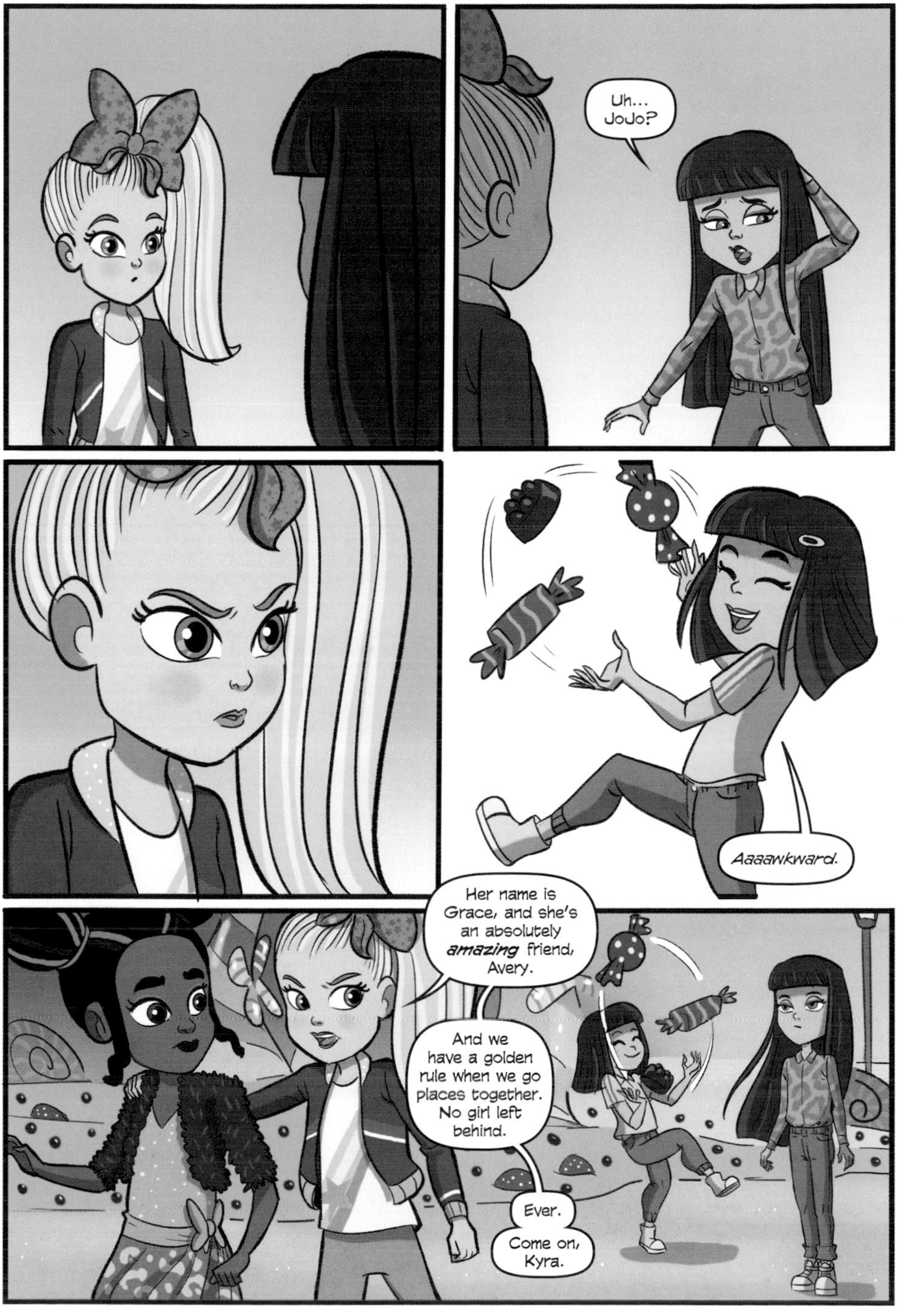
Uh... JoJo?
Aaaawkward.
Her name is Grace, and she's an absolutely **amazing** friend, Avery.
And we have a golden rule when we go places together. No girl left behind.
Ever.
Come on, Kyra.

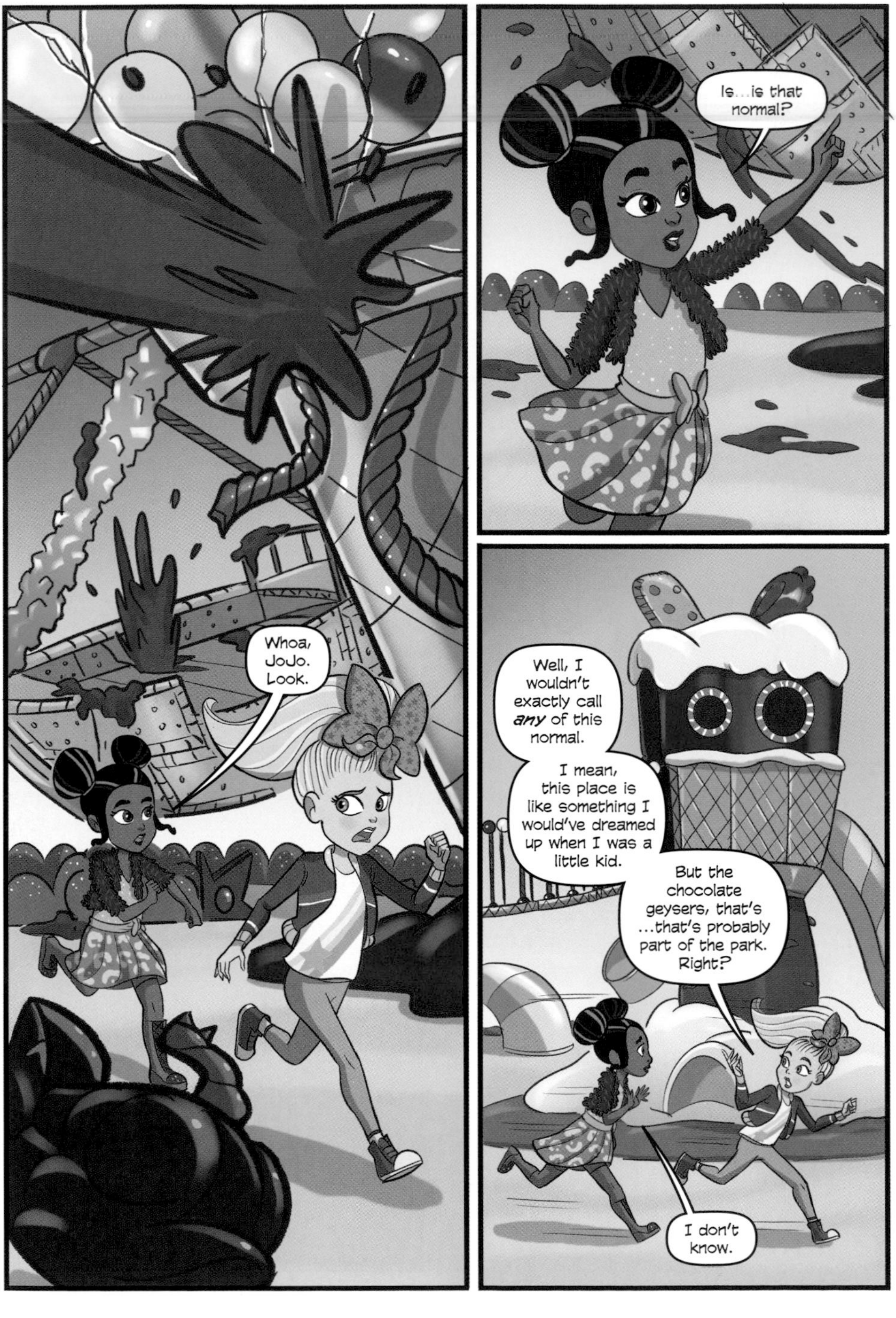
Is…is that normal?
Whoa, JoJo. Look.
Well, I wouldn't exactly call *any* of this normal.
I mean, this place is like something I would've dreamed up when I was a little kid.
But the chocolate geysers, that's …that's probably part of the park. Right?
I don't know.

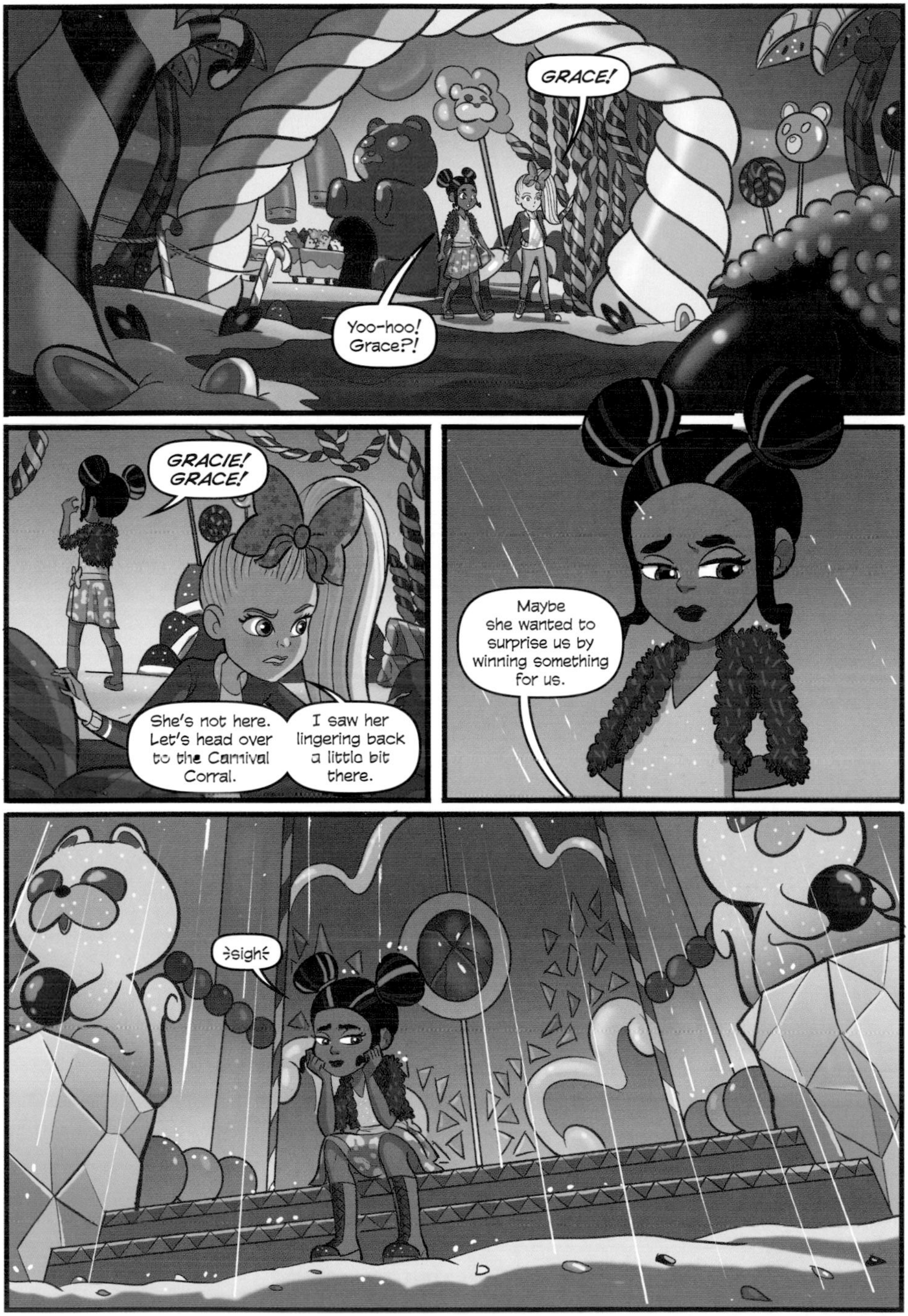
GRACE!
Yoo-hoo! Grace?!
GRACIE! GRACE!
I saw her lingering back a little bit there.
She's not here. Let's head over to the Carnival Corral.
Maybe she wanted to surprise us by winning something for us.
sigh

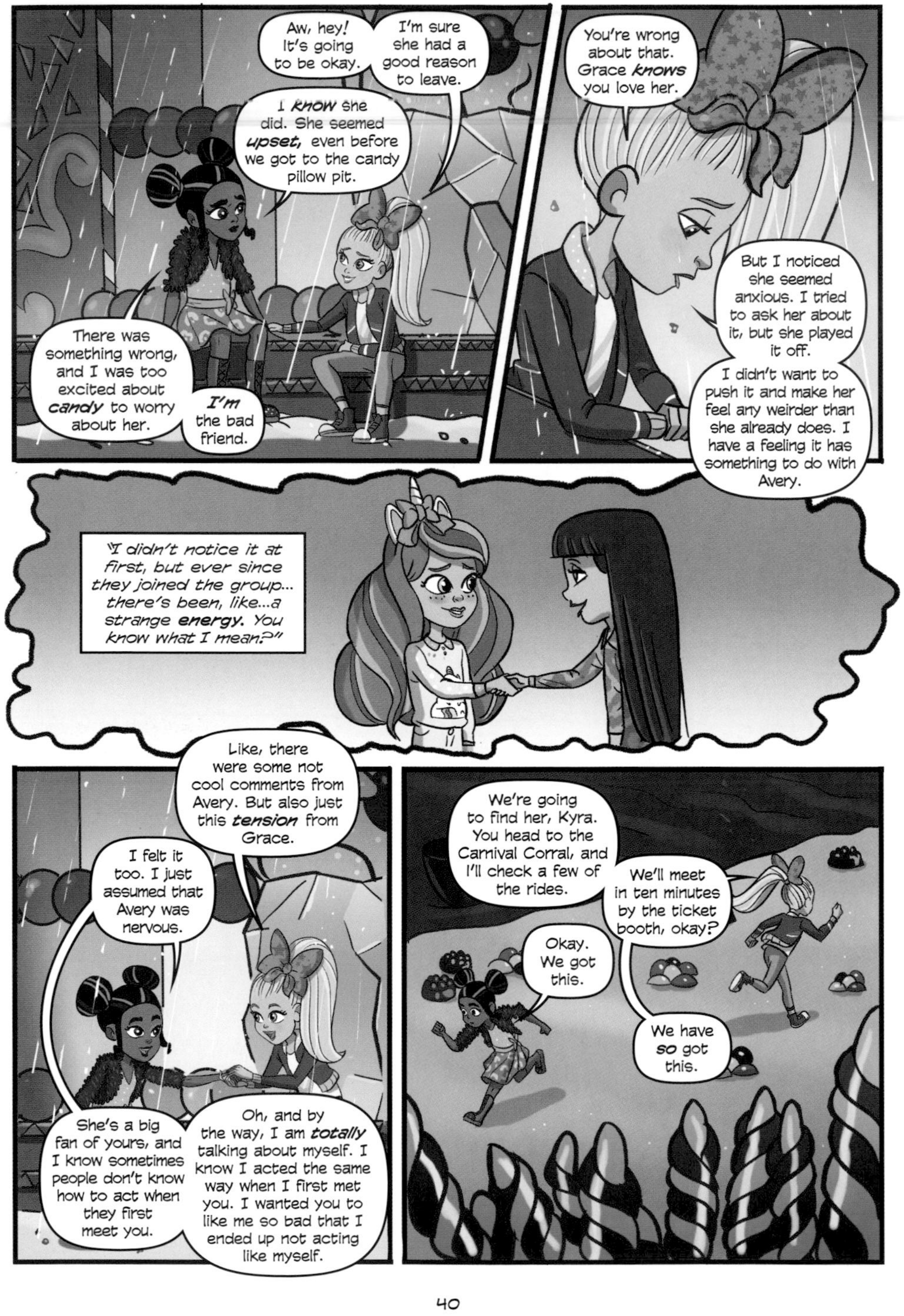
Aw, hey! It's going to be okay.
I'm sure she had a good reason to leave.
I *know* she did. She seemed *upset*, even before we got to the candy pillow pit.
There was something wrong, and I was too excited about *candy* to worry about her.
I'm the bad friend.
You're wrong about that. Grace *knows* you love her.
But I noticed she seemed anxious. I tried to ask her about it, but she played it off.
I didn't want to push it and make her feel any weirder than she already does. I have a feeling it has something to do with Avery.
"I didn't notice it at first, but ever since they joined the group... there's been, like...a strange *energy*. You know what I mean?"
Like, there were some not cool comments from Avery. But also just this *tension* from Grace.
I felt it too. I just assumed that Avery was nervous.
She's a big fan of yours, and I know sometimes people don't know how to act when they first meet you.
Oh, and by the way, I am *totally* talking about myself. I know I acted the same way when I first met you. I wanted you to like me so bad that I ended up not acting like myself.
We're going to find her, Kyra. You head to the Carnival Corral, and I'll check a few of the rides.
We'll meet in ten minutes by the ticket booth, okay?
Okay. We got this.
We have *so* got this.

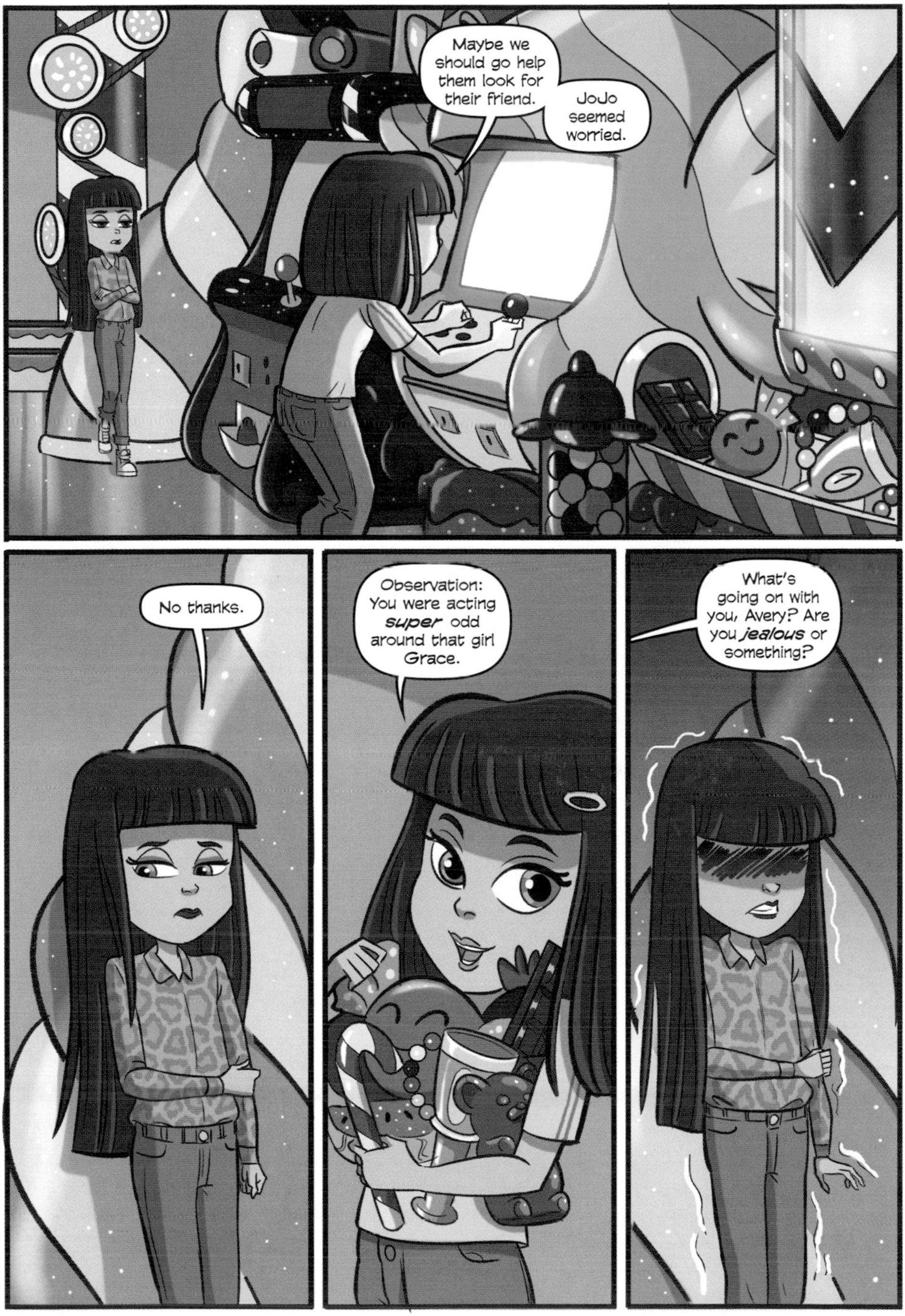
Maybe we should go help them look for their friend.
JoJo seemed worried.
No thanks.
Observation: You were acting *super* odd around that girl Grace.
What's going on with you, Avery? Are you *jealous* or something?

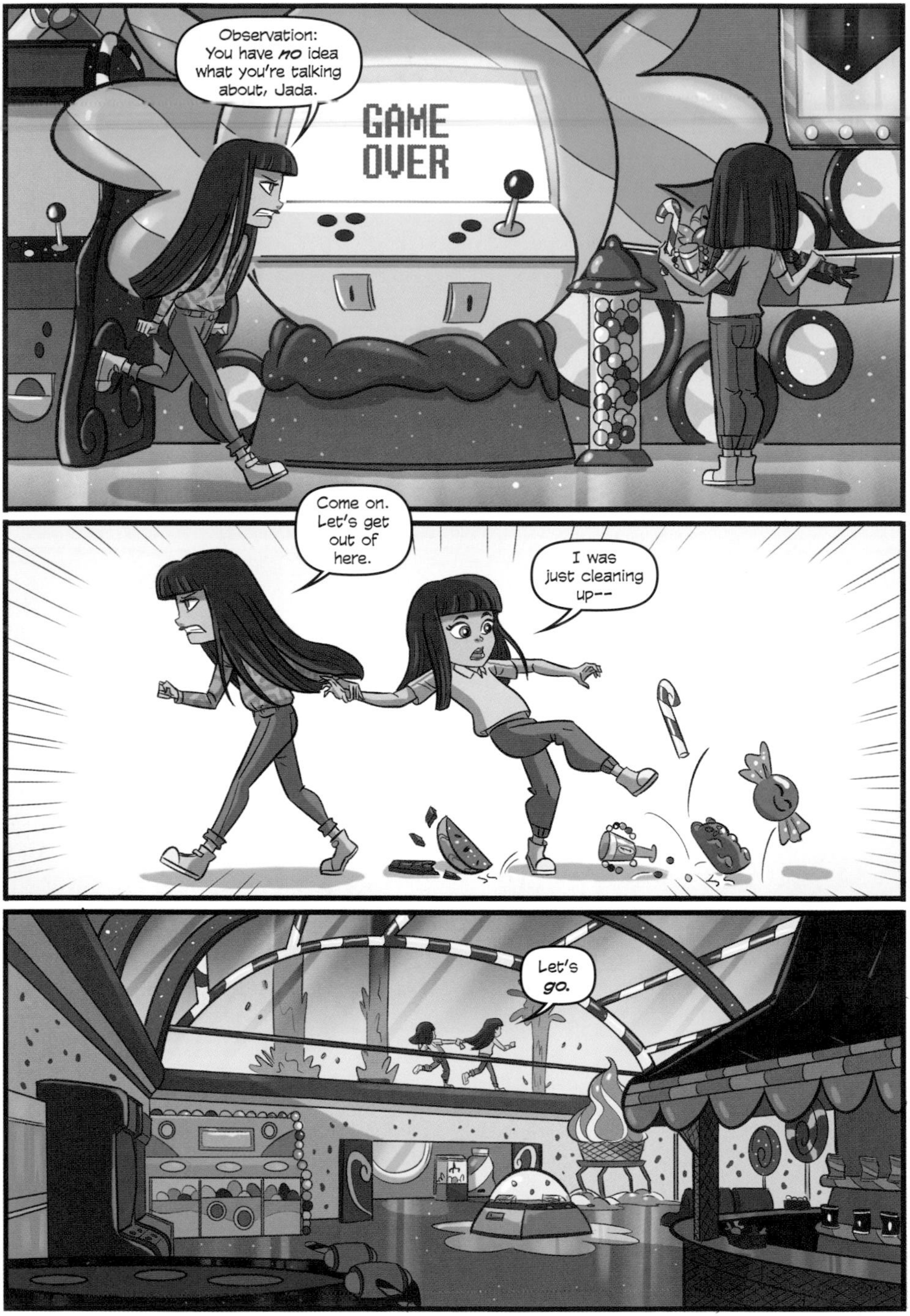
Observation: You have *no* idea what you're talking about, Jada.
GAME OVER
Come on. Let's get out of here.
I was just cleaning up--
Let's *go.*

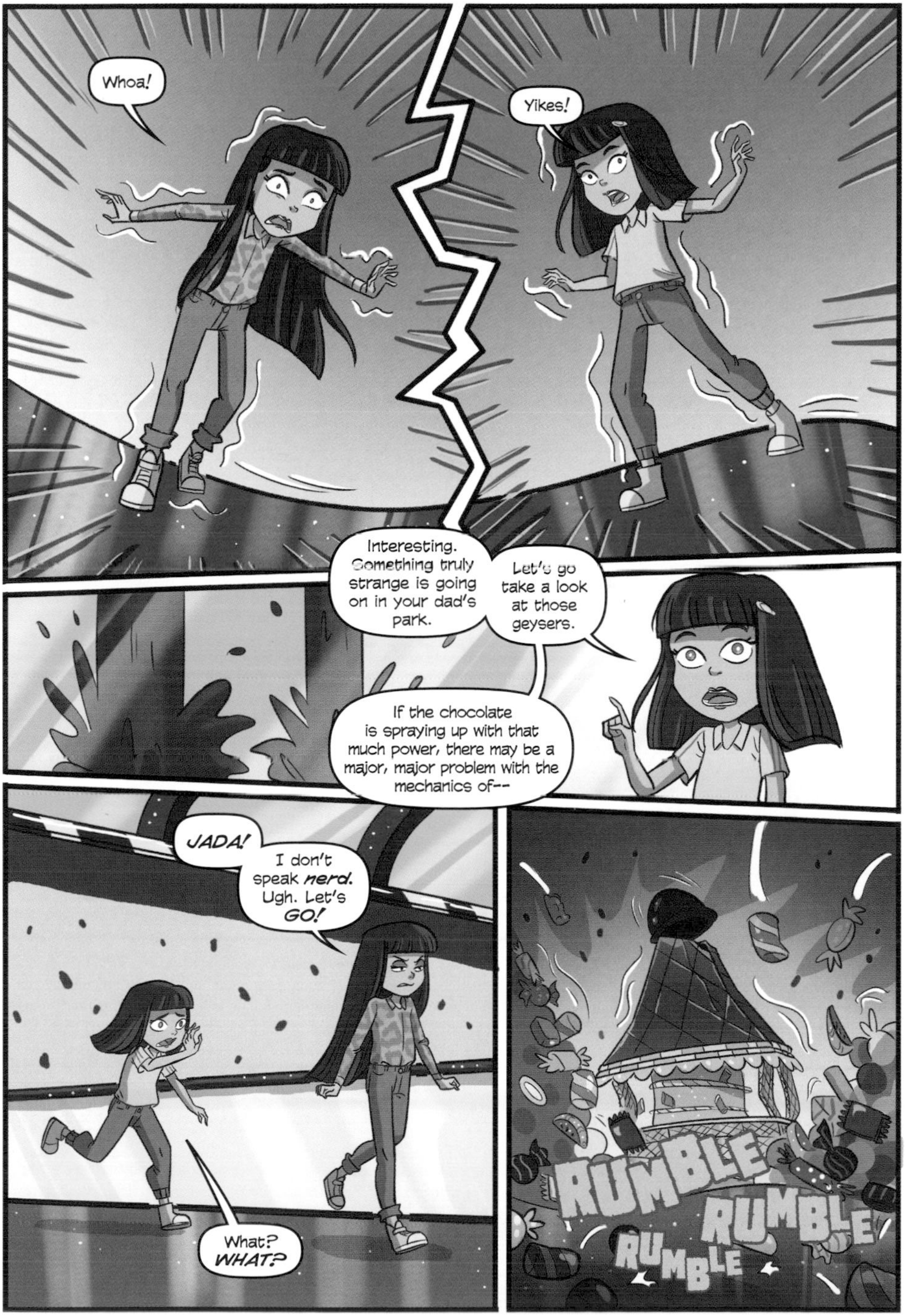
Whoa!
Yikes!
Interesting. Something truly strange is going on in your dad's park.
Let's go take a look at those geysers.
If the chocolate is spraying up with that much power, there may be a major, major problem with the mechanics of--
JADA!
I don't speak *nerd.* Ugh. Let's *GO!*
What? *WHAT?*
RUMBLE
RUMBLE
RUMBLE

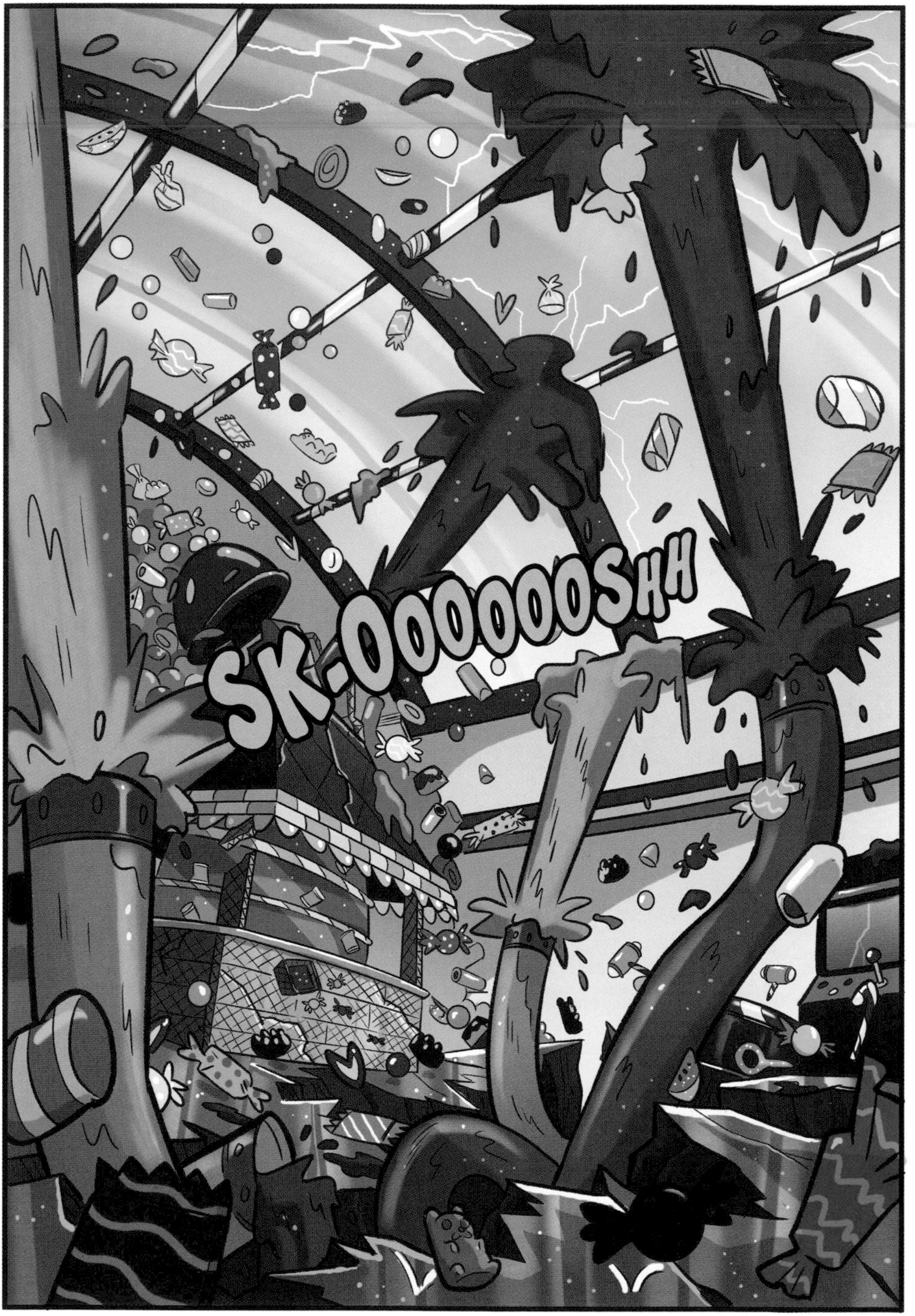
SK-OOOOOOOSHH

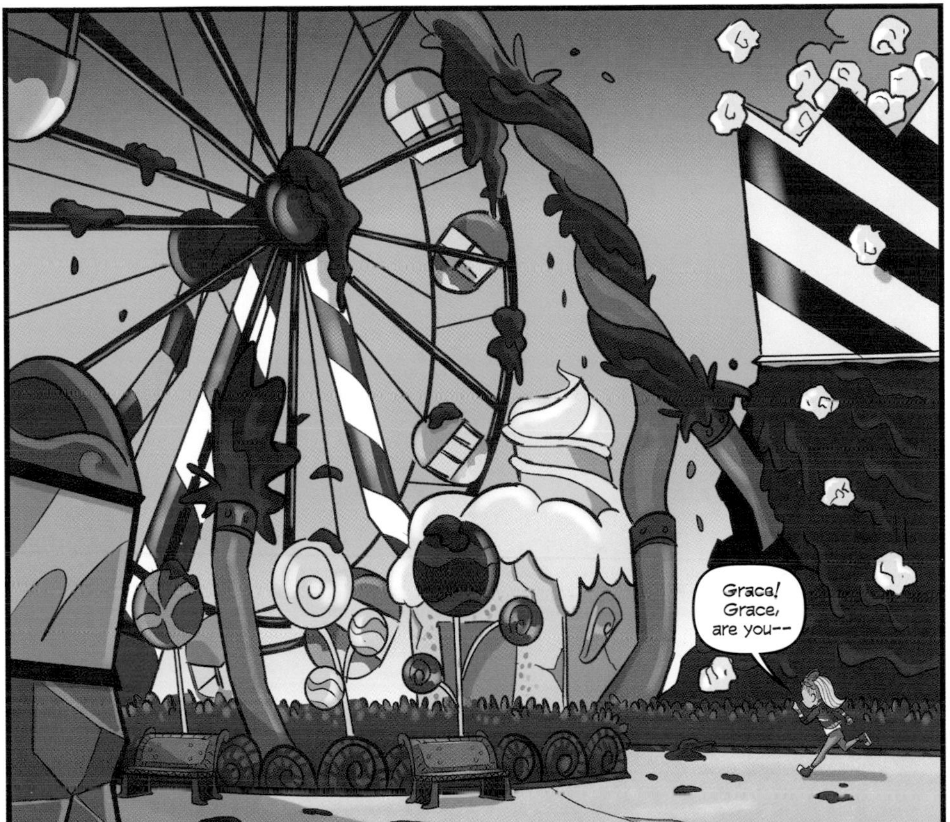
Grace! Grace, are you--

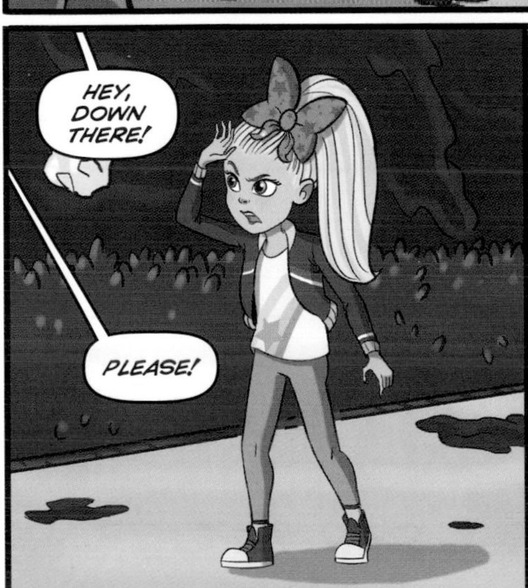
HEY, DOWN THERE!
PLEASE!

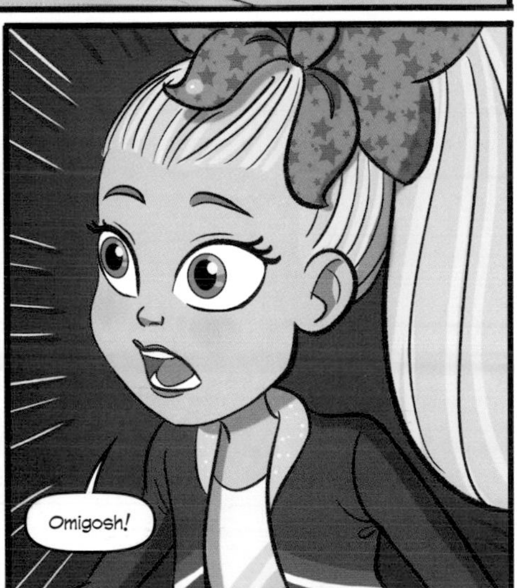
Omigosh!

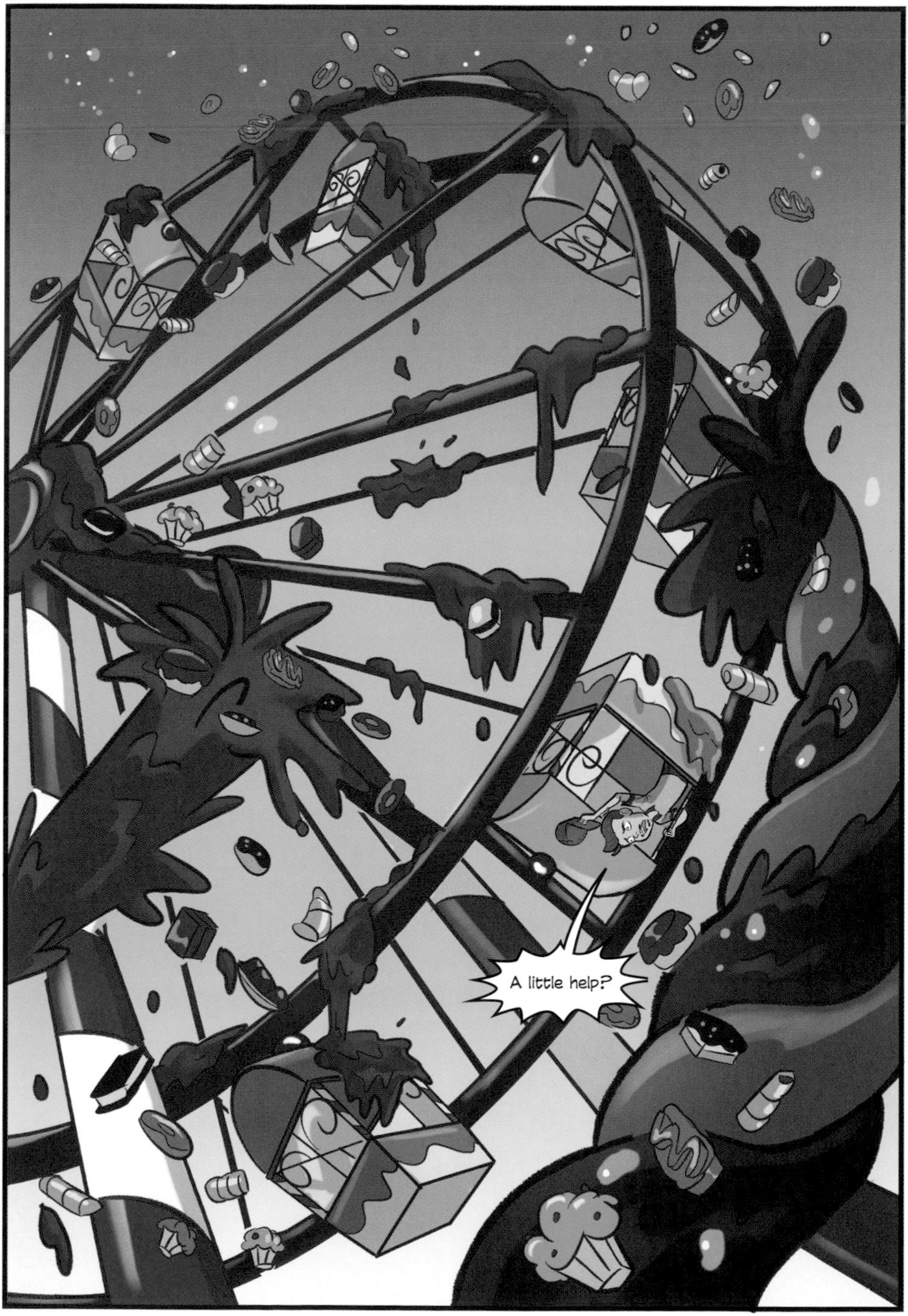
A little help?

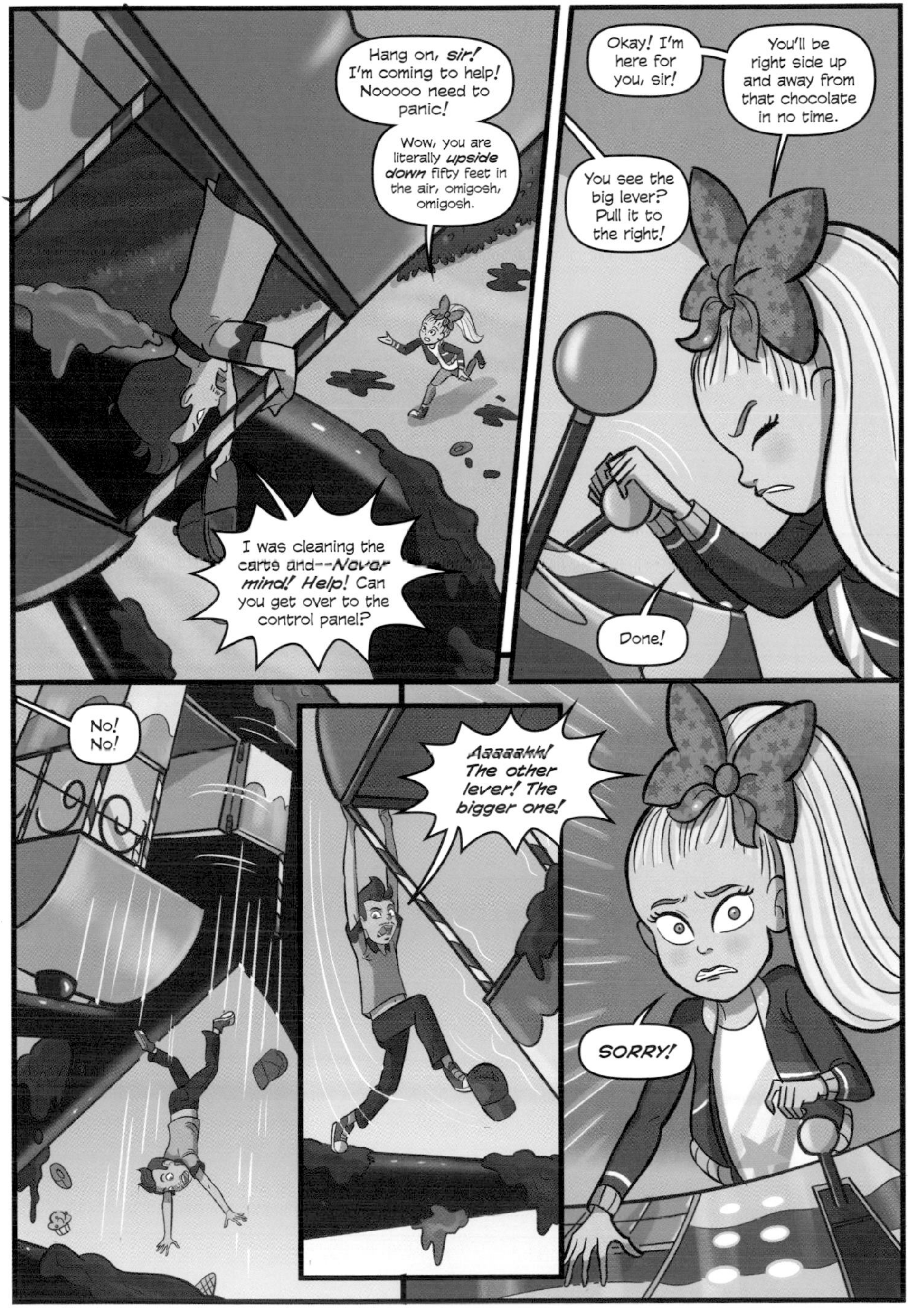
Hang on, sir! I'm coming to help! Nooooo need to panic!
Wow, you are literally upside down fifty feet in the air, omigosh, omigosh.
I was cleaning the carts and--Never mind! Help! Can you get over to the control panel?
Okay! I'm here for you, sir!
You'll be right side up and away from that chocolate in no time.
You see the big lever? Pull it to the right!
Done!
No! No!
Aaaaakk! The other lever! The bigger one!
SORRY!

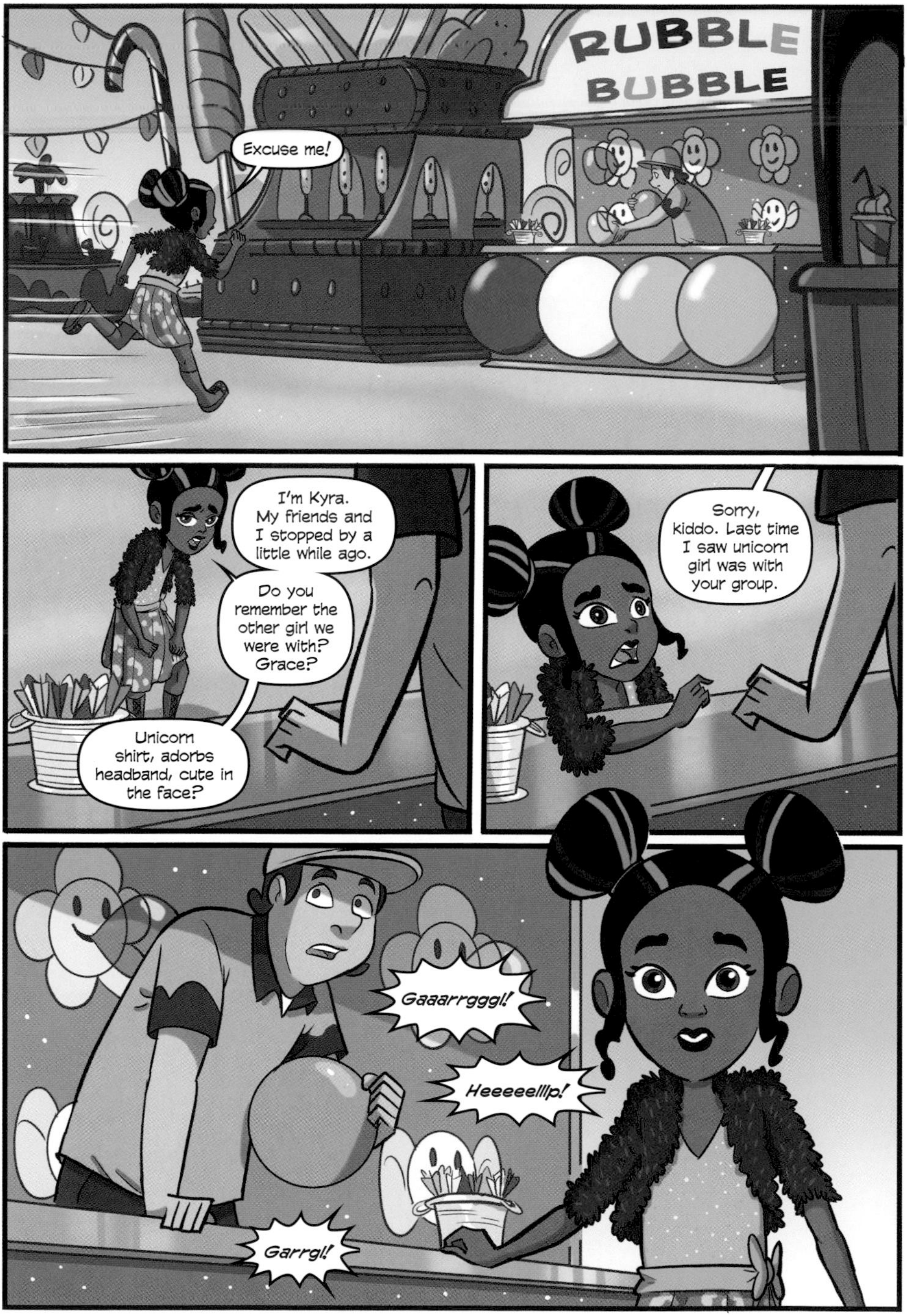
RUBBLE BUBBLE
Excuse me!
I'm Kyra. My friends and I stopped by a little while ago.
Do you remember the other girl we were with? Grace?
Unicorn shirt, adorbs headband, cute in the face?
Sorry, kiddo. Last time I saw unicorn girl was with your group.
Gaaarrgggl!
Heeeeelllp!
Garrgl!

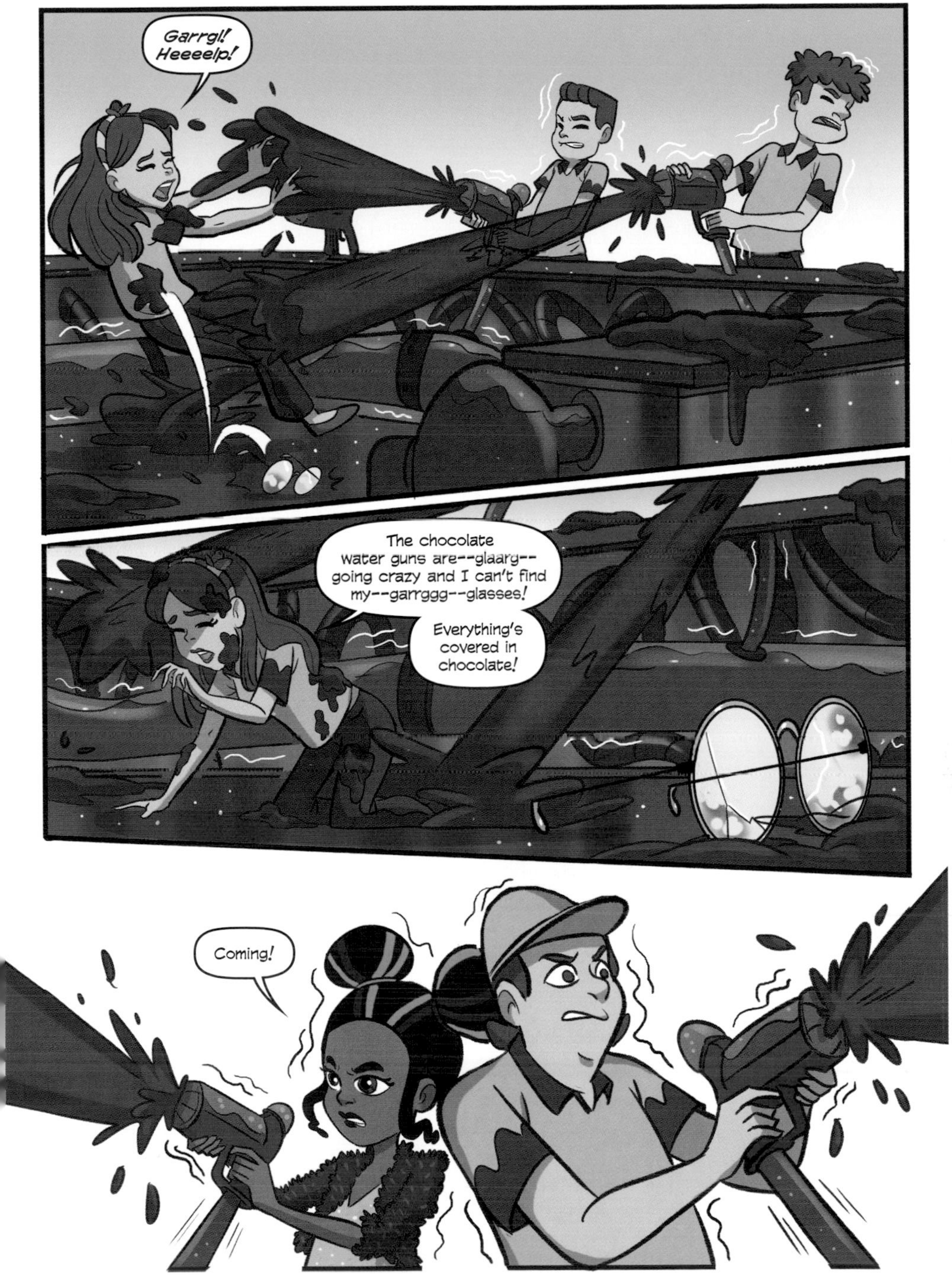
Garrgl! Heeeelp!
The chocolate water guns are--glaarg--going crazy and I can't find my--garrggg--glasses!
Everything's covered in chocolate!
Coming!

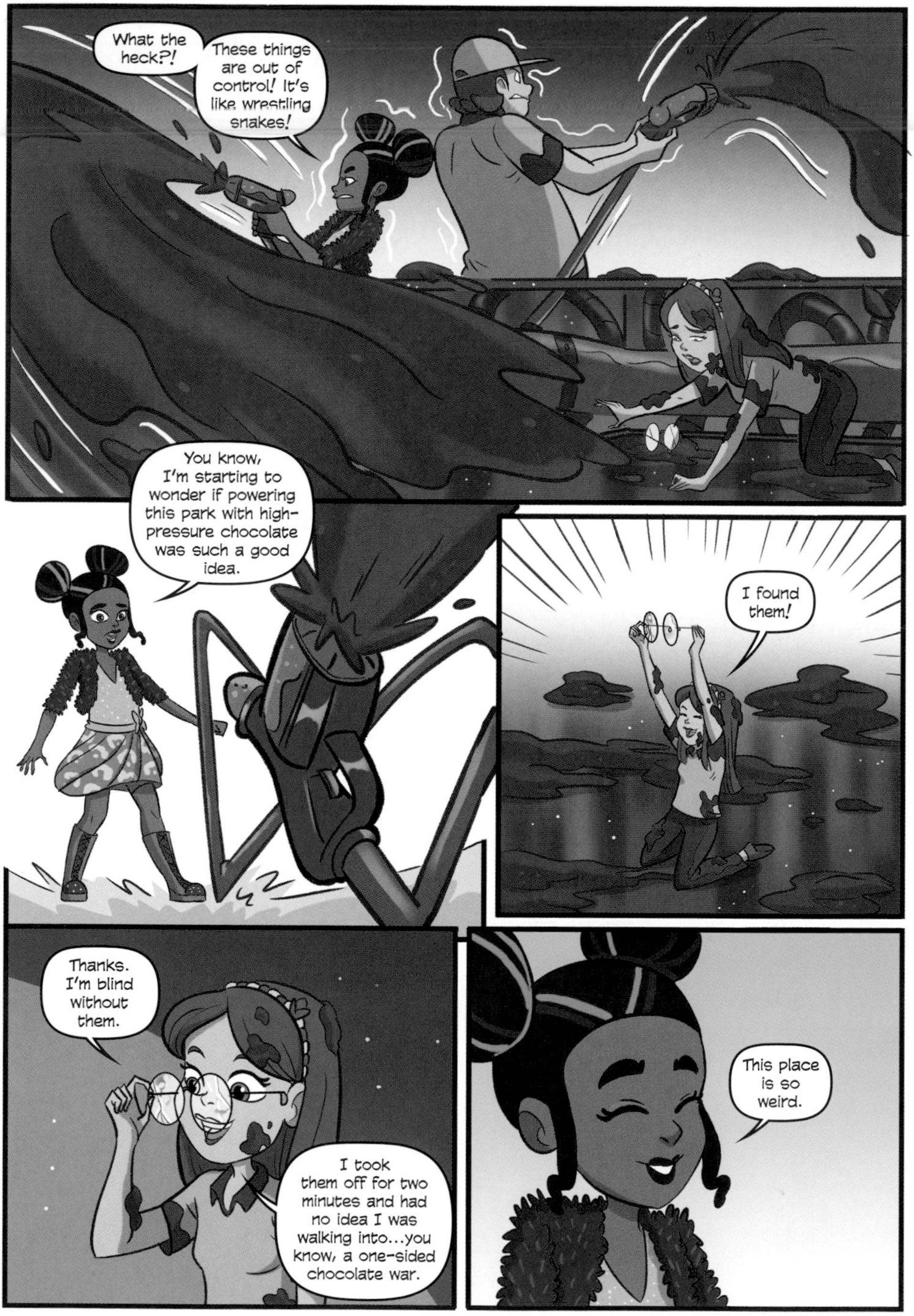
What the heck?!
These things are out of control! It's like wrestling snakes!
You know, I'm starting to wonder if powering this park with high-pressure chocolate was such a good idea.
I found them!
Thanks. I'm blind without them.
I took them off for two minutes and had no idea I was walking into...you know, a one-sided chocolate war.
This place is so weird.

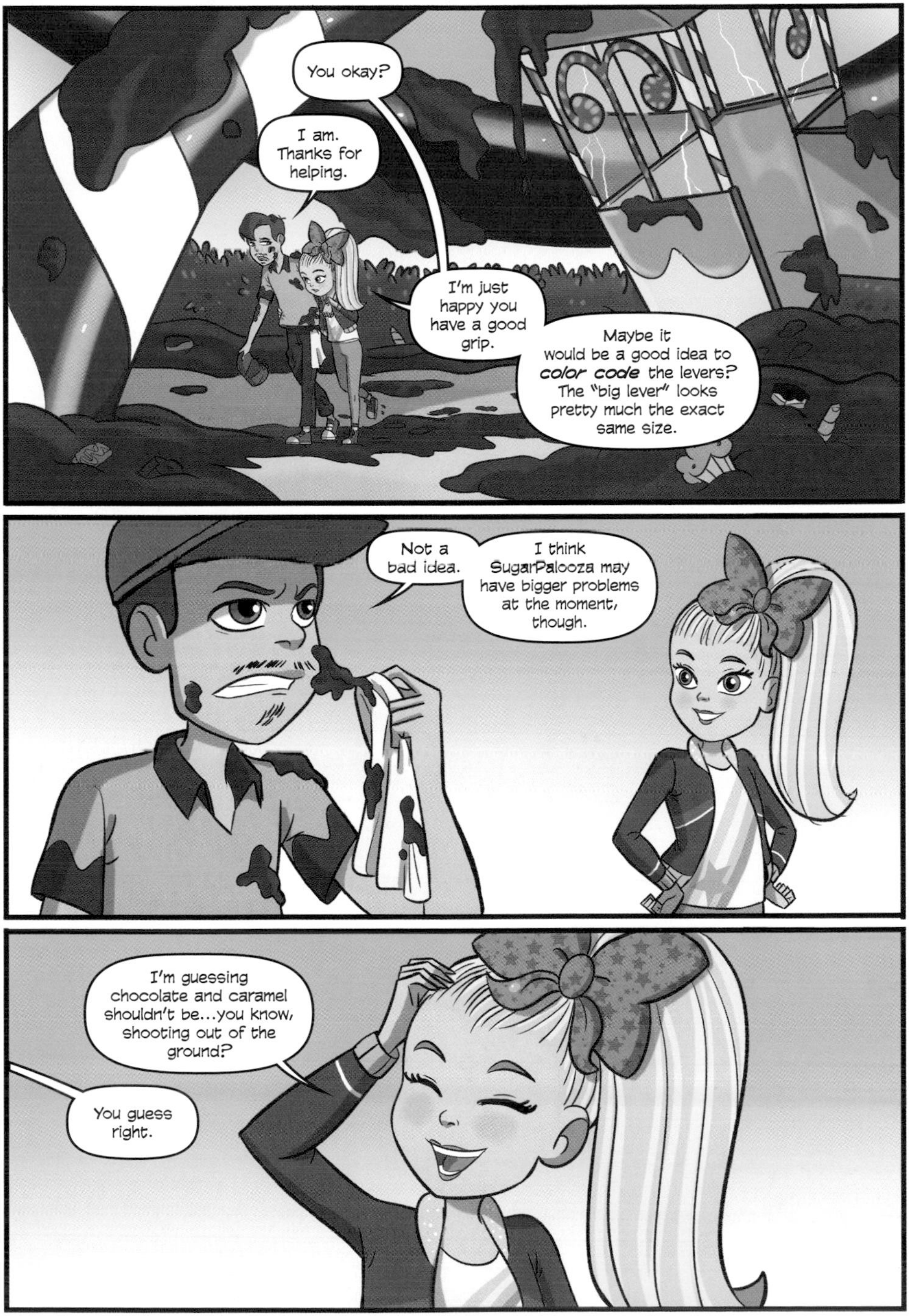
You okay?
I am. Thanks for helping.
I'm just happy you have a good grip.
Maybe it would be a good idea to ***color code*** the levers? The "big lever" looks pretty much the exact same size.
Not a bad idea.
I think SugarPalooza may have bigger problems at the moment, though.
I'm guessing chocolate and caramel shouldn't be...you know, shooting out of the ground?
You guess right.

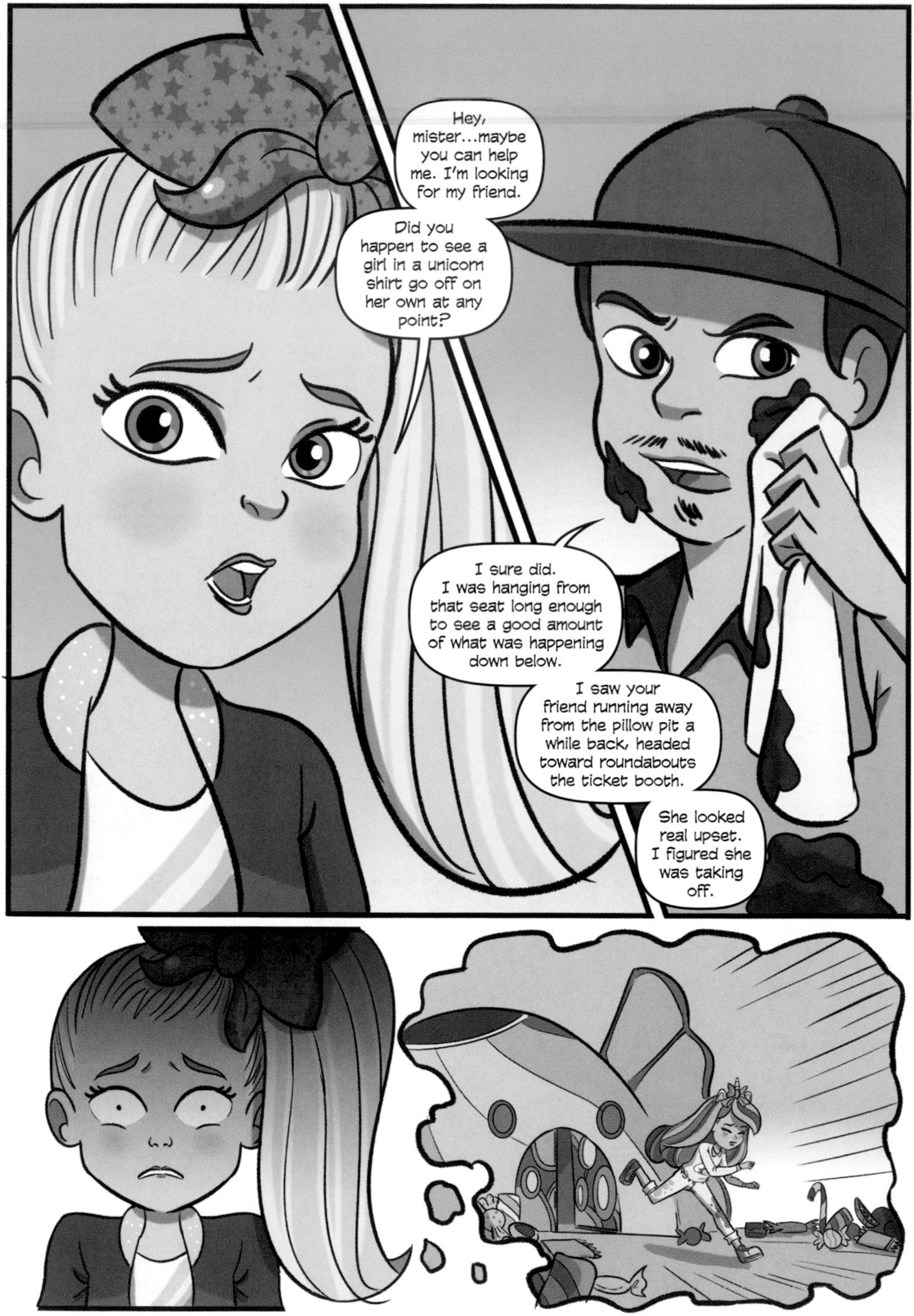
Hey, mister...maybe you can help me. I'm looking for my friend.
Did you happen to see a girl in a unicorn shirt go off on her own at any point?
I sure did. I was hanging from that seat long enough to see a good amount of what was happening down below.
I saw your friend running away from the pillow pit a while back, headed toward roundabouts the ticket booth.
She looked real upset. I figured she was taking off.

CHAPTER THREE

A STICKY SITUATION

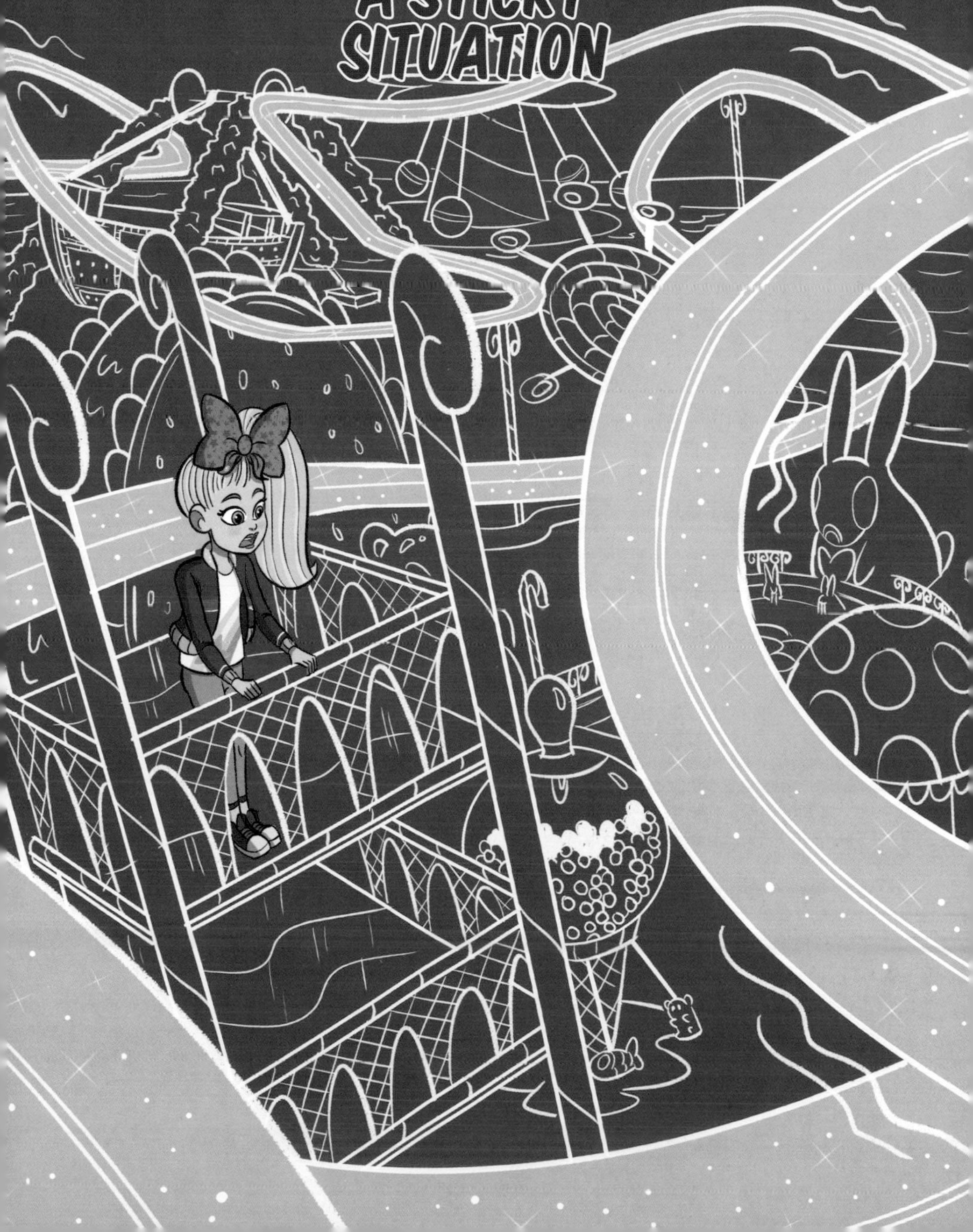

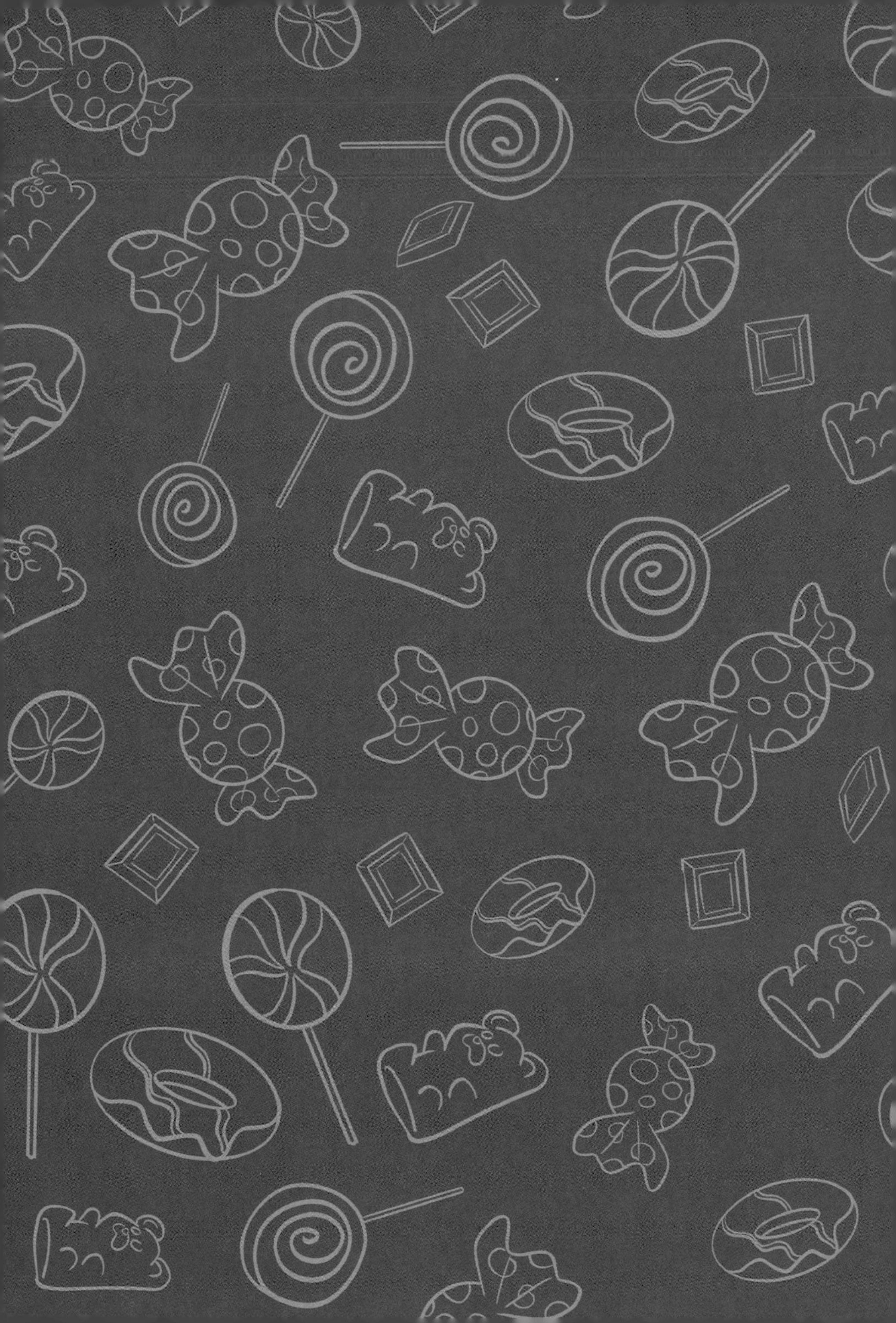

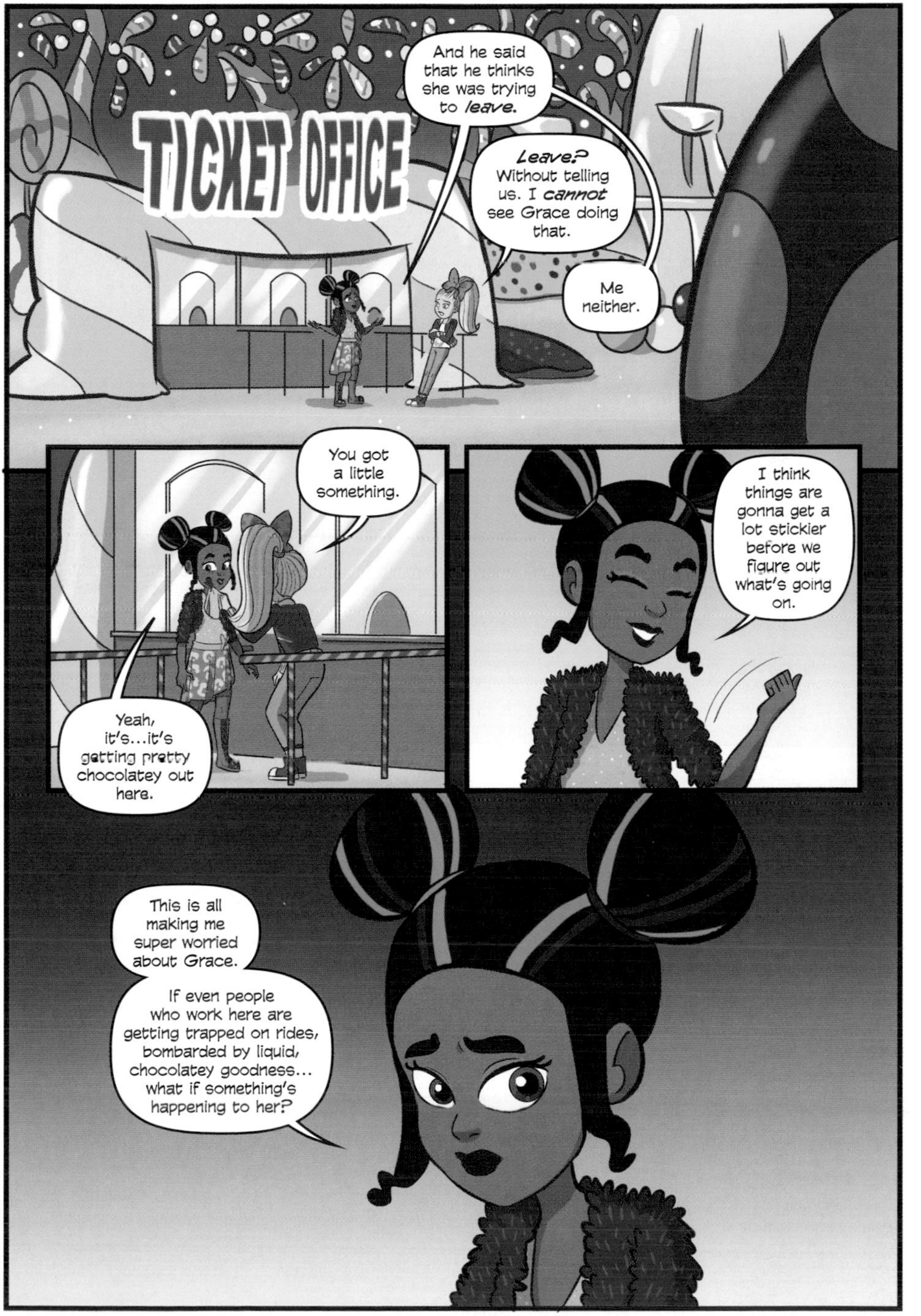

And he said that he thinks she was trying to *leave.*
TICKET OFFICE
Leave? Without telling us. I *cannot* see Grace doing that.
Me neither.
You got a little something.
Yeah, it's...it's getting pretty chocolatey out here.
I think things are gonna get a lot stickier before we figure out what's going on.
This is all making me super worried about Grace.
If even people who work here are getting trapped on rides, bombarded by liquid, chocolatey goodness... what if something's happening to her?

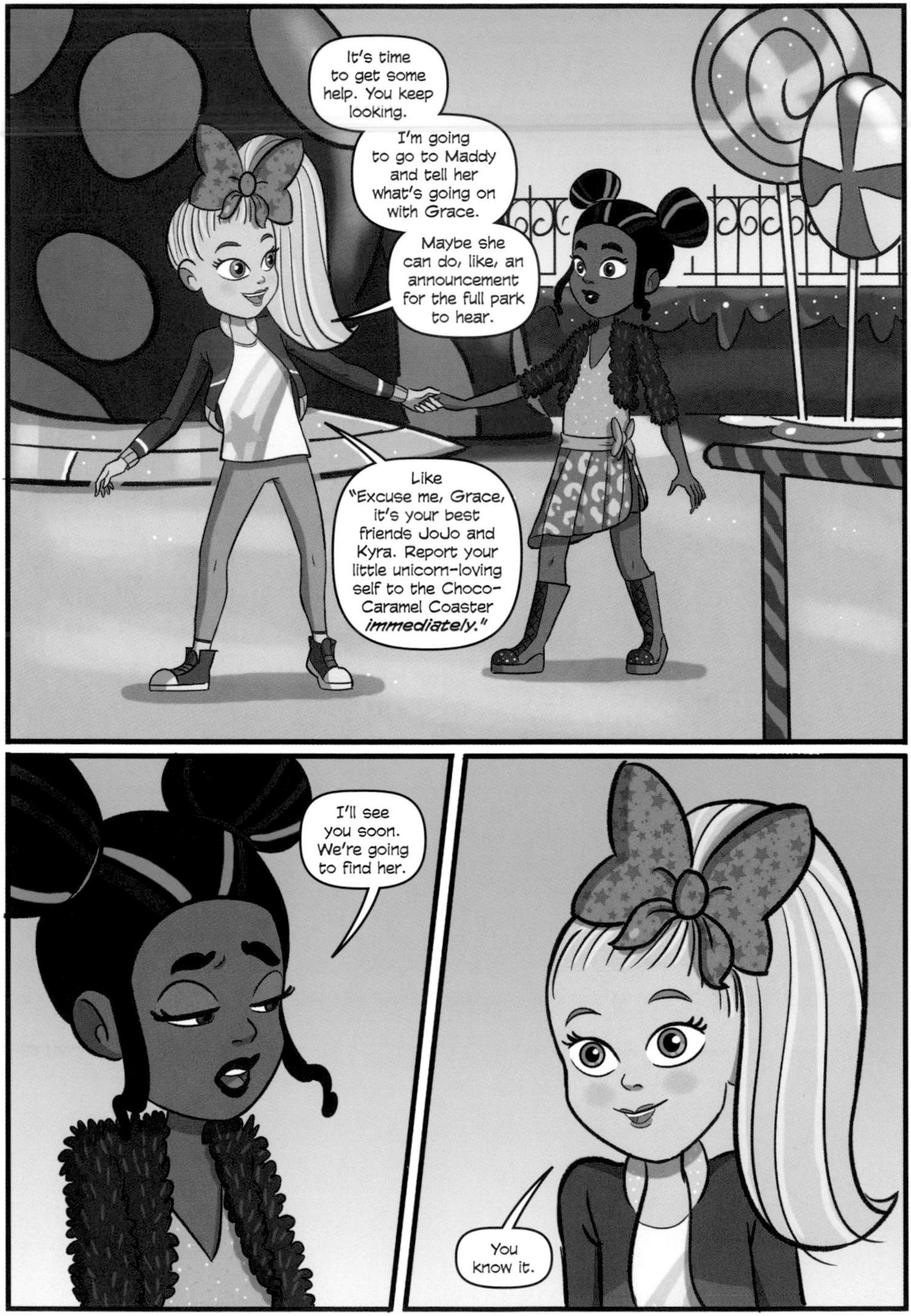
It's time to get some help. You keep looking.
I'm going to go to Maddy and tell her what's going on with Grace.
Maybe she can do, like, an announcement for the full park to hear.
Like "Excuse me, Grace, it's your best friends JoJo and Kyra. Report your little unicorn-loving self to the Choco-Caramel Coaster *immediately*."
I'll see you soon. We're going to find her.
You know it.

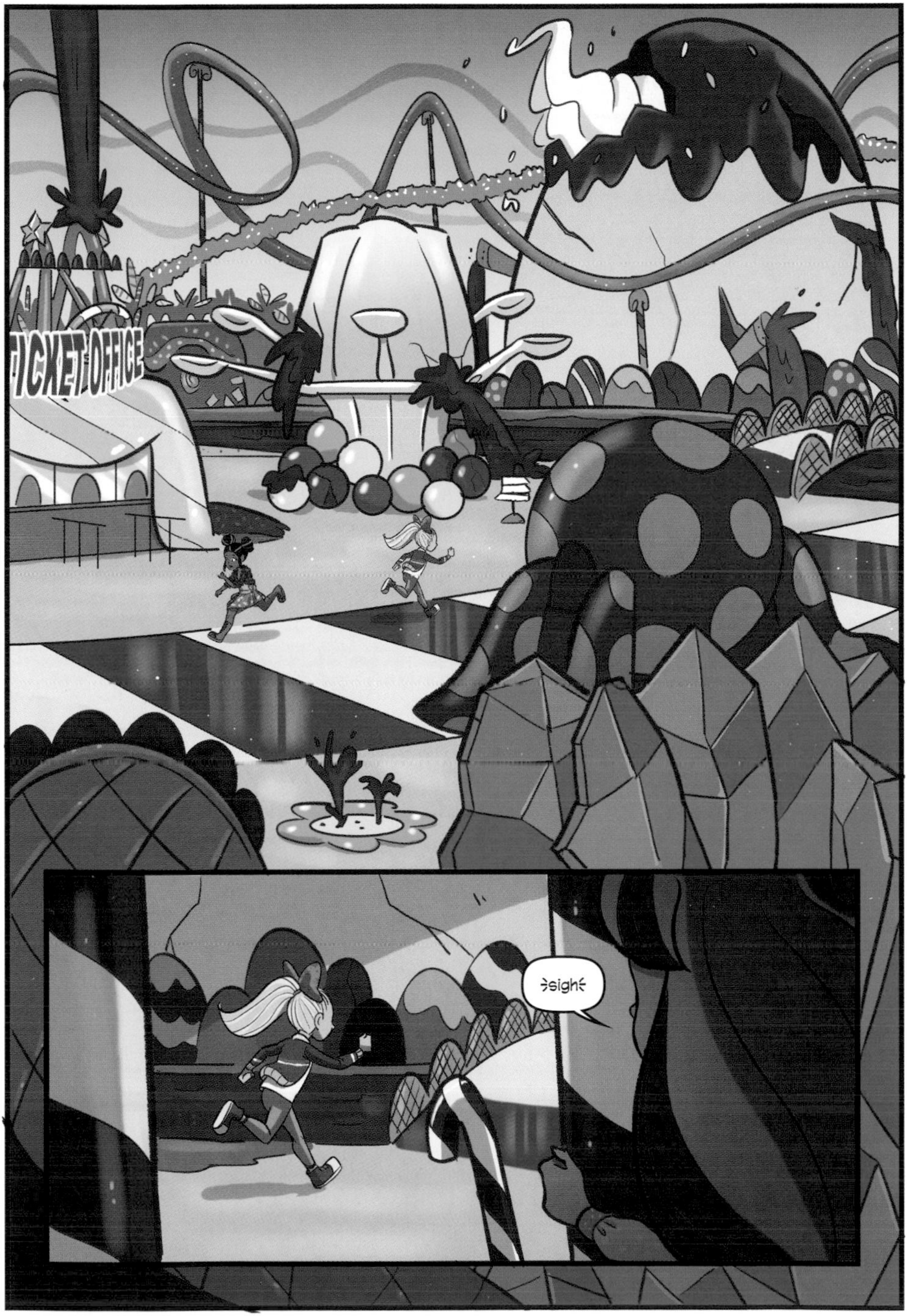
TICKET OFFICE
⸗sigh⸗

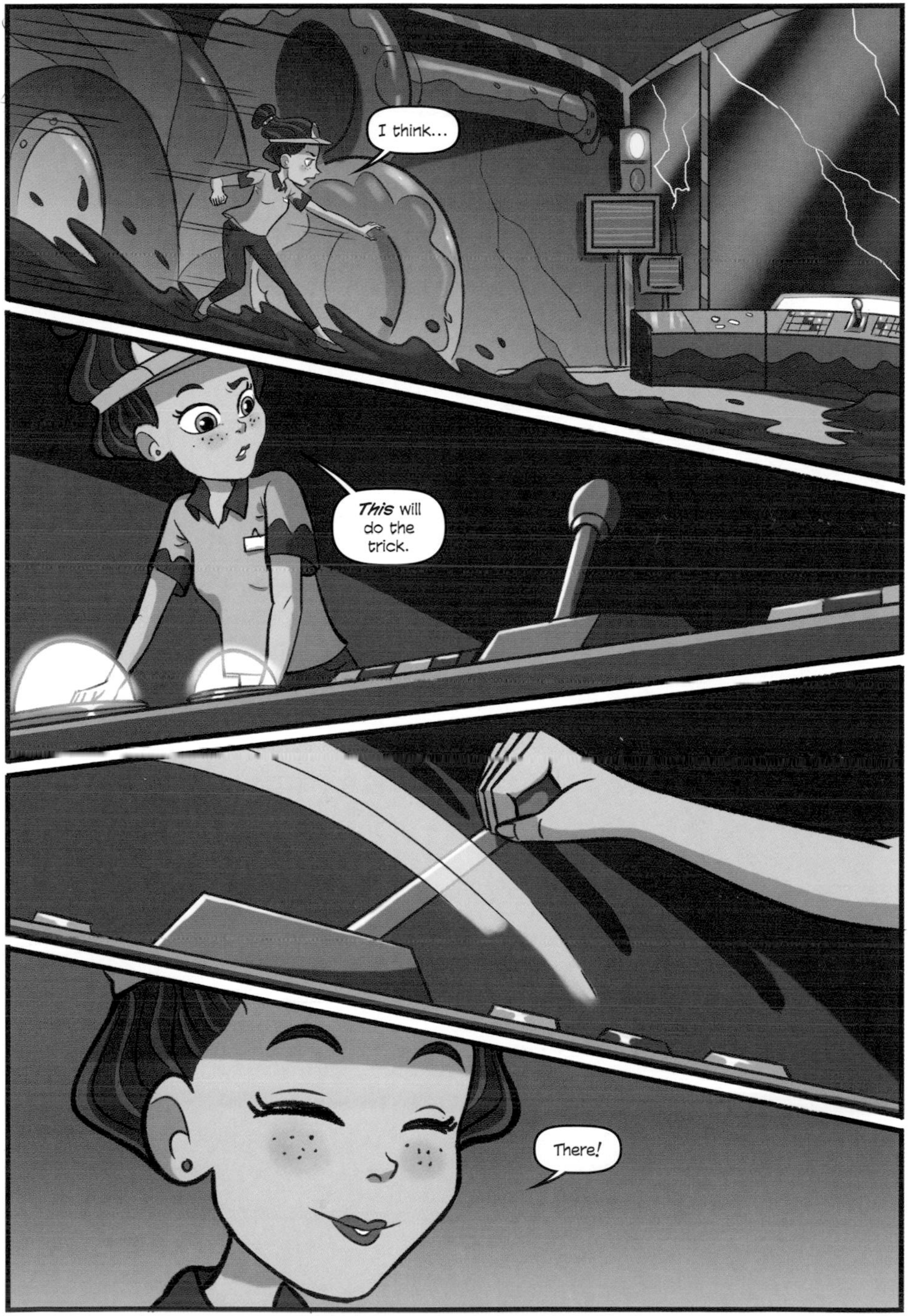
I think...
This will do the trick.
There!

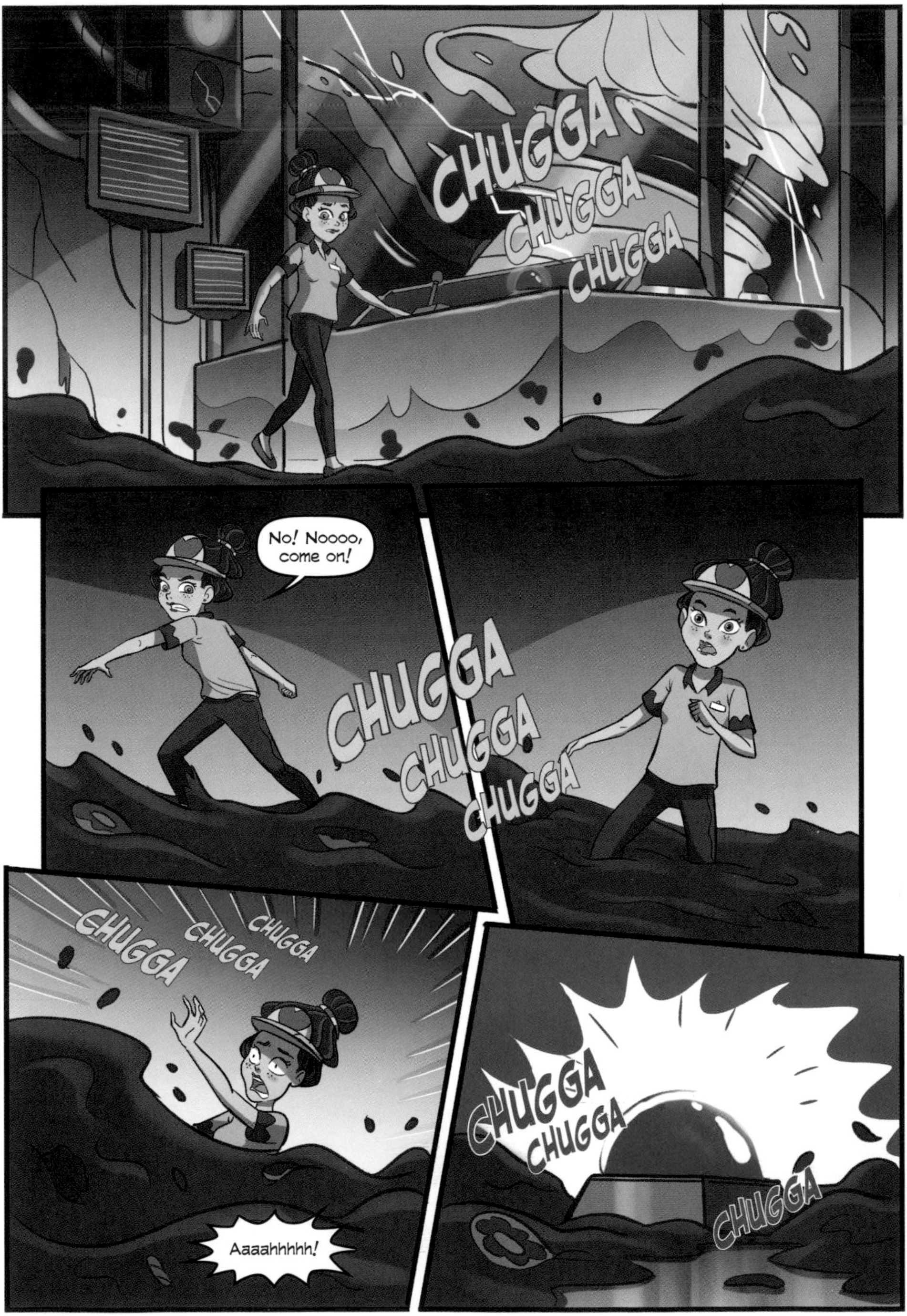

CHUGGA
CHUGGA
CHUGGA
No! Noooo, come on!
CHUGGA
CHUGGA
CHUGGA
CHUGGA
CHUGGA
CHUGGA
Aaaahhhhh!
CHUGGA
CHUGGA
CHUGGA

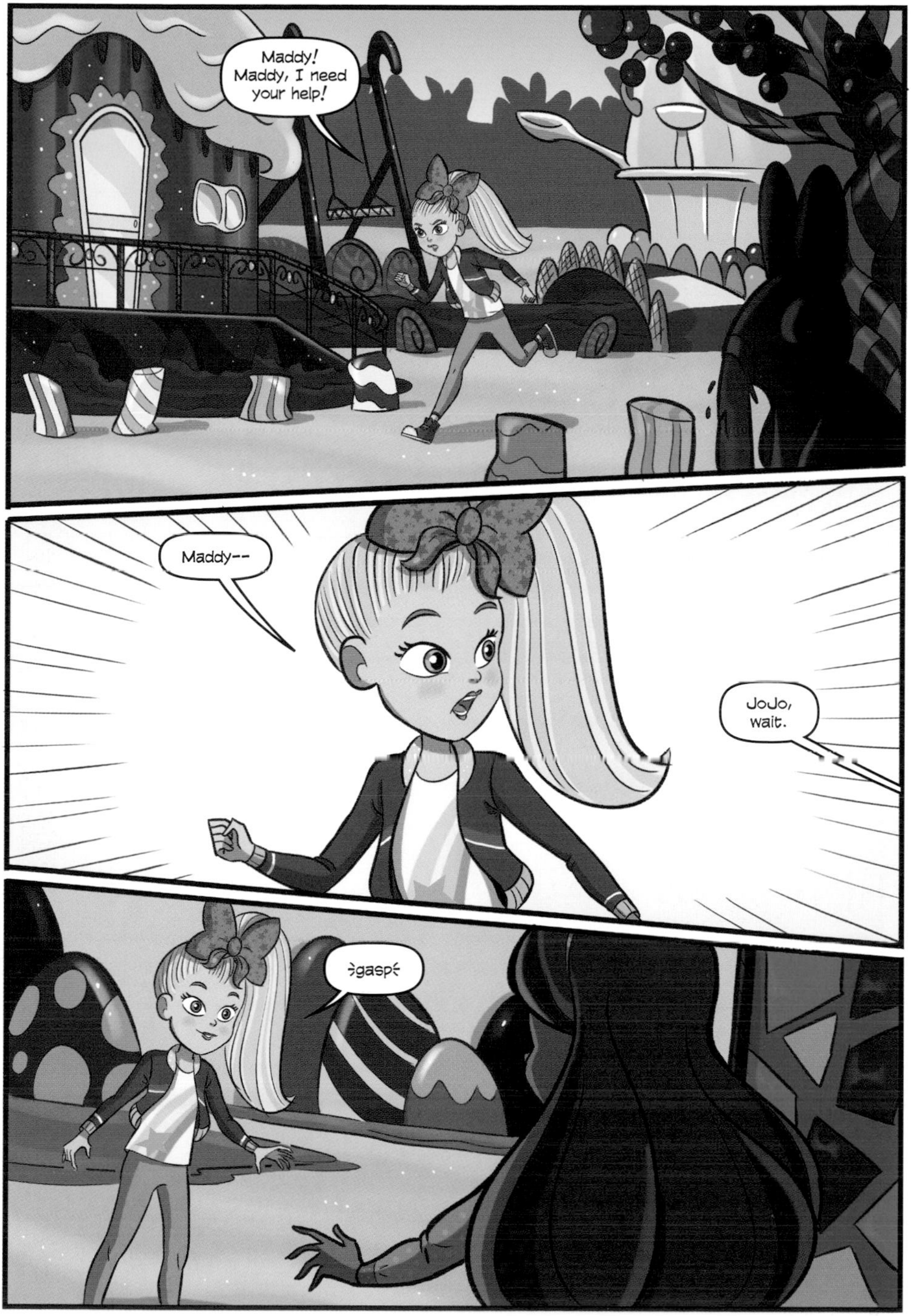
Maddy! Maddy, I need your help!
Maddy--
JoJo, wait.
≻gasp≺

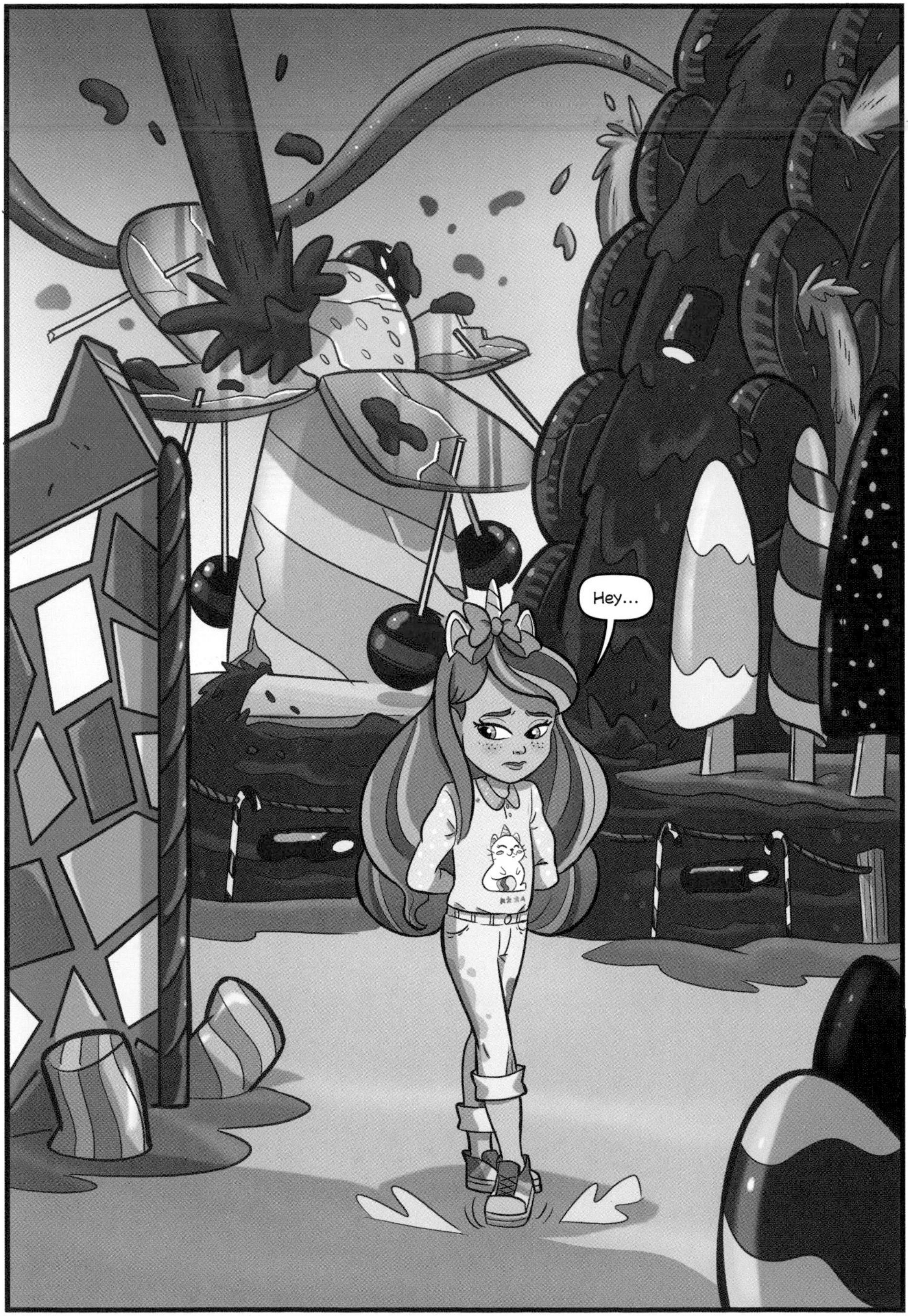
Hey...

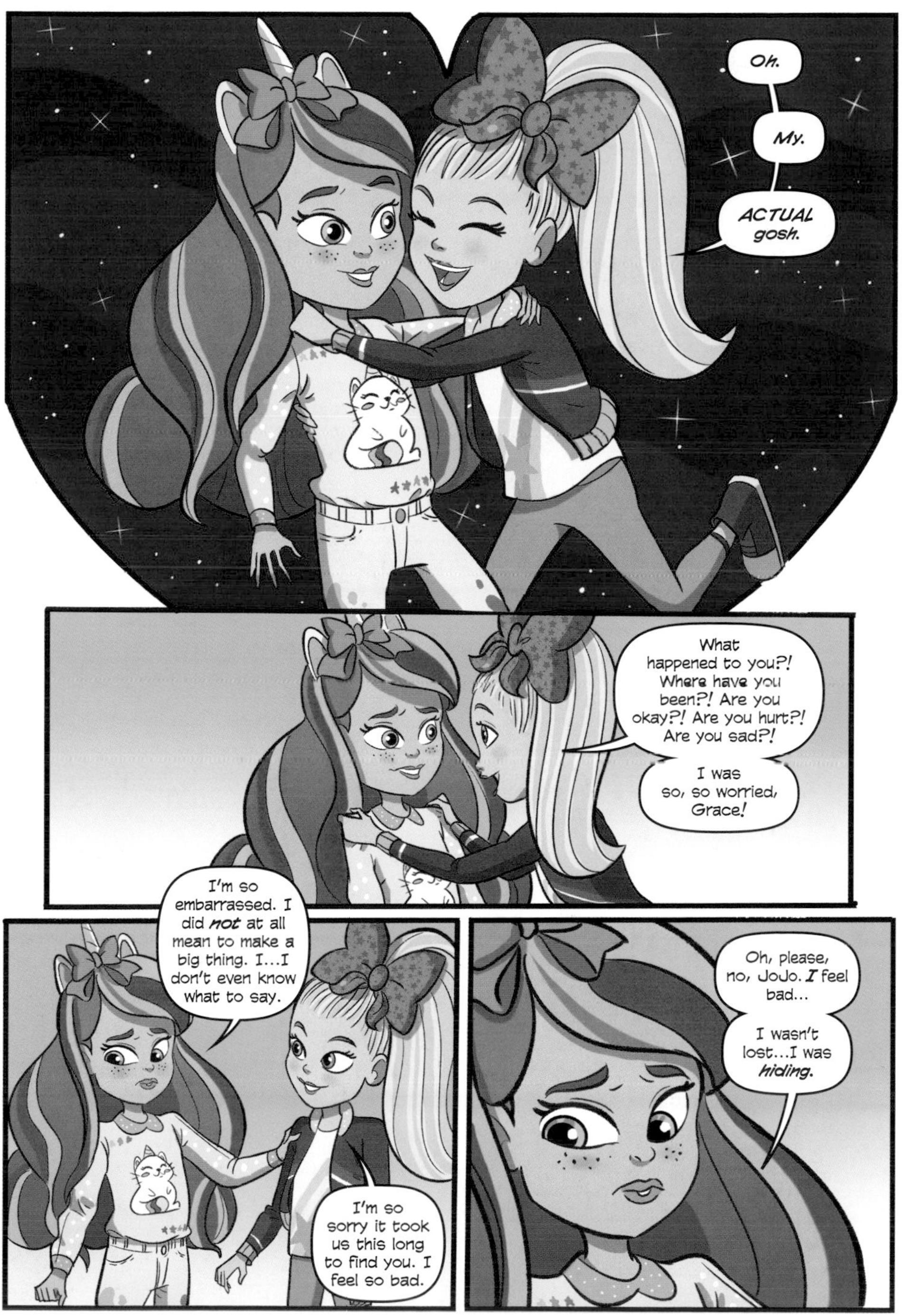
Oh.
My.
ACTUAL gosh.
What happened to you?! Where have you been?! Are you okay?! Are you hurt?! Are you sad?!
I was so, so worried, Grace!
I'm so embarrassed. I did *not* at all mean to make a big thing. I...I don't even know what to say.
I'm so sorry it took us this long to find you. I feel so bad.
Oh, please, no, JoJo. *I* feel bad...
I wasn't lost...I was *hiding*.

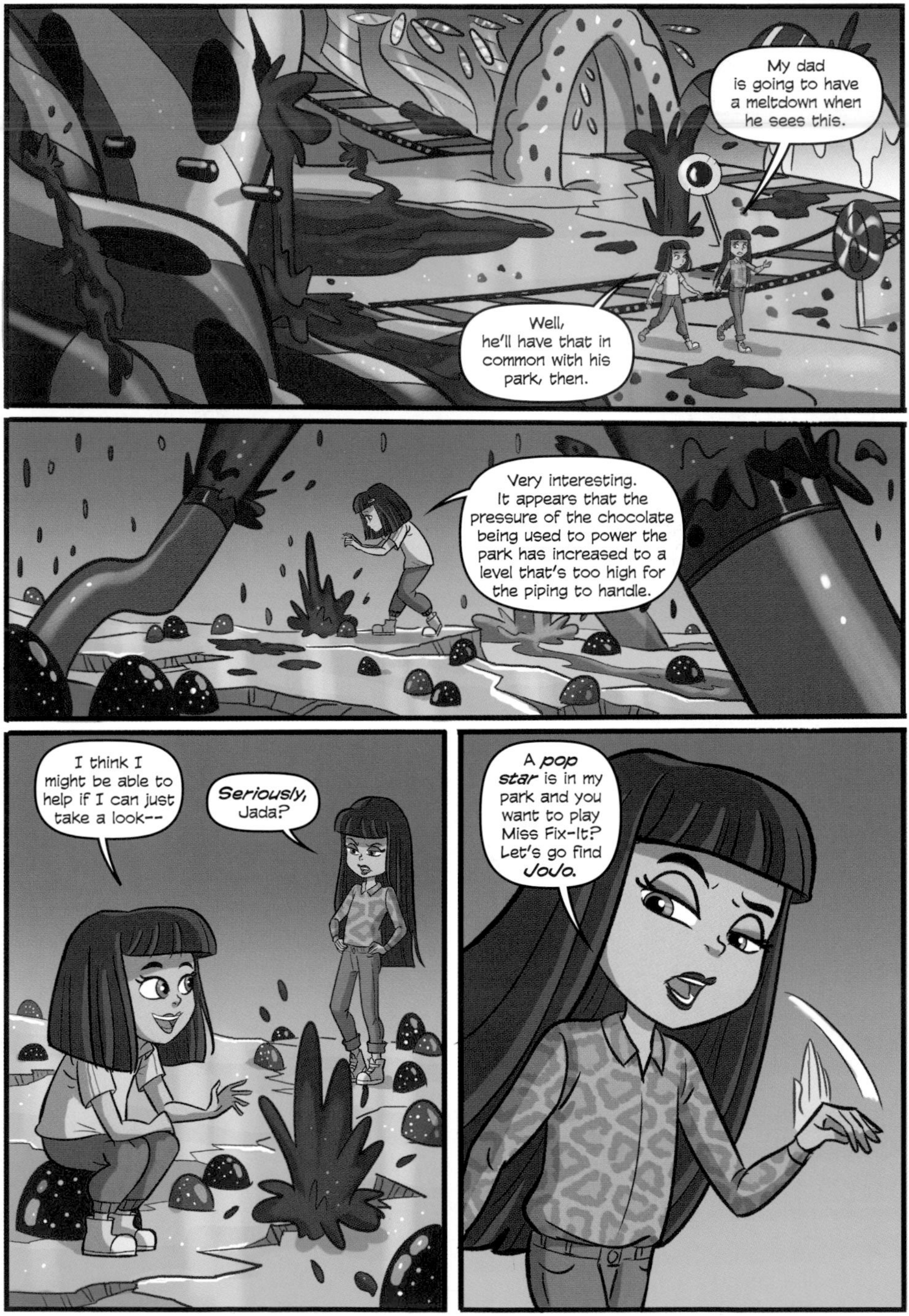
My dad is going to have a meltdown when he sees this.
Well, he'll have that in common with his park, then.
Very interesting. It appears that the pressure of the chocolate being used to power the park has increased to a level that's too high for the piping to handle.
I think I might be able to help if I can just take a look--
Seriously, Jada?
A *pop star* is in my park and you want to play Miss Fix-It? Let's go find *JoJo.*

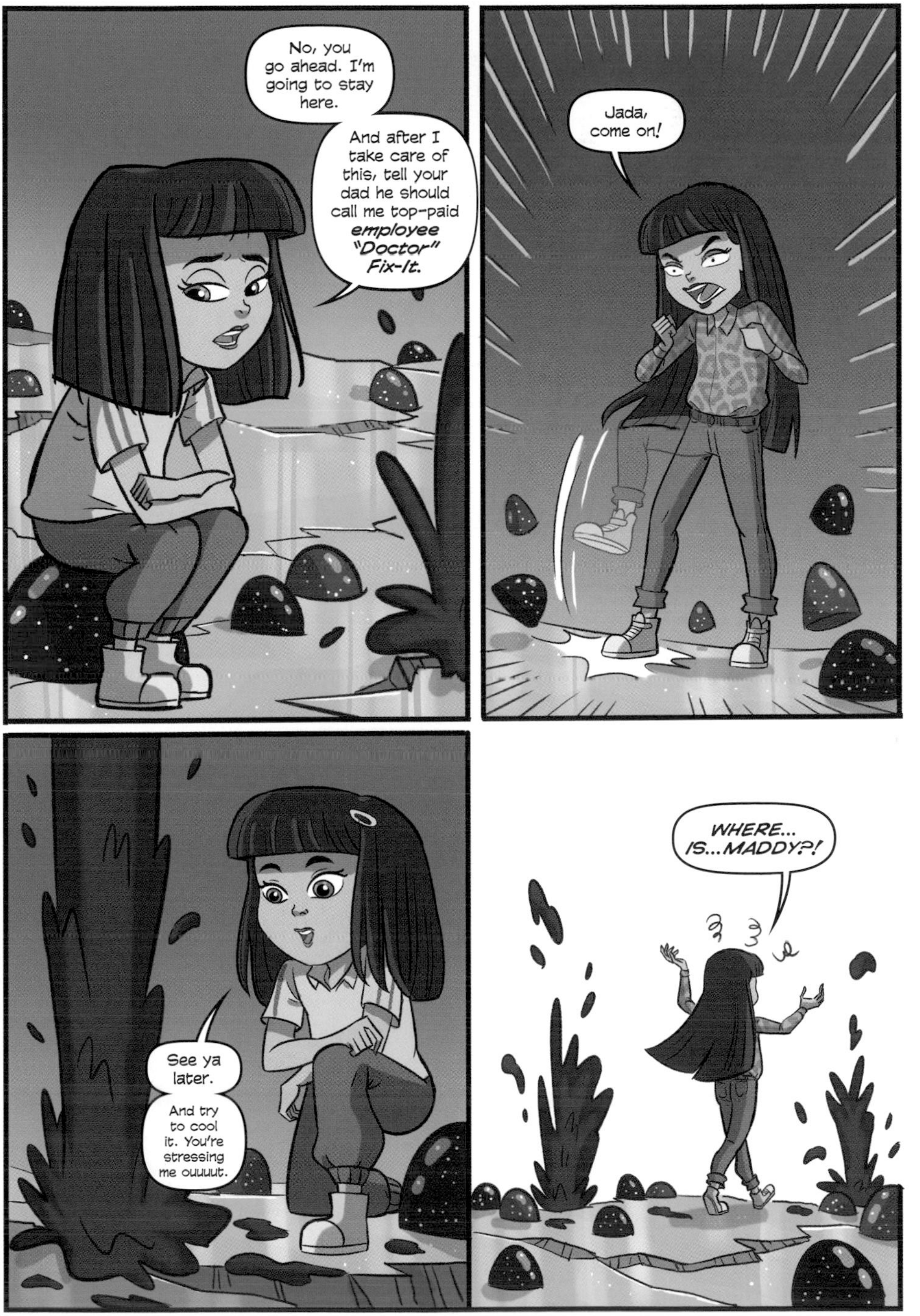
No, you go ahead. I'm going to stay here.
And after I take care of this, tell your dad he should call me top-paid *employee "Doctor" Fix-It.*
Jada, come on!
See ya later.
And try to cool it. You're stressing me ouuuut.
WHERE... IS...MADDY?!

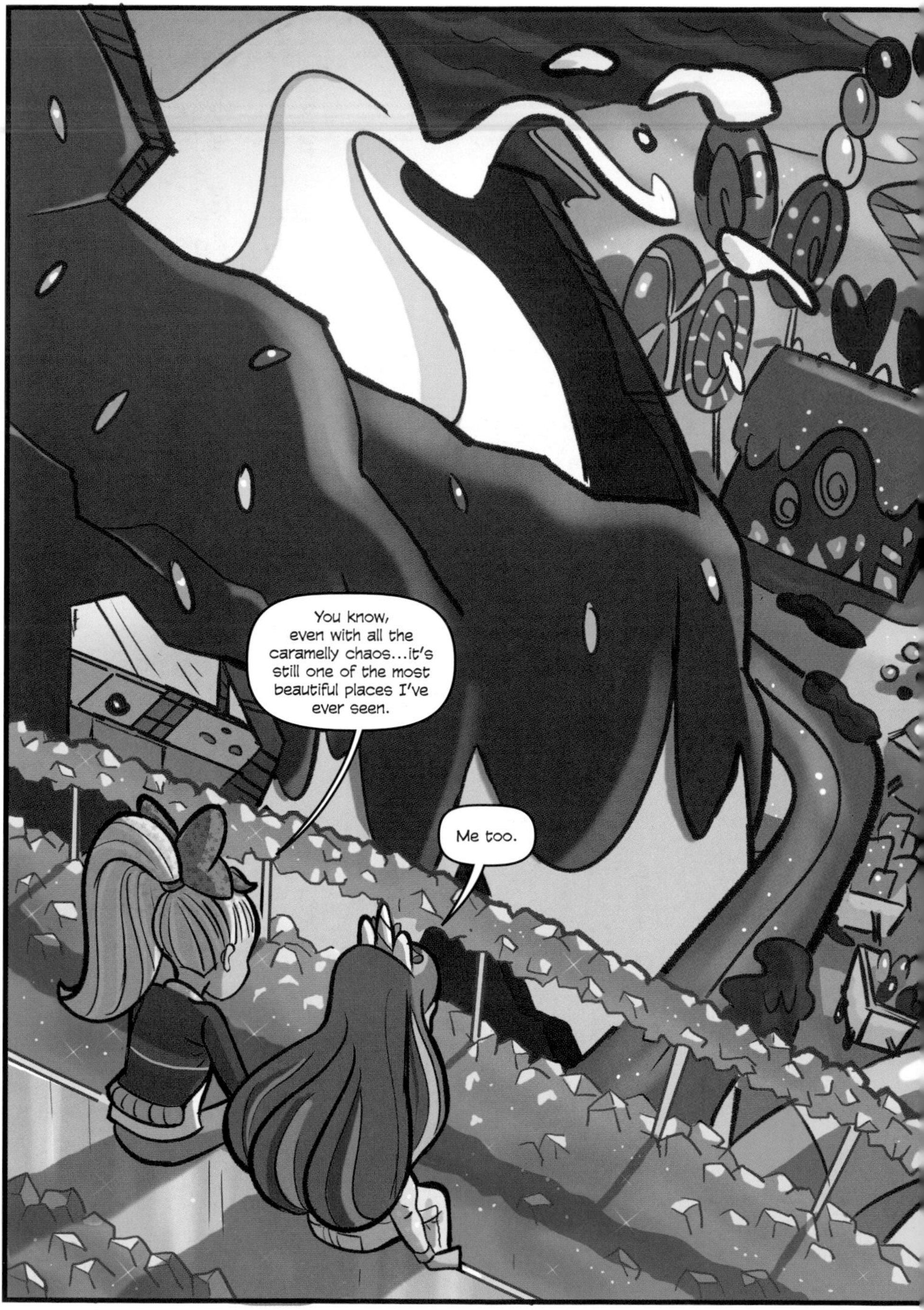
You know, even with all the caramelly chaos...it's still one of the most beautiful places I've ever seen.
Me too.

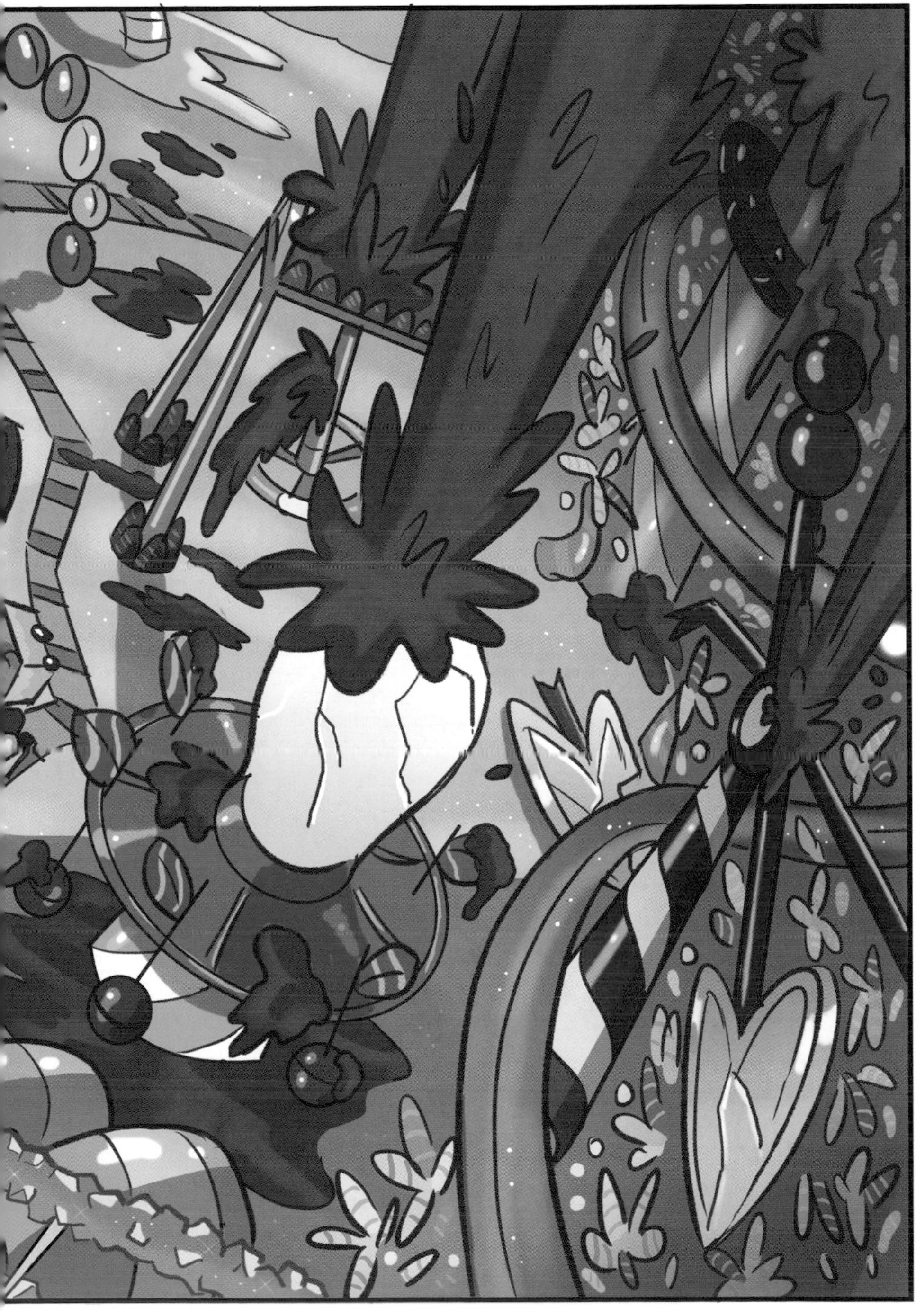

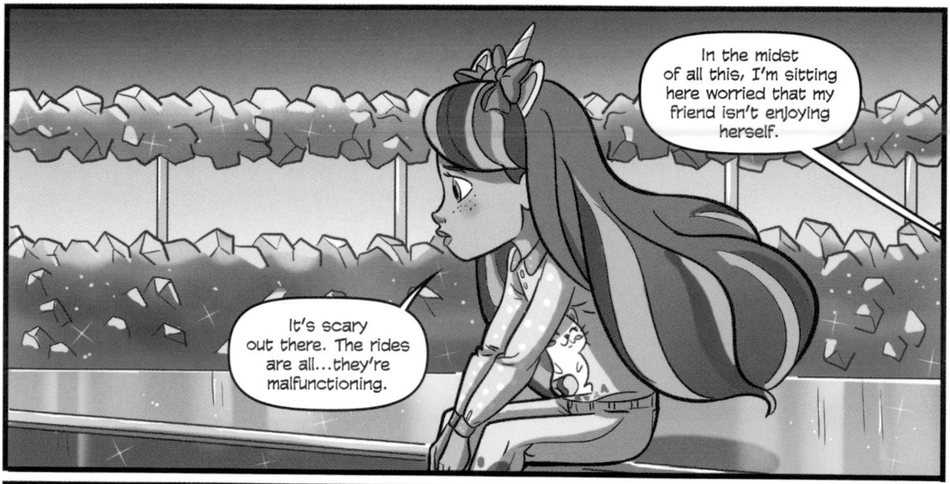
In the midst of all this, I'm sitting here worried that my friend isn't enjoying herself.
It's scary out there. The rides are all...they're malfunctioning.

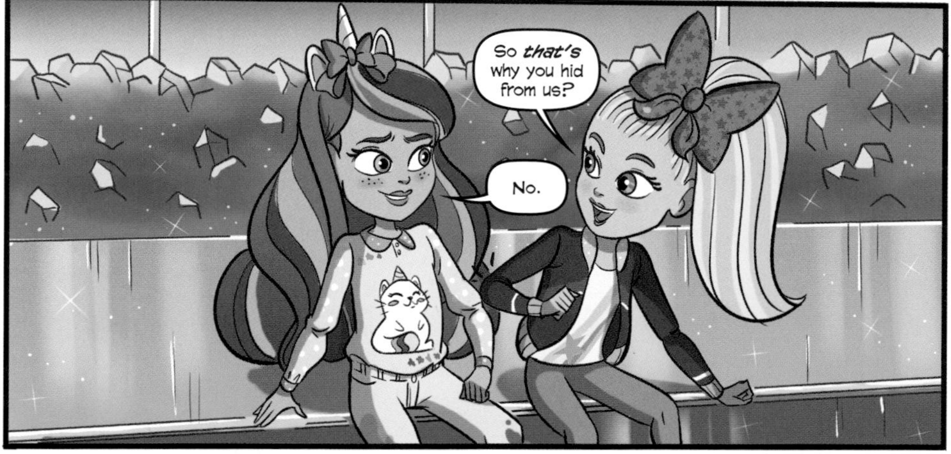
So *that's* why you hid from us?
No.

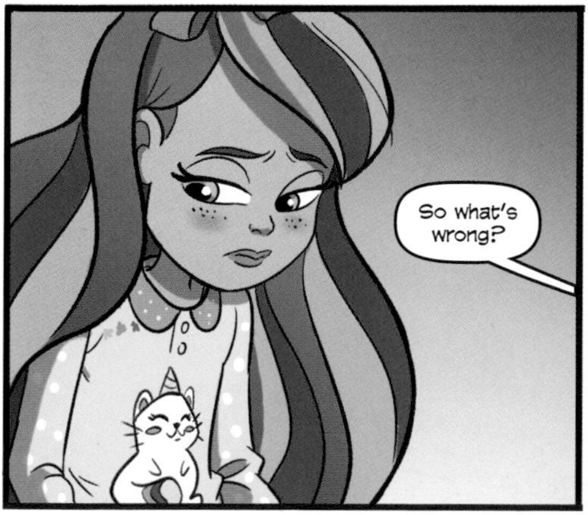
So what's wrong?

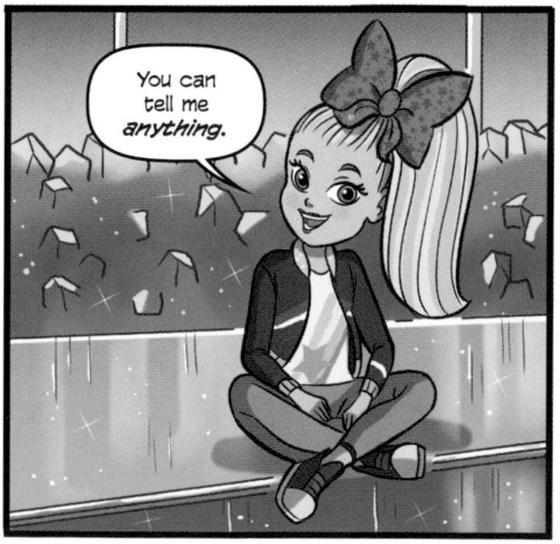
You can tell me *anything*.

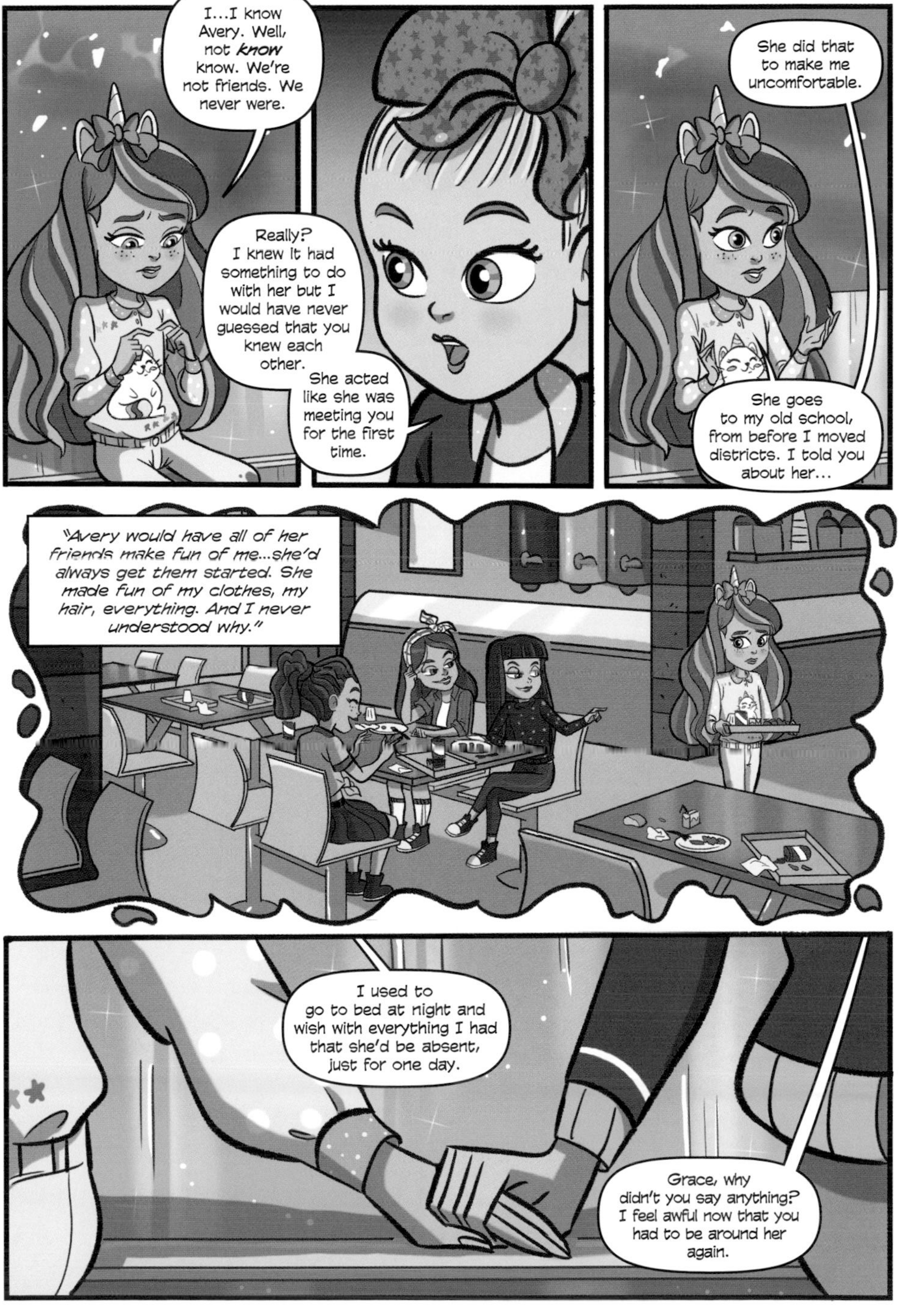

I...I know Avery. Well, not *know* know. We're not friends. We never were.
Really? I knew it had something to do with her but I would have never guessed that you knew each other.
She acted like she was meeting you for the first time.
She did that to make me uncomfortable.
She goes to my old school, from before I moved districts. I told you about her...
"Avery would have all of her friends make fun of me...she'd always get them started. She made fun of my clothes, my hair, everything. And I never understood why."
I used to go to bed at night and wish with everything I had that she'd be absent, just for one day.
Grace, why didn't you say anything? I feel awful now that you had to be around her again.

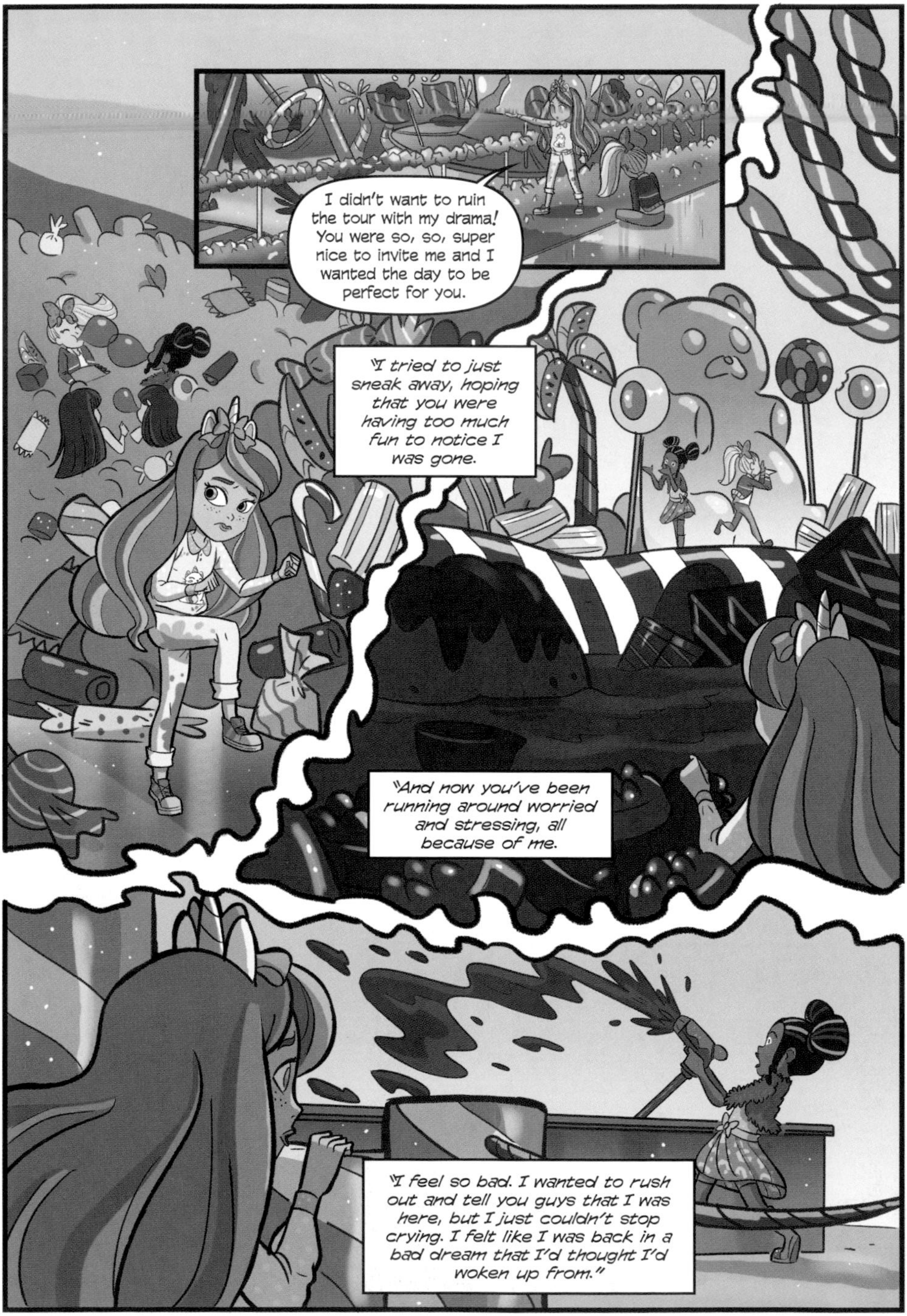

I didn't want to ruin the tour with my drama! You were so, so, super nice to invite me and I wanted the day to be perfect for you.
"I tried to just sneak away, hoping that you were having too much fun to notice I was gone.
"And now you've been running around worried and stressing, all because of me.
"I feel so bad. I wanted to rush out and tell you guys that I was here, but I just couldn't stop crying. I felt like I was back in a bad dream that I'd thought I'd woken up from."

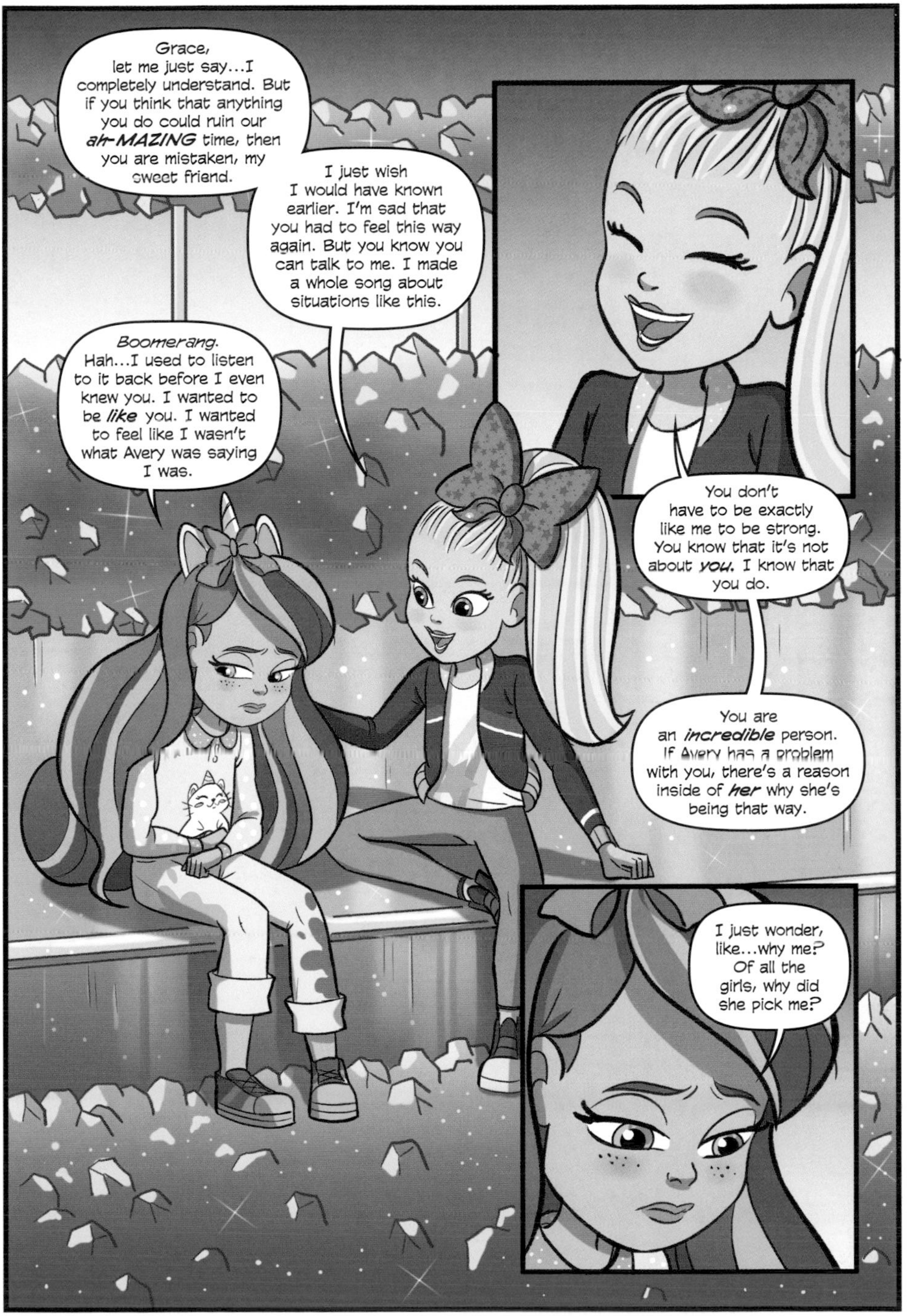

Grace, let me just say...I completely understand. But if you think that anything you do could ruin our ah-MAZING time, then you are mistaken, my sweet friend.
I just wish I would have known earlier. I'm sad that you had to feel this way again. But you know you can talk to me. I made a whole song about situations like this.
Boomerang. Hah...I used to listen to it back before I even knew you. I wanted to be like you. I wanted to feel like I wasn't what Avery was saying I was.
You don't have to be exactly like me to be strong. You know that it's not about you. I know that you do.
You are an incredible person. If Avery has a problem with you, there's a reason inside of her why she's being that way.
I just wonder, like...why me? Of all the girls, why did she pick me?

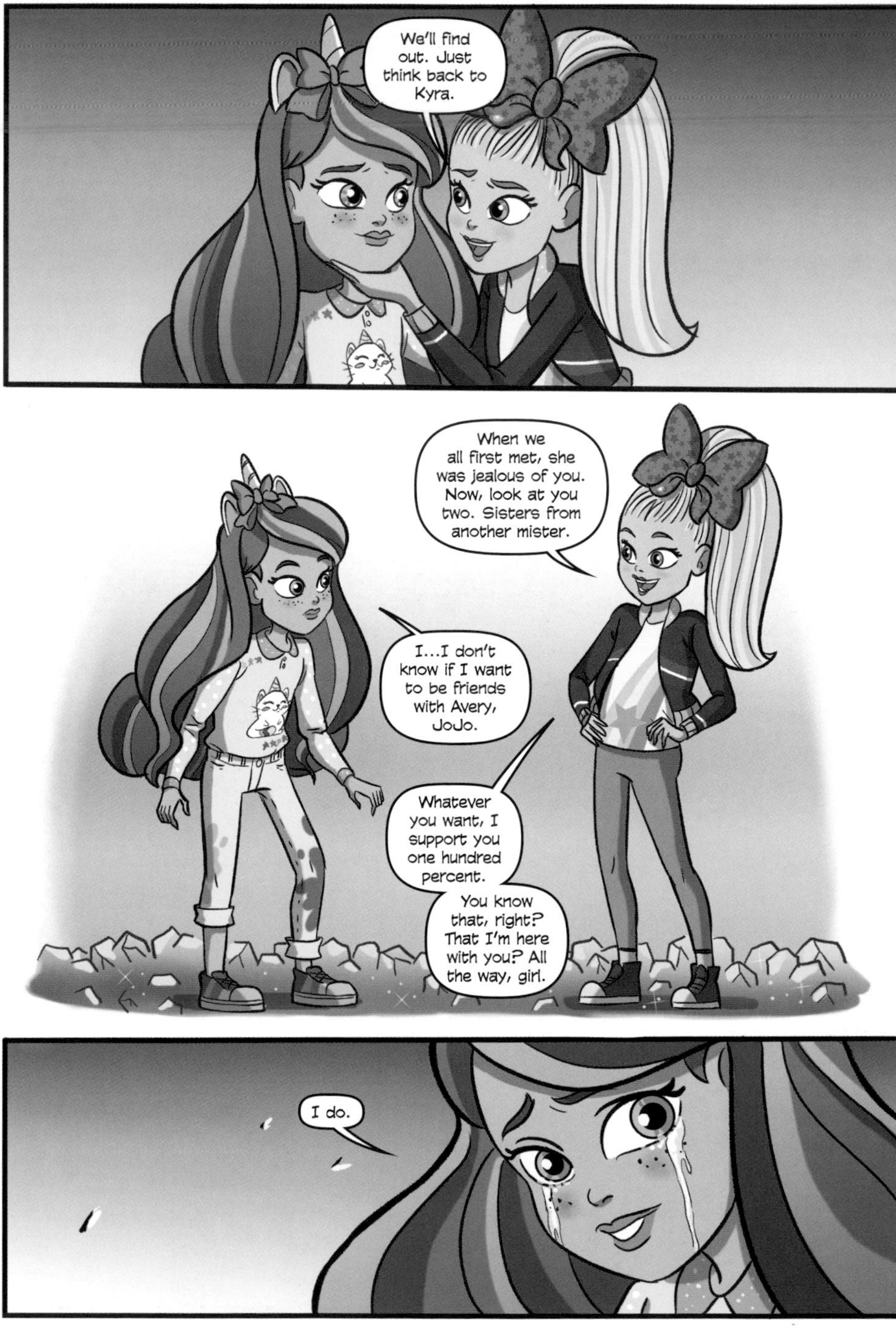
We'll find out. Just think back to Kyra.
When we all first met, she was jealous of you. Now, look at you two. Sisters from another mister.
I...I don't know if I want to be friends with Avery, JoJo.
Whatever you want, I support you one hundred percent.
You know that, right? That I'm here with you? All the way, girl.
I do.

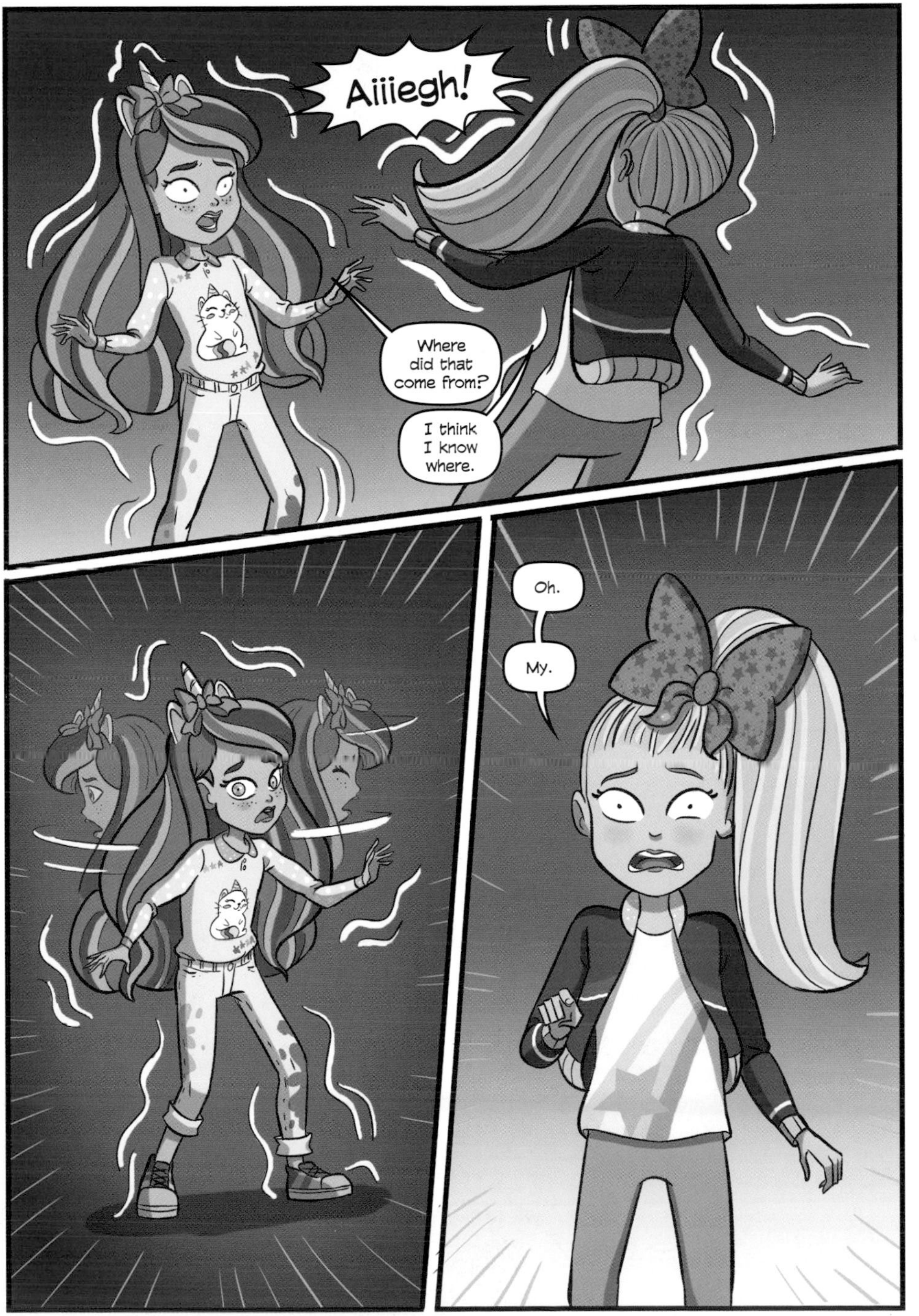
Aiiiegh!
Where did that come from?
I think I know where.
Oh.
My.

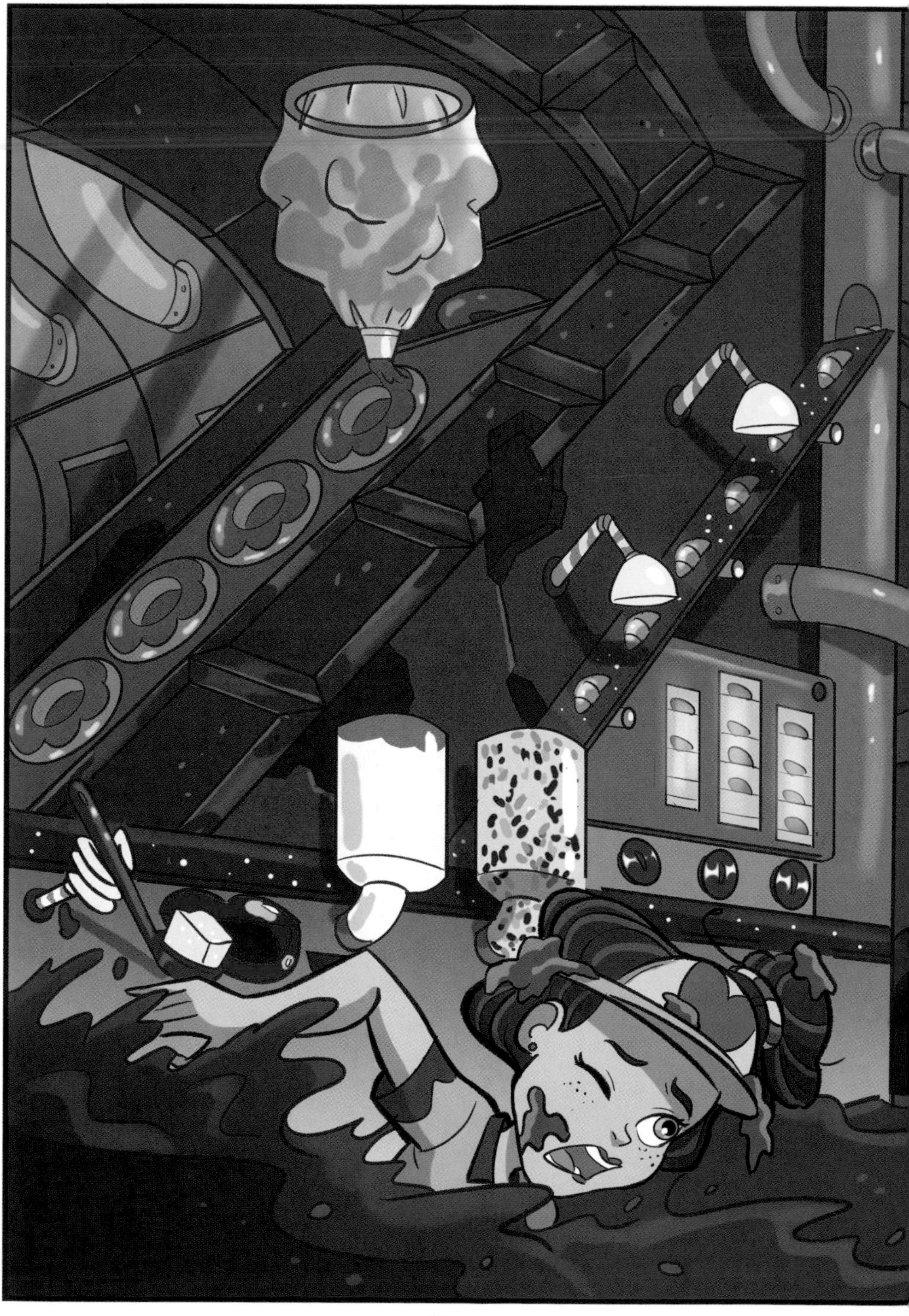

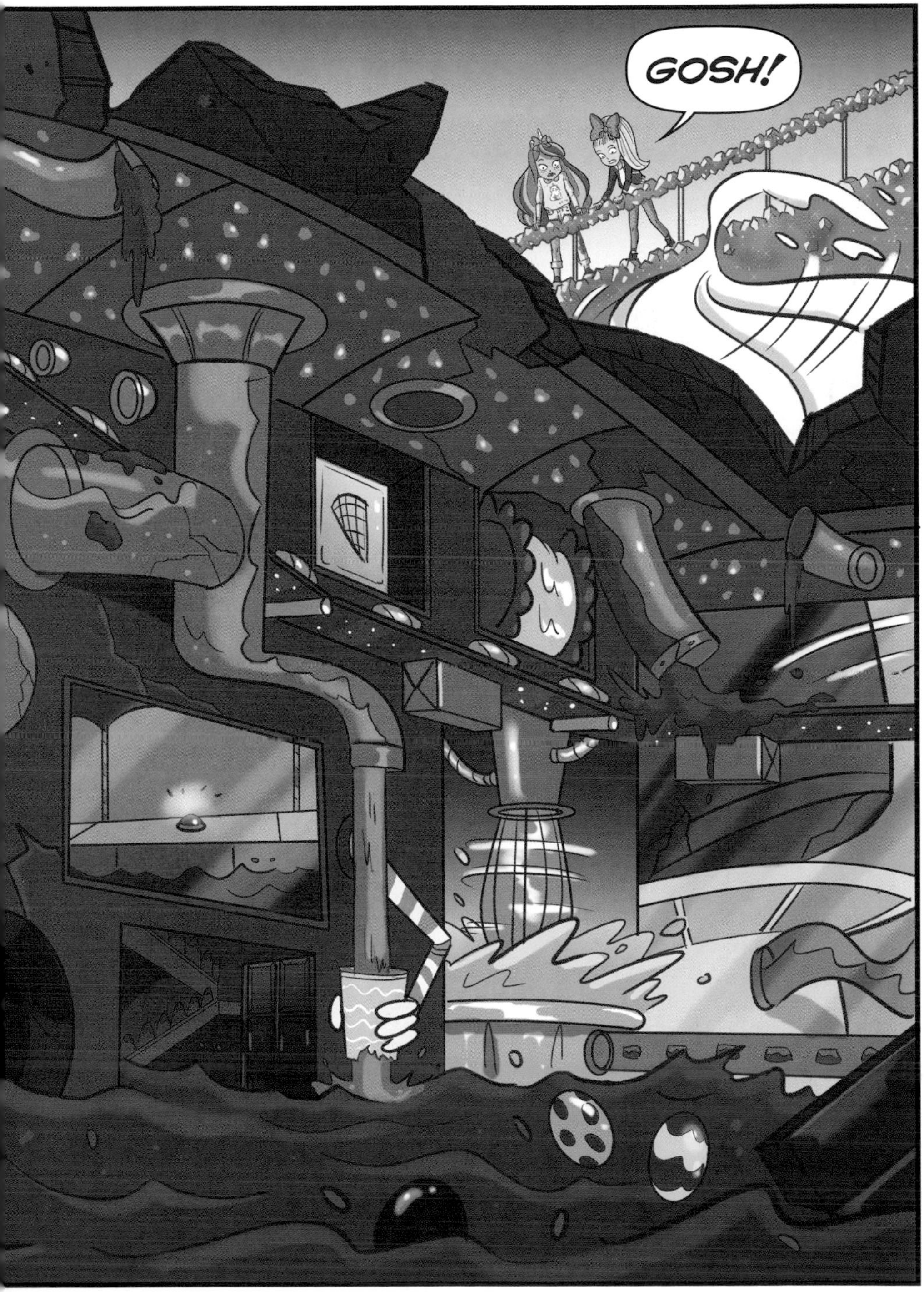
GOSH!

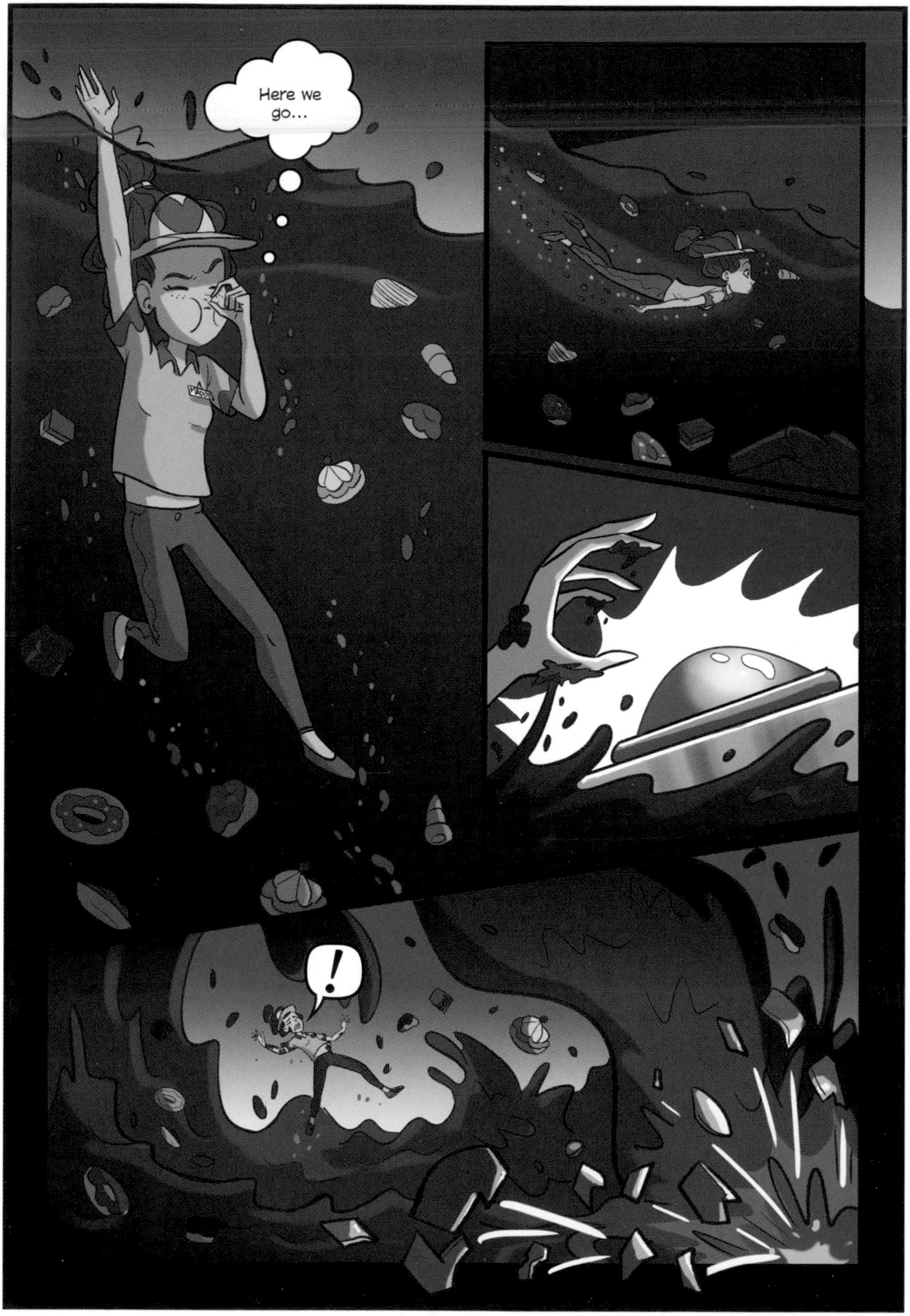

Here we go...
!

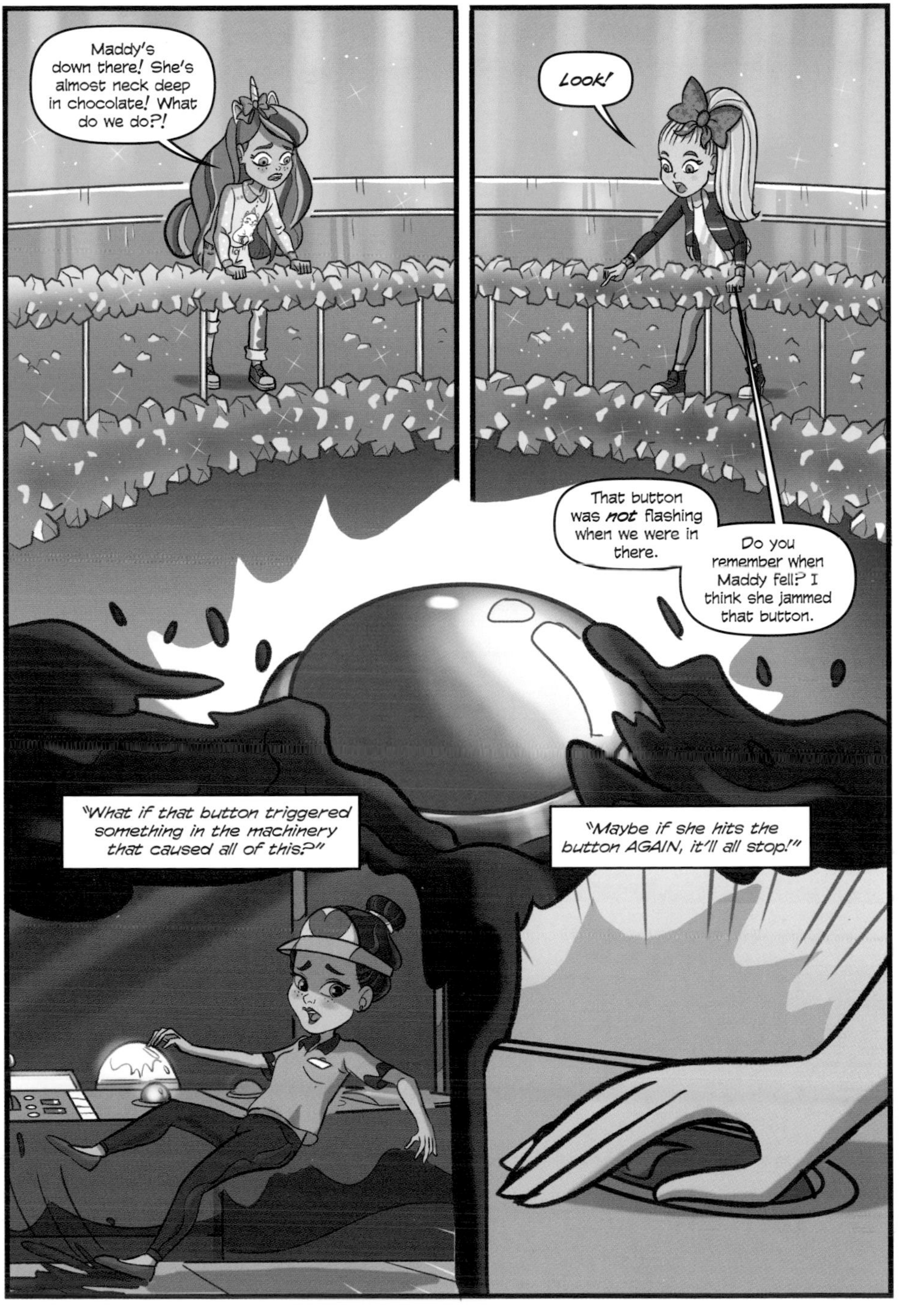

Maddy's down there! She's almost neck deep in chocolate! What do we do?!
Look!
That button was *not* flashing when we were in there.
Do you remember when Maddy fell? I think she jammed that button.
"What if that button triggered something in the machinery that caused all of this?"
"Maybe if she hits the button AGAIN, it'll all stop!"

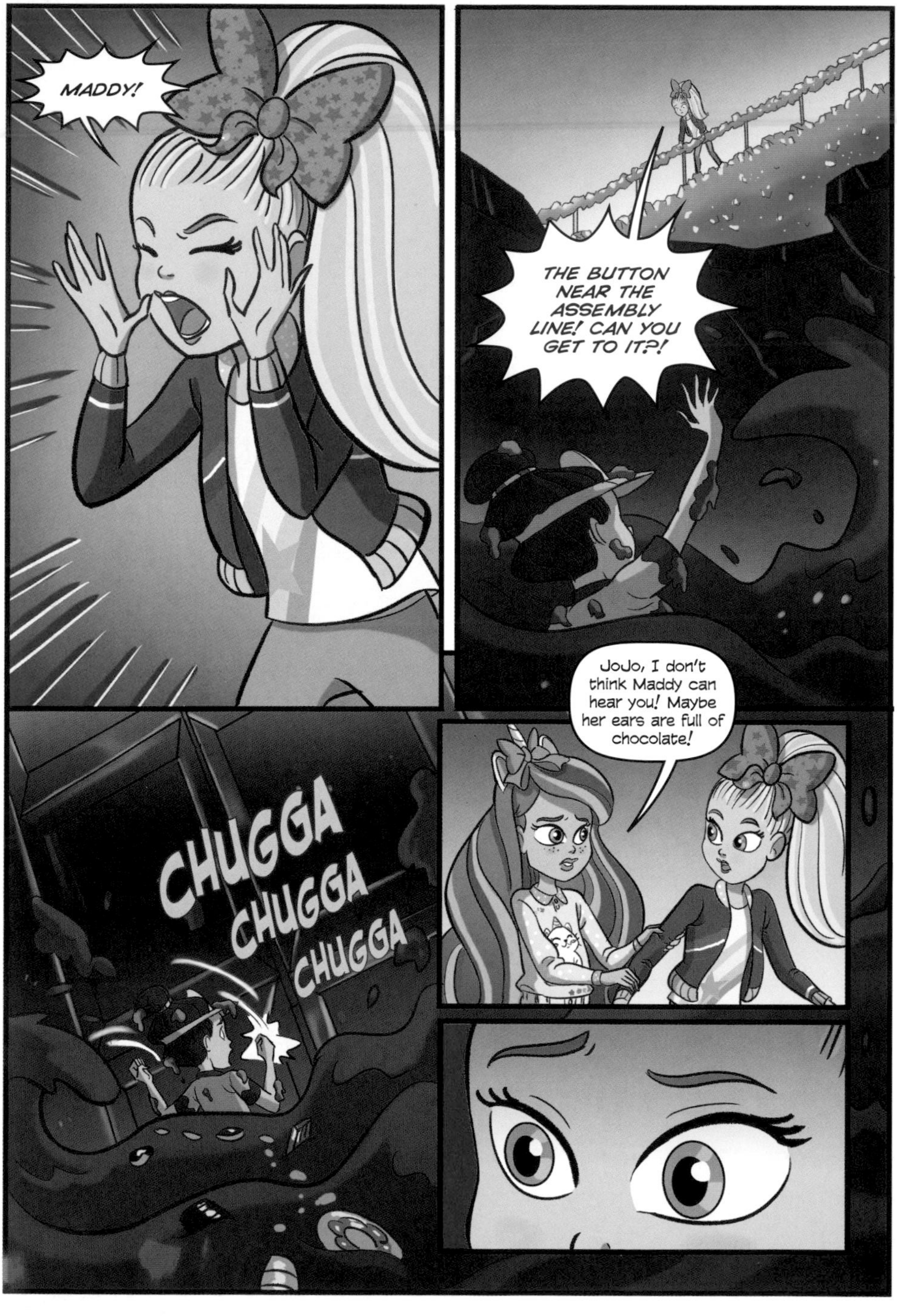
MADDY!
THE BUTTON NEAR THE ASSEMBLY LINE! CAN YOU GET TO IT?!
CHUGGA CHUGGA CHUGGA
JoJo, I don't think Maddy can hear you! Maybe her ears are full of chocolate!

CHAPTER FOUR

JUST DESSERTS

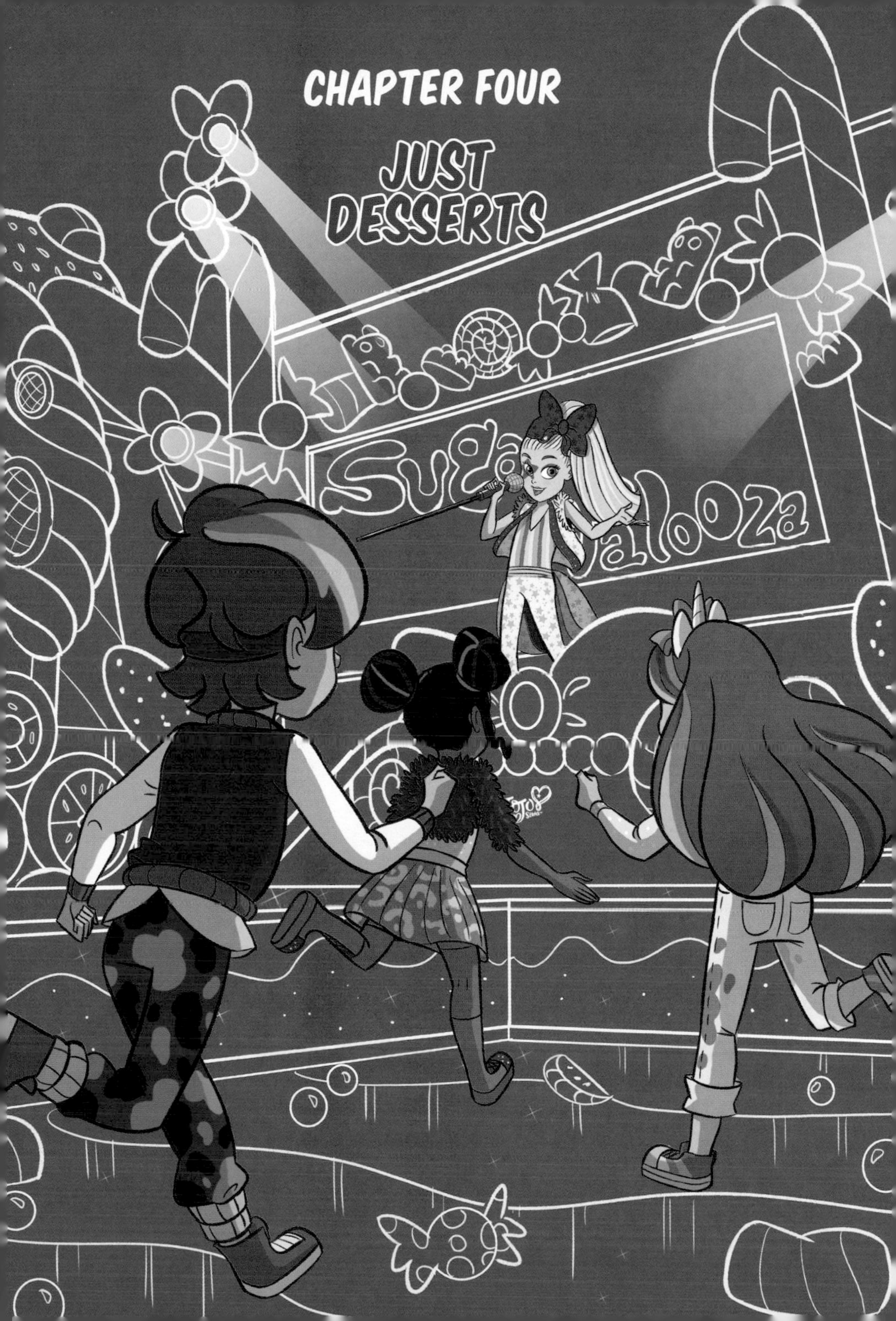

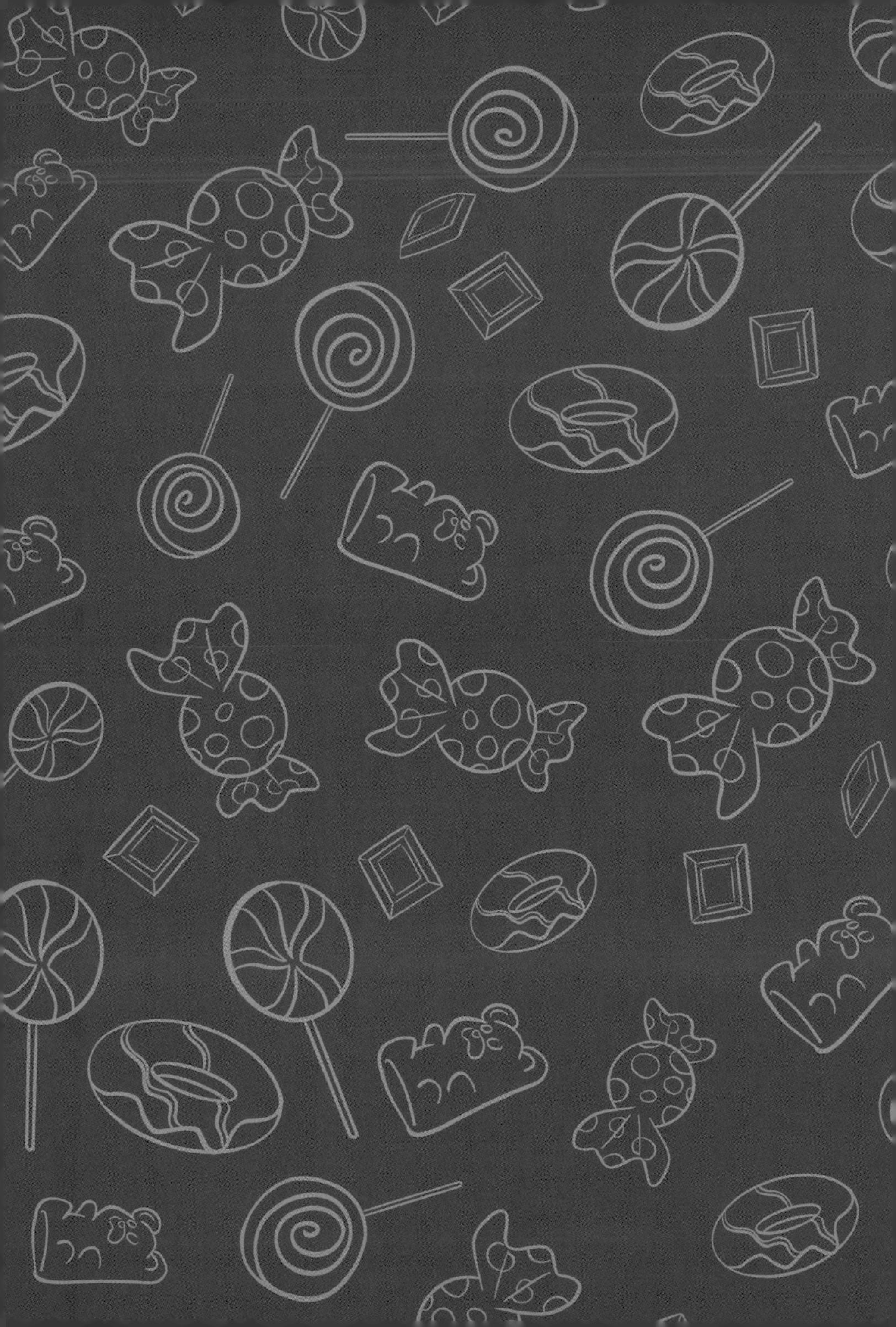

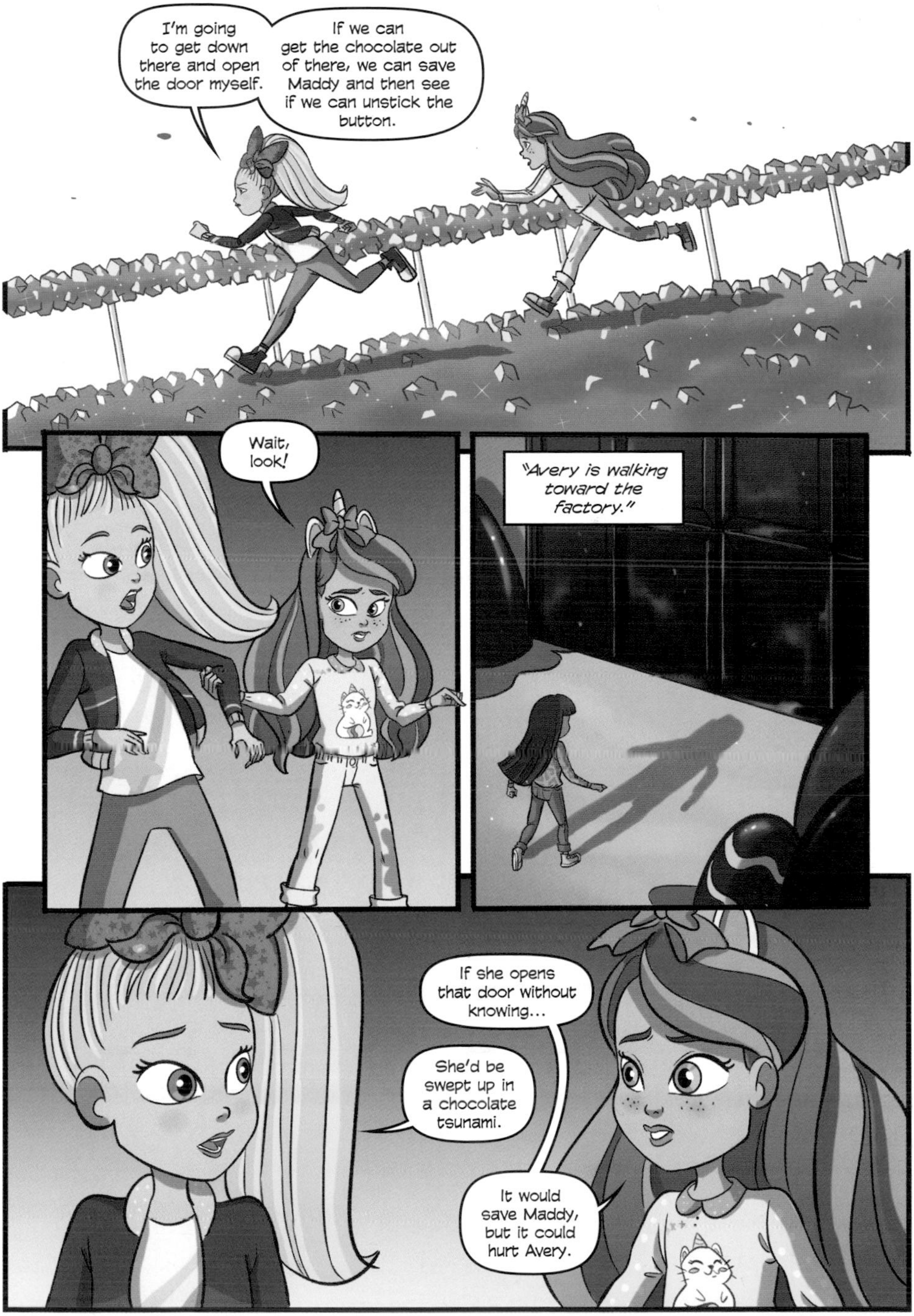

I'm going to get down there and open the door myself.
If we can get the chocolate out of there, we can save Maddy and then see if we can unstick the button.
Wait, look!
"Avery is walking toward the factory."
If she opens that door without knowing...
She'd be swept up in a chocolate tsunami.
It would save Maddy, but it could hurt Avery.

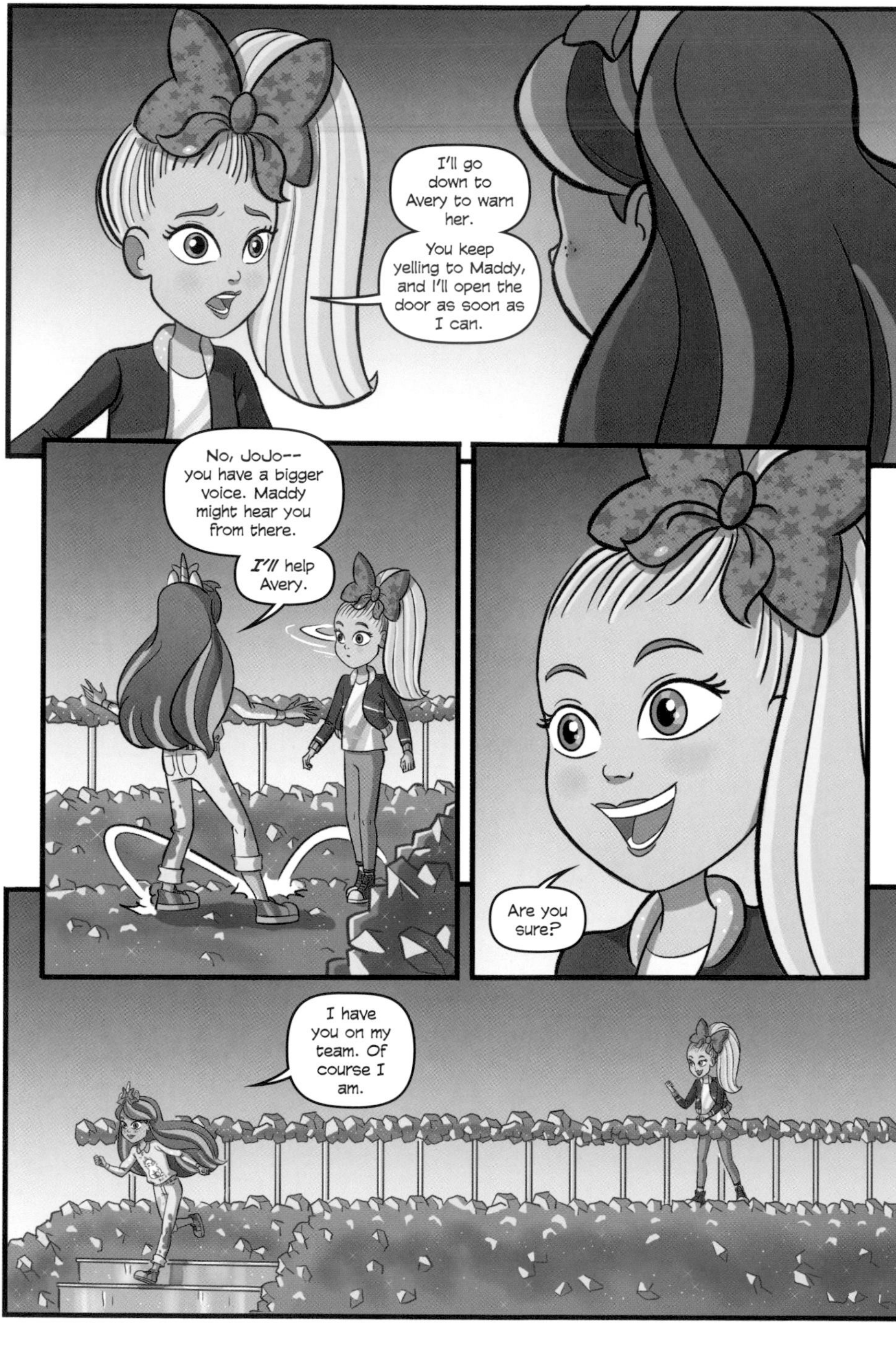
I'll go down to Avery to warn her.
You keep yelling to Maddy, and I'll open the door as soon as I can.
No, JoJo-- you have a bigger voice. Maddy might hear you from there.
I'll help Avery.
Are you sure?
I have you on my team. Of course I am.

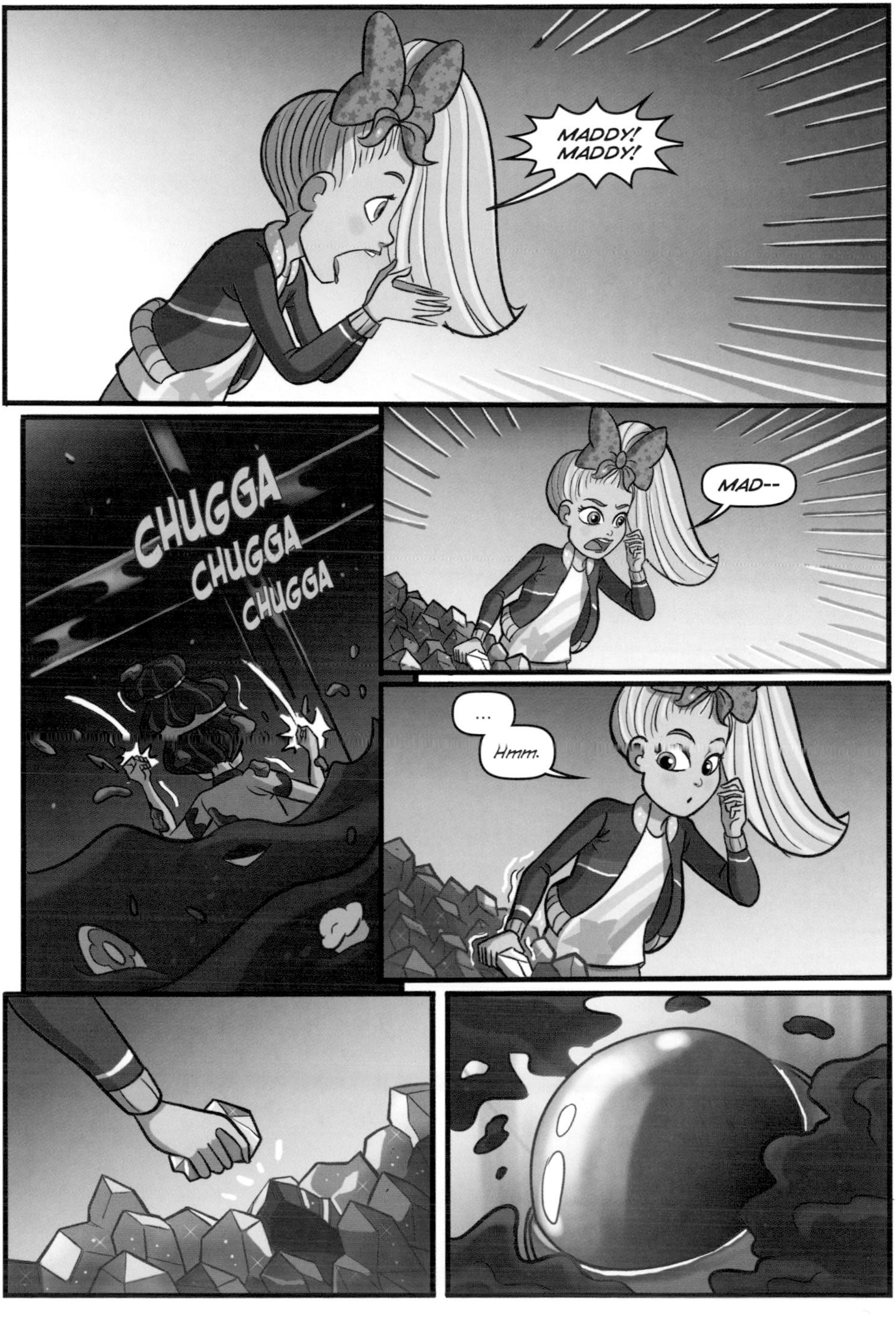

MADDY! MADDY!
CHUGGA
CHUGGA
CHUGGA
MAD--
...
Hmm.

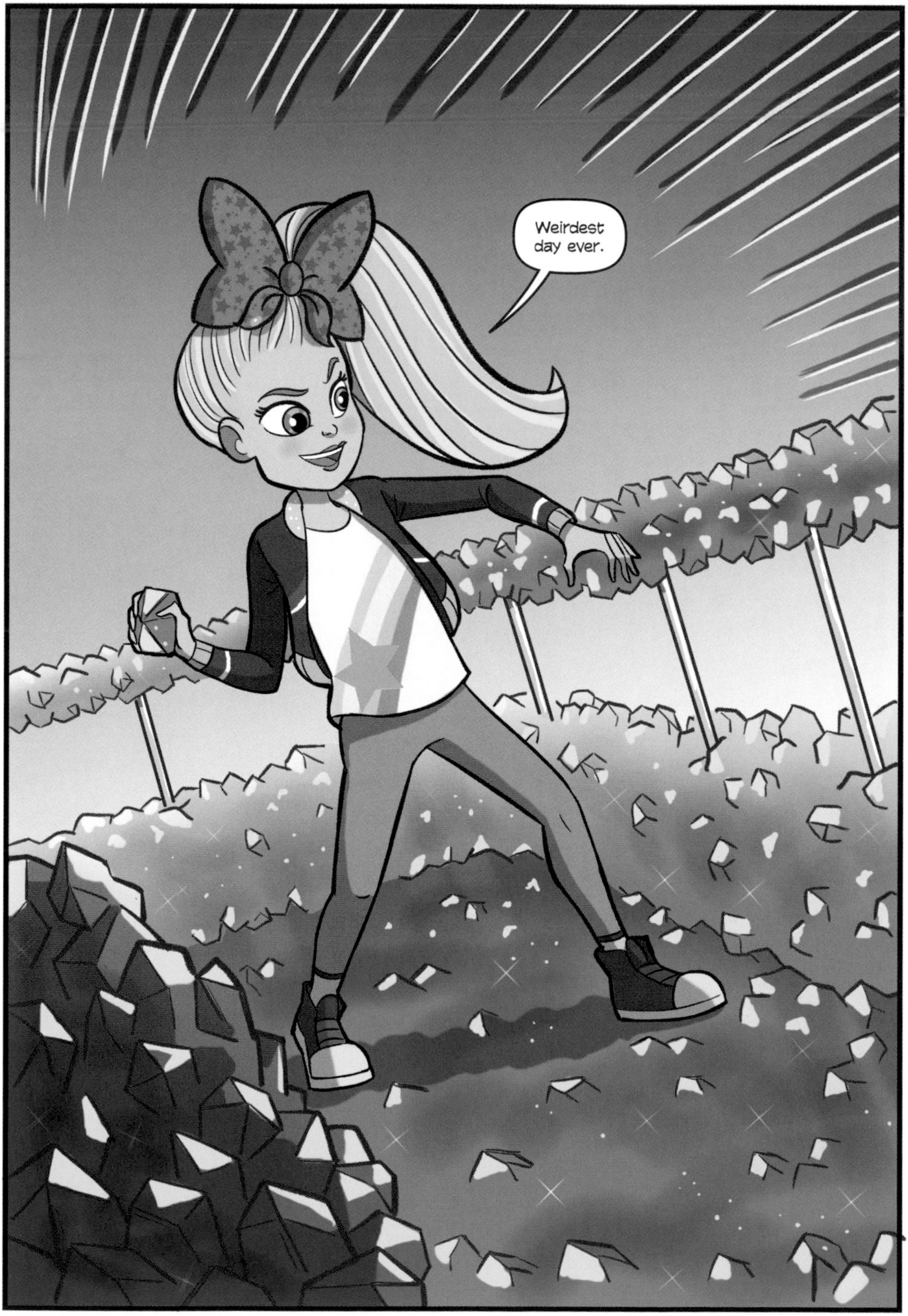
Weirdest day ever.

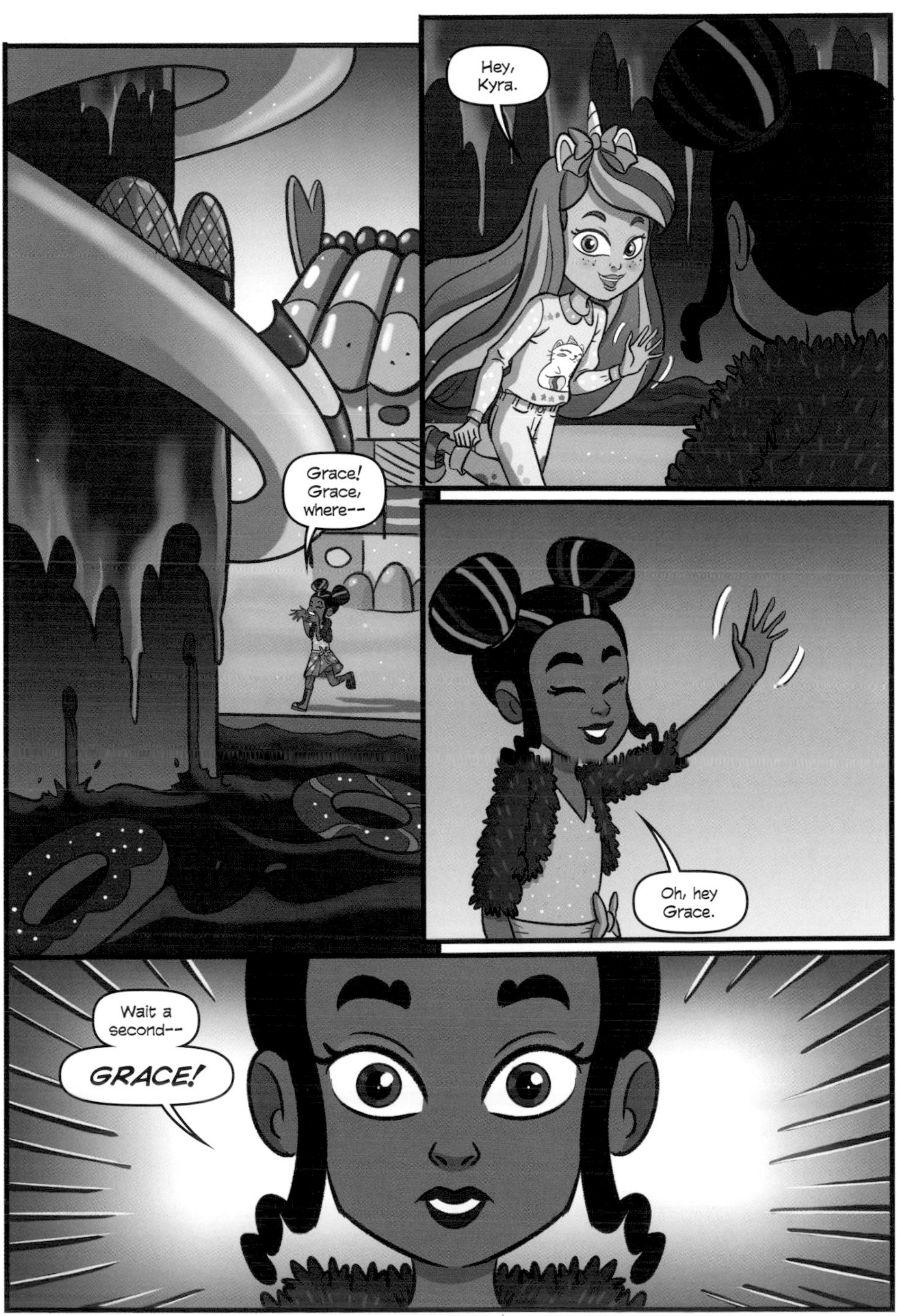
Hey, Kyra.
Grace! Grace, where--
Oh, hey Grace.
Wait a second--
GRACE!

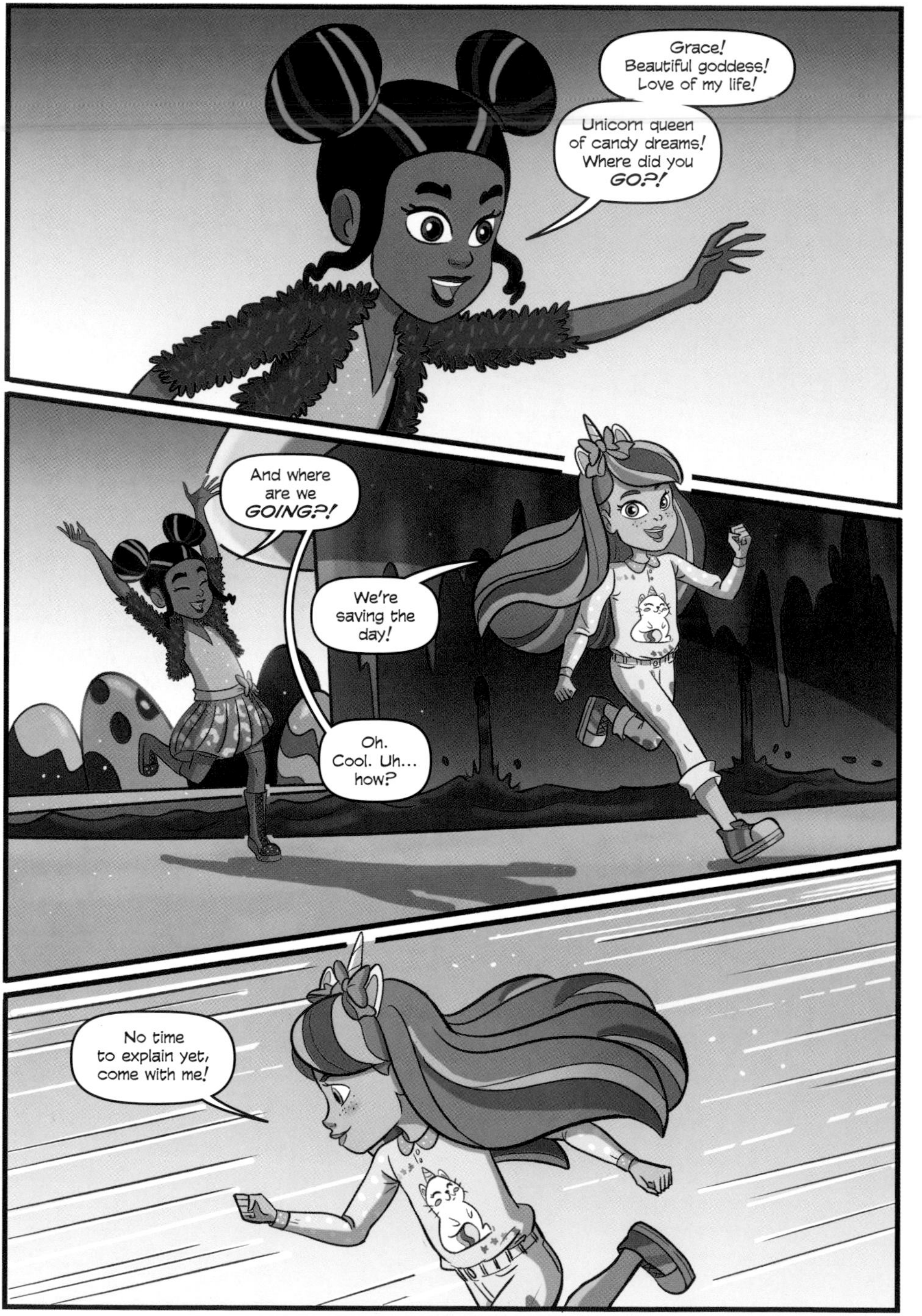
Grace! Beautiful goddess! Love of my life!
Unicorn queen of candy dreams! Where did you GO?!
And where are we GOING?!
We're saving the day!
Oh. Cool. Uh... how?
No time to explain yet, come with me!

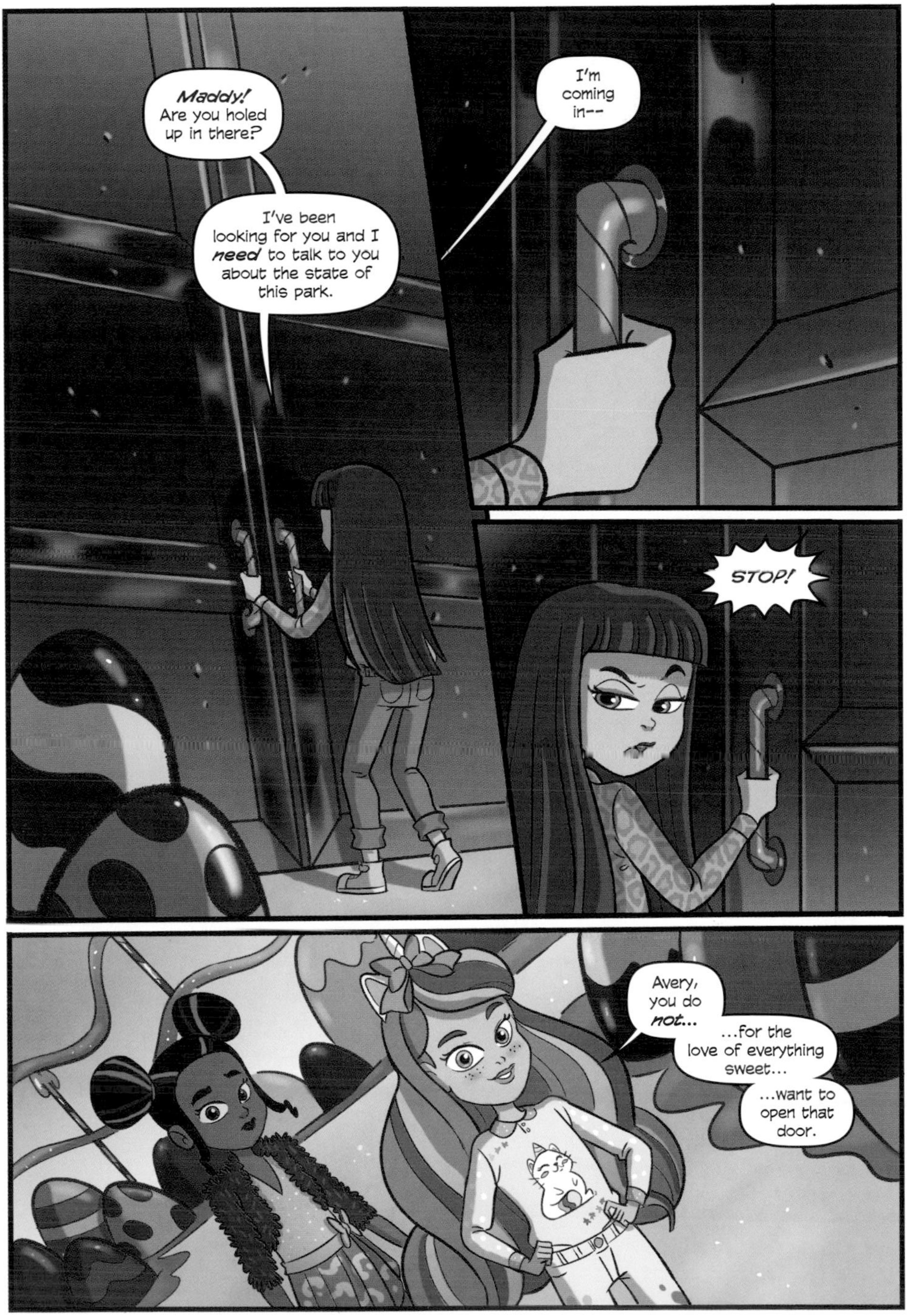

Maddy! Are you holed up in there?
I've been looking for you and I need to talk to you about the state of this park.
I'm coming in--
STOP!
Avery, you do not...
...for the love of everything sweet...
...want to open that door.

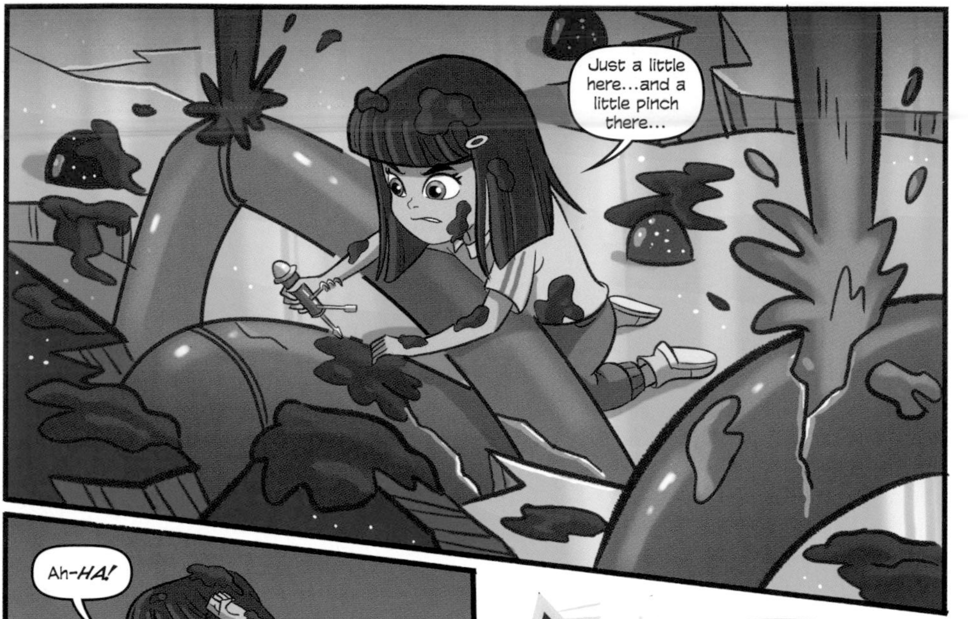
Just a little here...and a little pinch there...

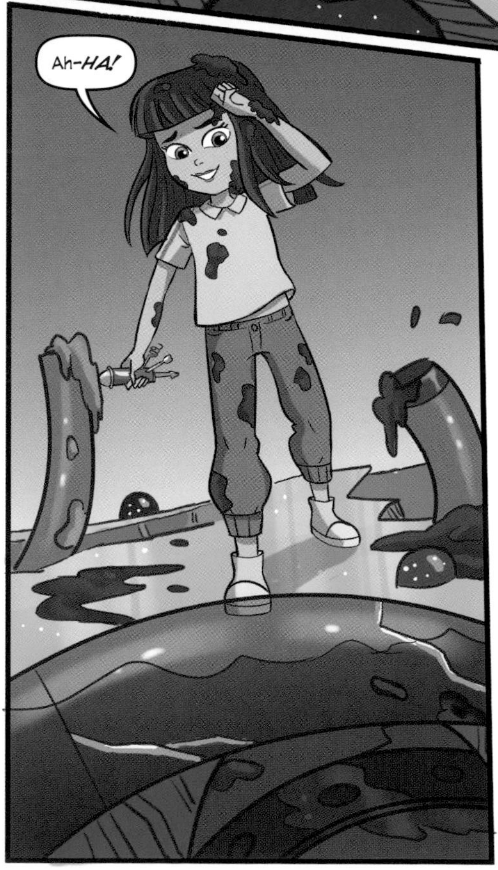
Ah-*HA!*

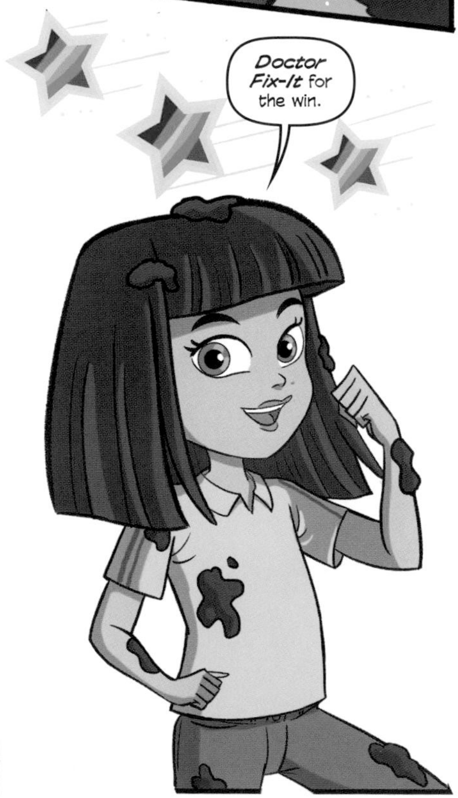
Doctor Fix-It for the win.

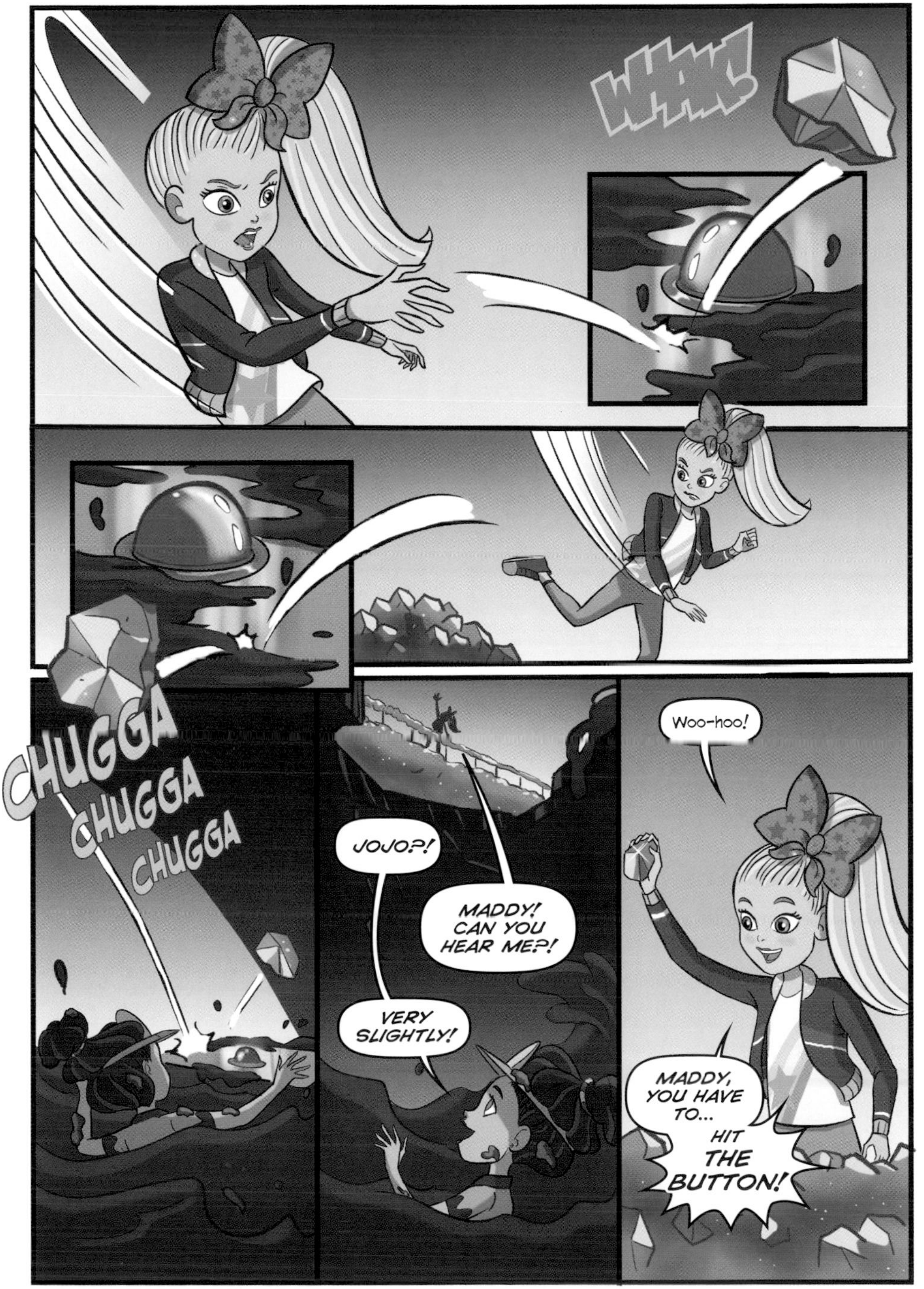
WHAK!
CHUGGA
CHUGGA
CHUGGA
JOJO?!
MADDY! CAN YOU HEAR ME?!
VERY SLIGHTLY!
Woo-hoo!
MADDY, YOU HAVE TO... HIT THE BUTTON!

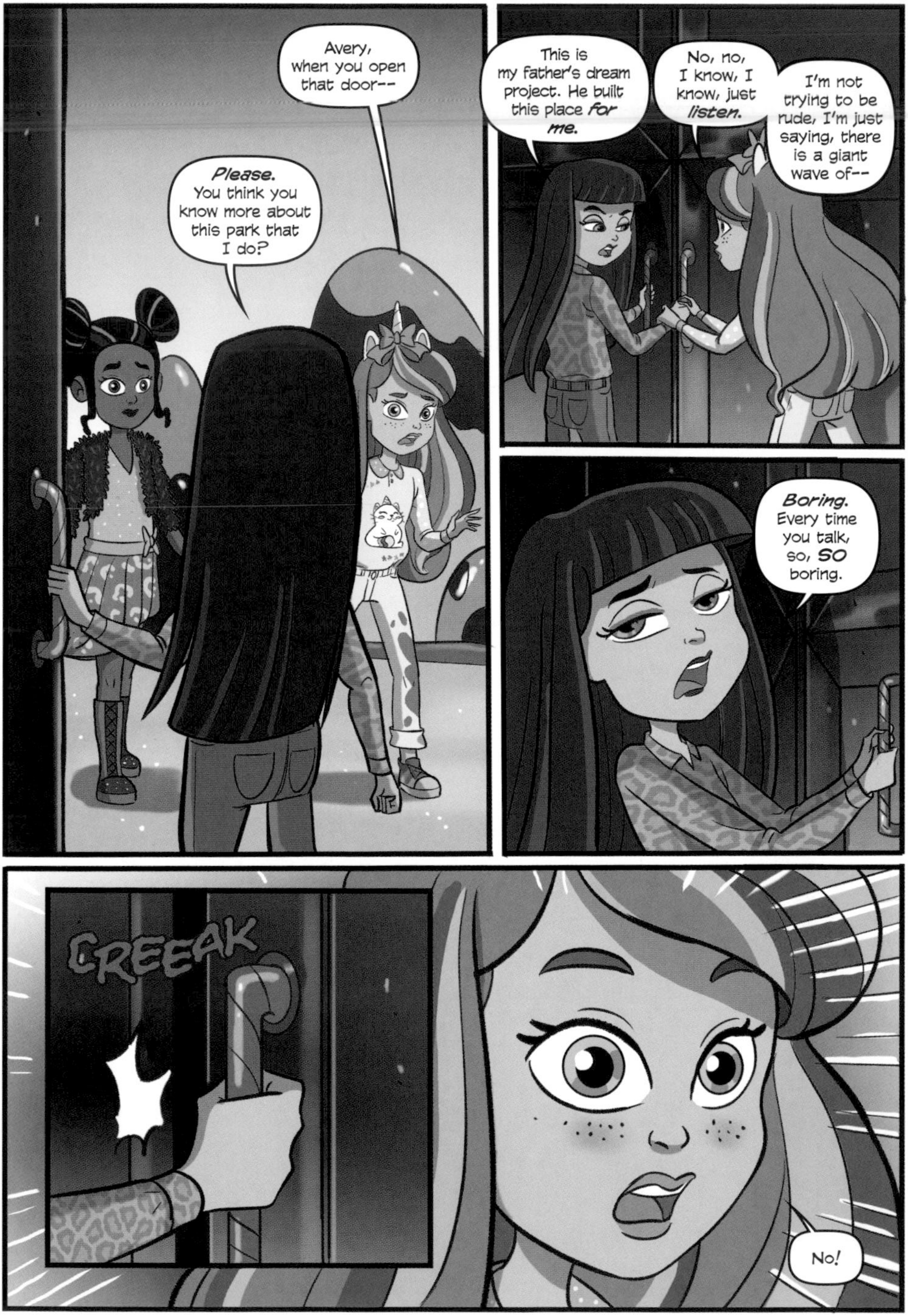
Avery, when you open that door--
Please. You think you know more about this park that I do?
This is my father's dream project. He built this place *for me.*
No, no, I know, I know, just *listen.*
I'm not trying to be rude, I'm just saying, there is a giant wave of--
Boring. Every time you talk, so, *SO* boring.
CREEAK
No!

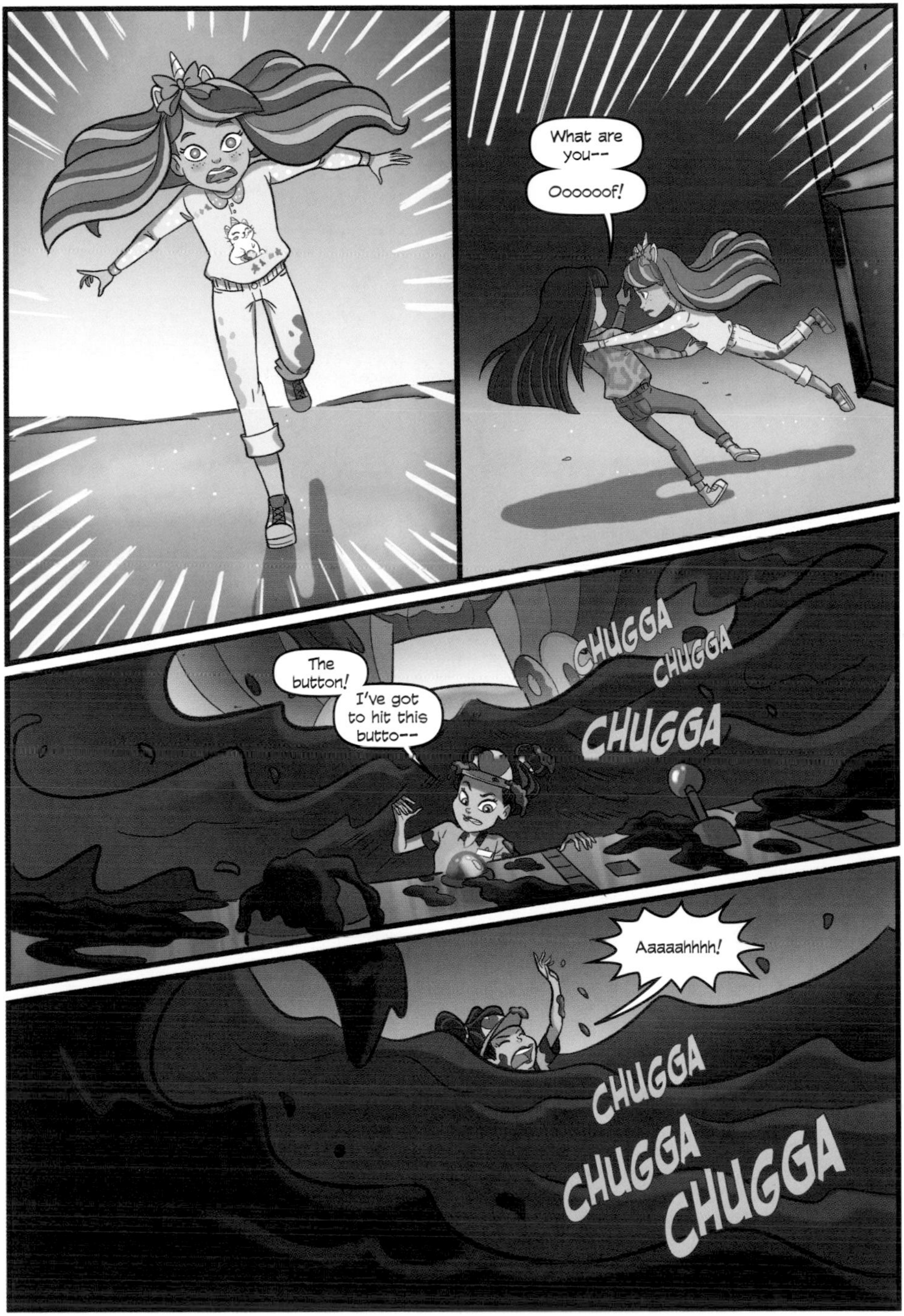
What are you--
Oooooof!
The button!
I've got to hit this butto--
CHUGGA
CHUGGA
CHUGGA
Aaaaahhhh!
CHUGGA
CHUGGA
CHUGGA

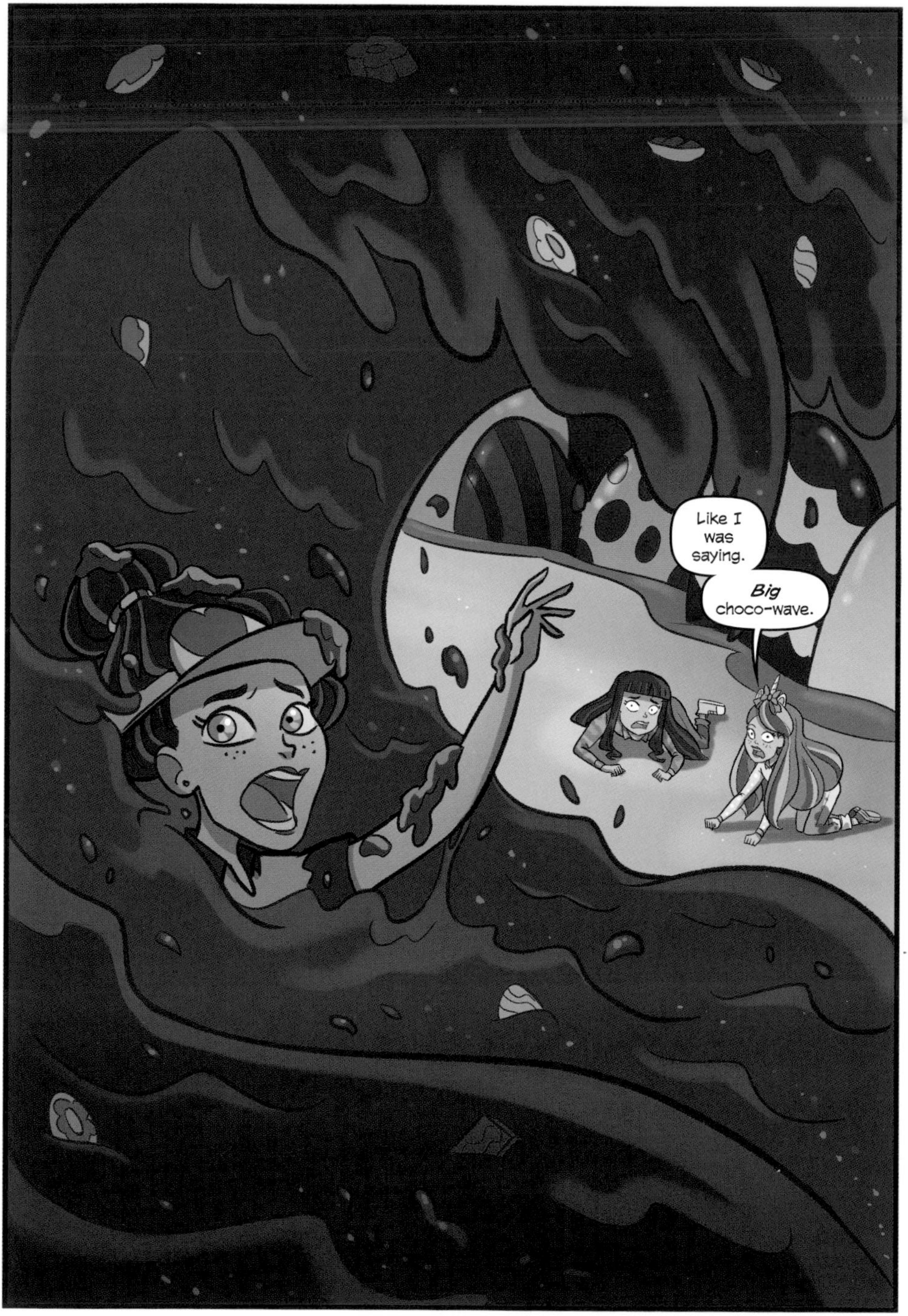
Like I was saying.
Big choco-wave.

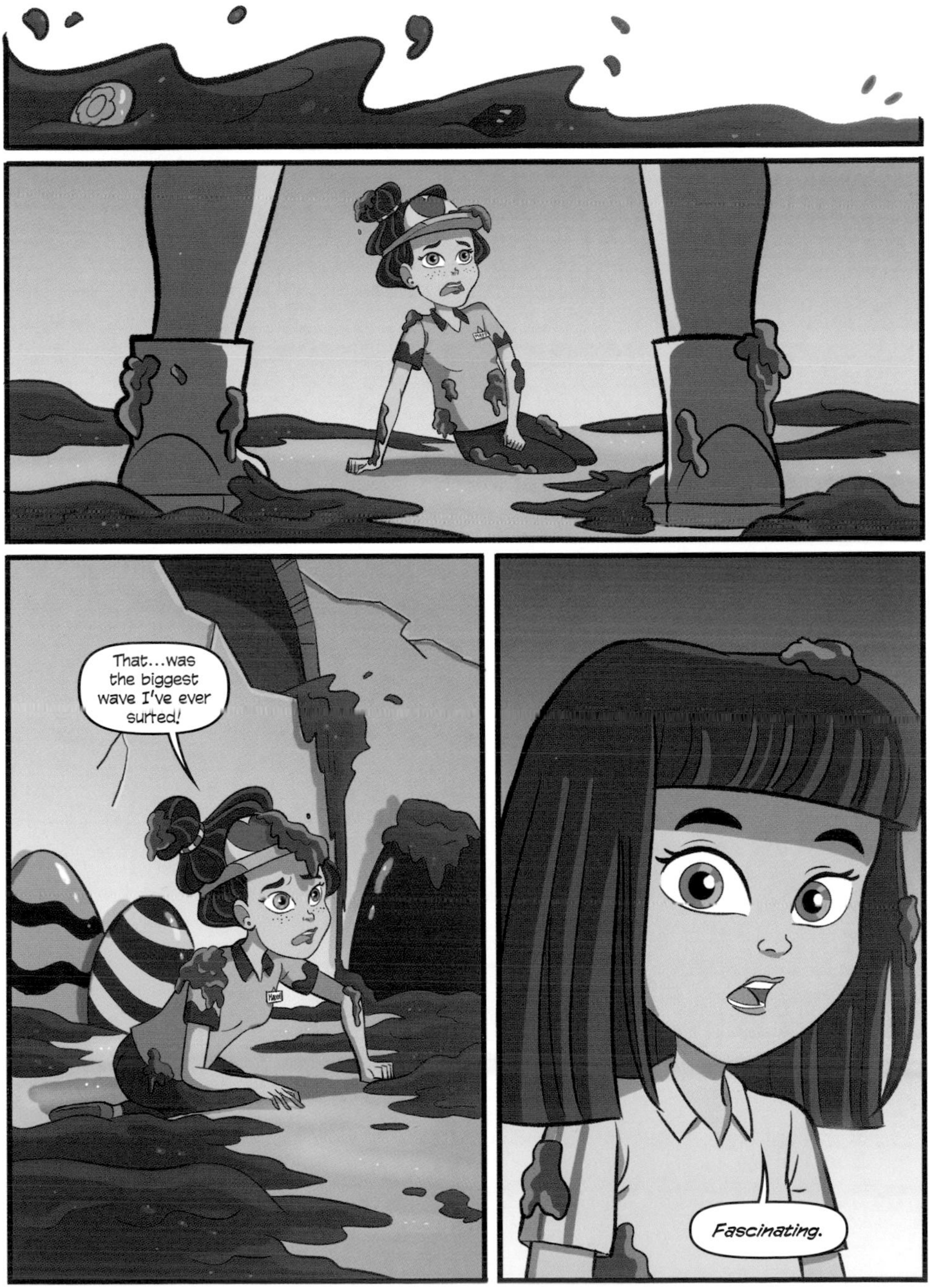
That...was the biggest wave I've ever surfed!
Fascinating.

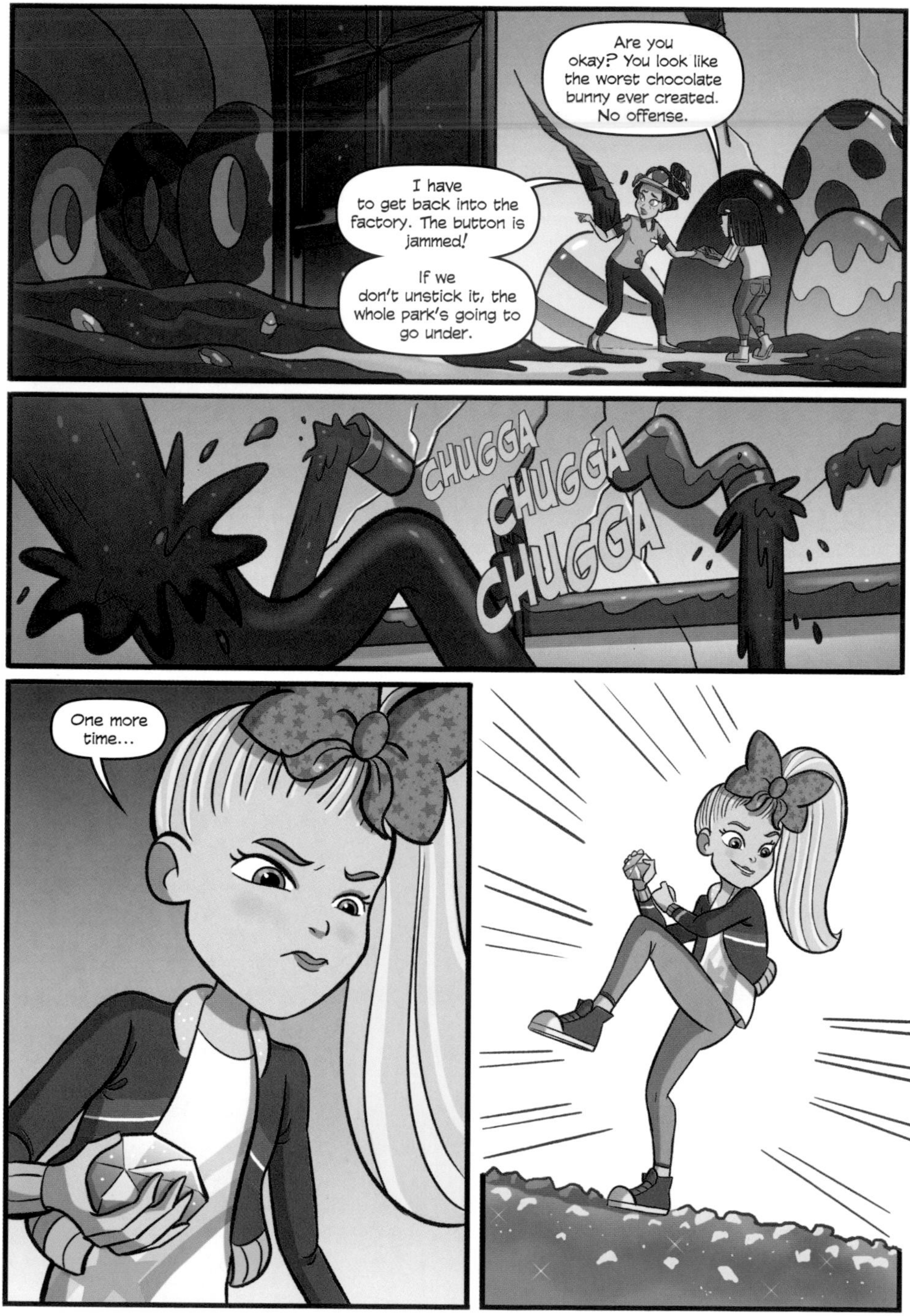
Are you okay? You look like the worst chocolate bunny ever created. No offense.
I have to get back into the factory. The button is jammed!
If we don't unstick it, the whole park's going to go under.
CHUGGA CHUGGA CHUGGA
One more time...

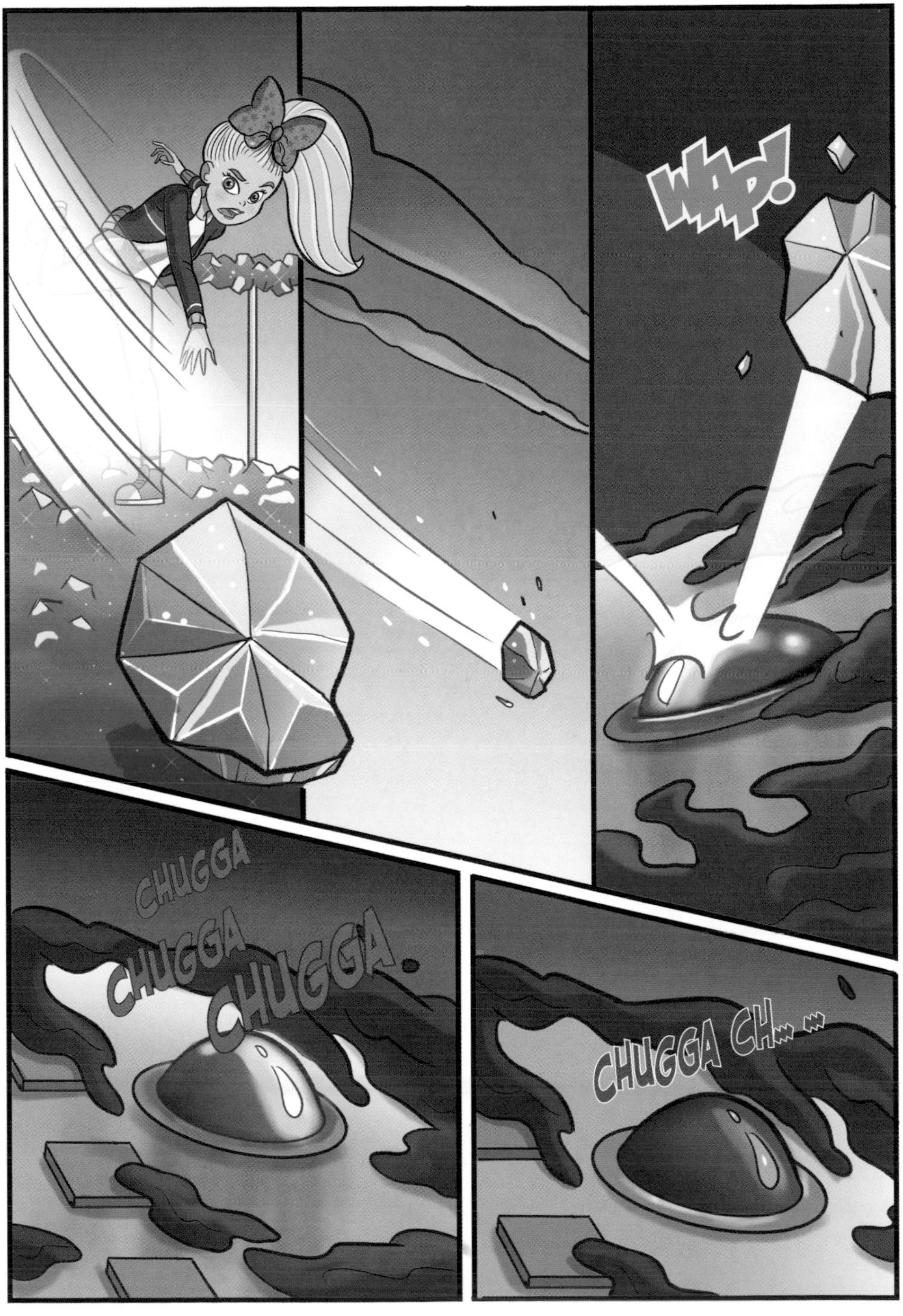
WAP!
CHUGGA
CHUGGA
CHUGGA.
CHUGGA CH...

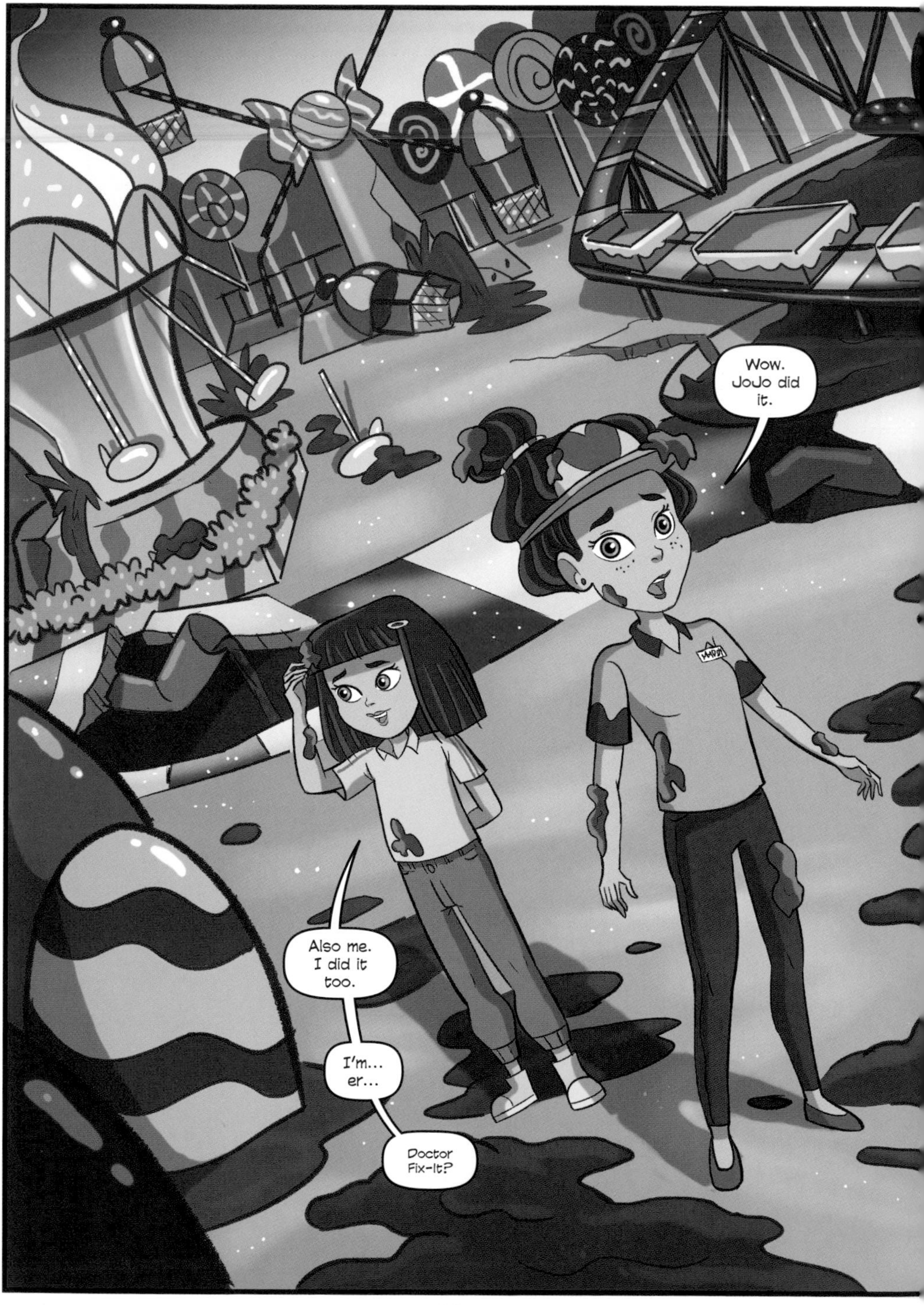
Wow. JoJo did it.
Also me. I did it too.
I'm... er...
Doctor Fix-It?

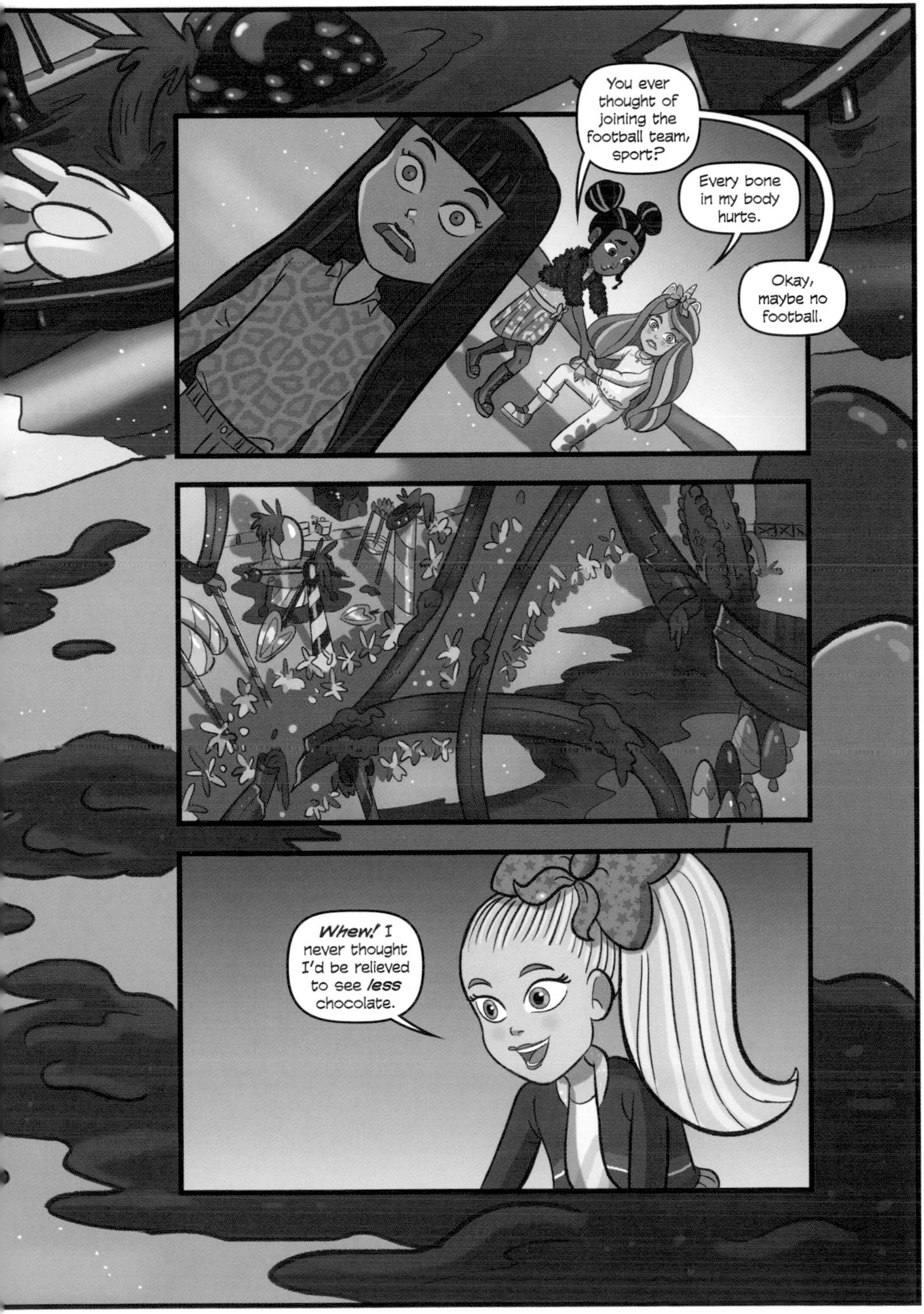
You ever thought of joining the football team, sport?
Every bone in my body hurts.
Okay, maybe no football.
Whew! I never thought I'd be relieved to see *less* chocolate.

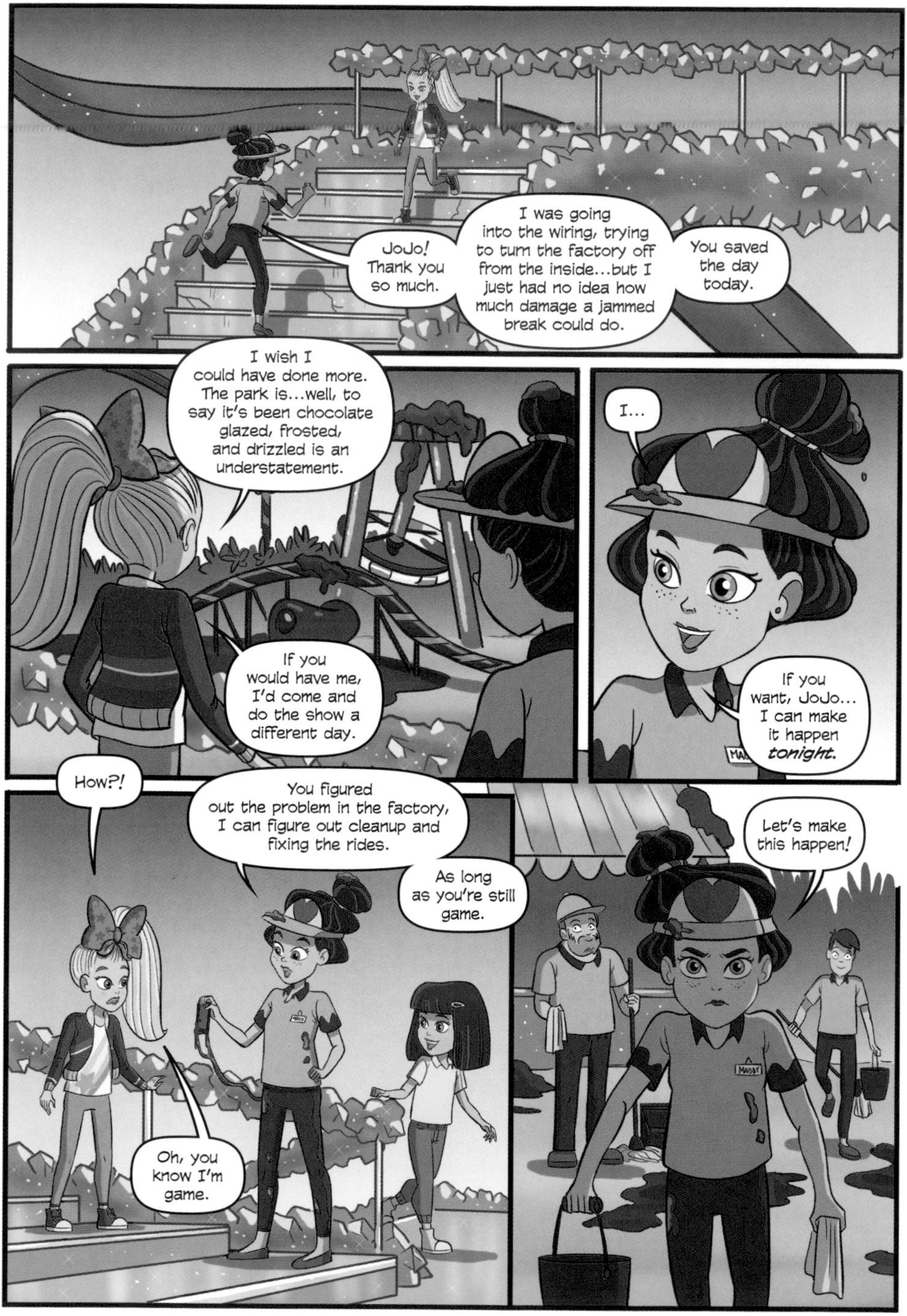
JoJo! Thank you so much.
I was going into the wiring, trying to turn the factory off from the inside...but I just had no idea how much damage a jammed break could do.
You saved the day today.
I wish I could have done more. The park is...well, to say it's been chocolate glazed, frosted, and drizzled is an understatement.
If you would have me, I'd come and do the show a different day.
I...
If you want, JoJo... I can make it happen *tonight.*
How?!
You figured out the problem in the factory, I can figure out cleanup and fixing the rides.
As long as you're still game.
Oh, you know I'm game.
Let's make this happen!

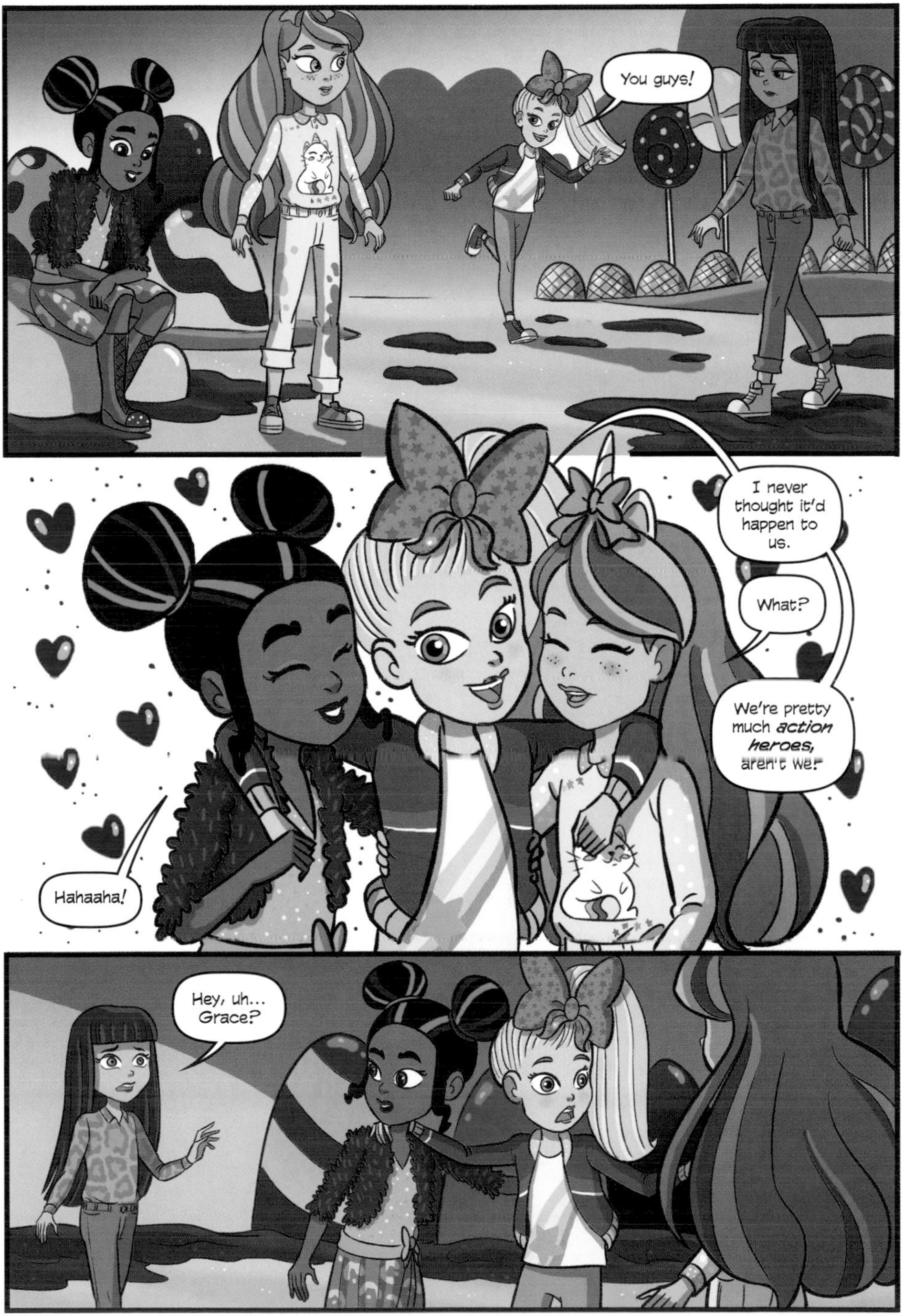
You guys!
I never thought it'd happen to us.
What?
We're pretty much *action heroes,* aren't we?
Hahaaha!
Hey, uh... Grace?

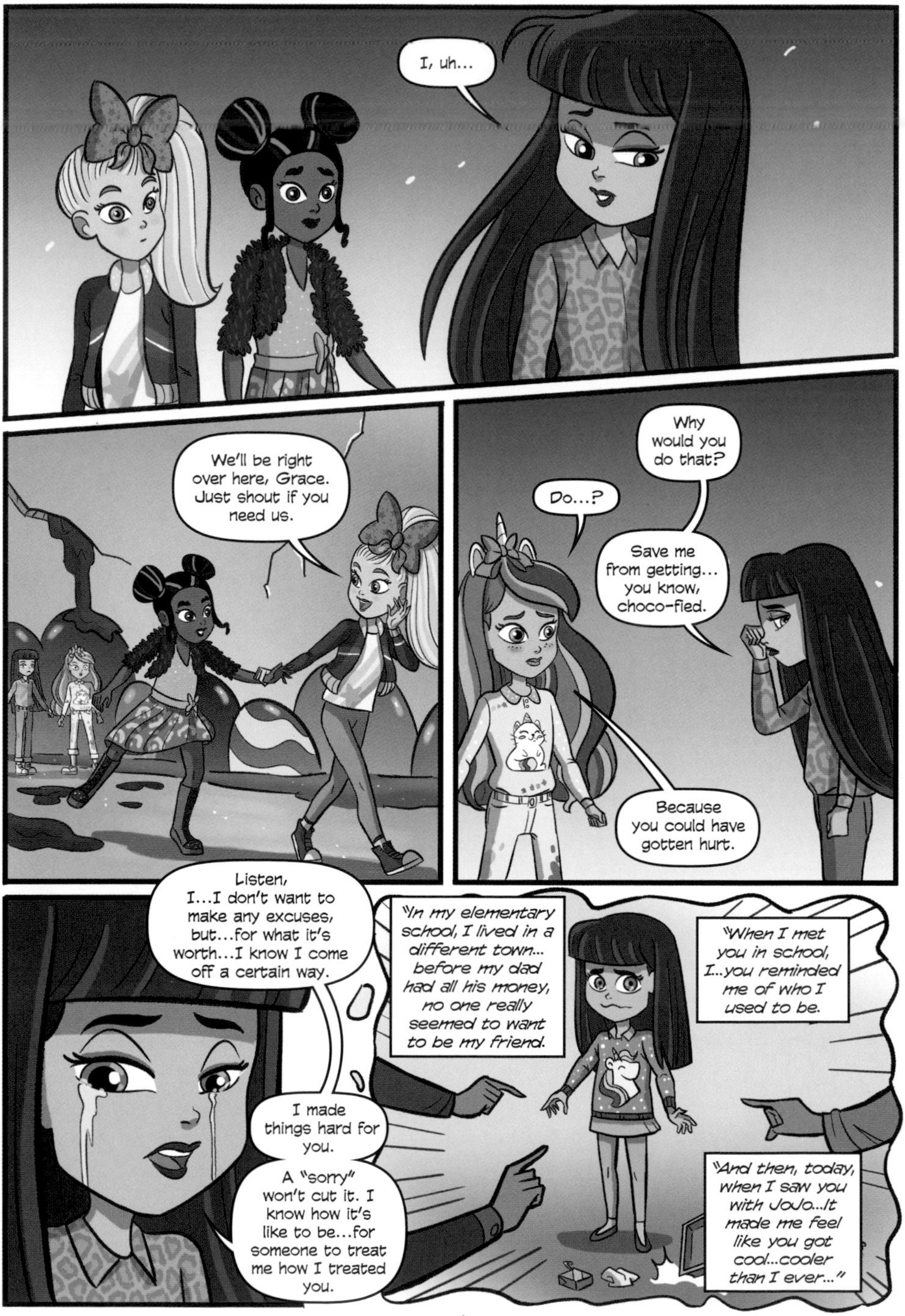

I, uh...
We'll be right over here, Grace. Just shout if you need us.
Why would you do that?
Do...?
Save me from getting... you know, choco-fied.
Because you could have gotten hurt.
Listen, I...I don't want to make any excuses, but...for what it's worth...I know I come off a certain way.
"In my elementary school, I lived in a different town... before my dad had all his money, no one really seemed to want to be my friend.
"When I met you in school, I...you reminded me of who I used to be.
I made things hard for you.
A "sorry" won't cut it. I know how it's like to be...for someone to treat me how I treated you.
"And then, today, when I saw you with JoJo...It made me feel like you got cool...cooler than I ever..."

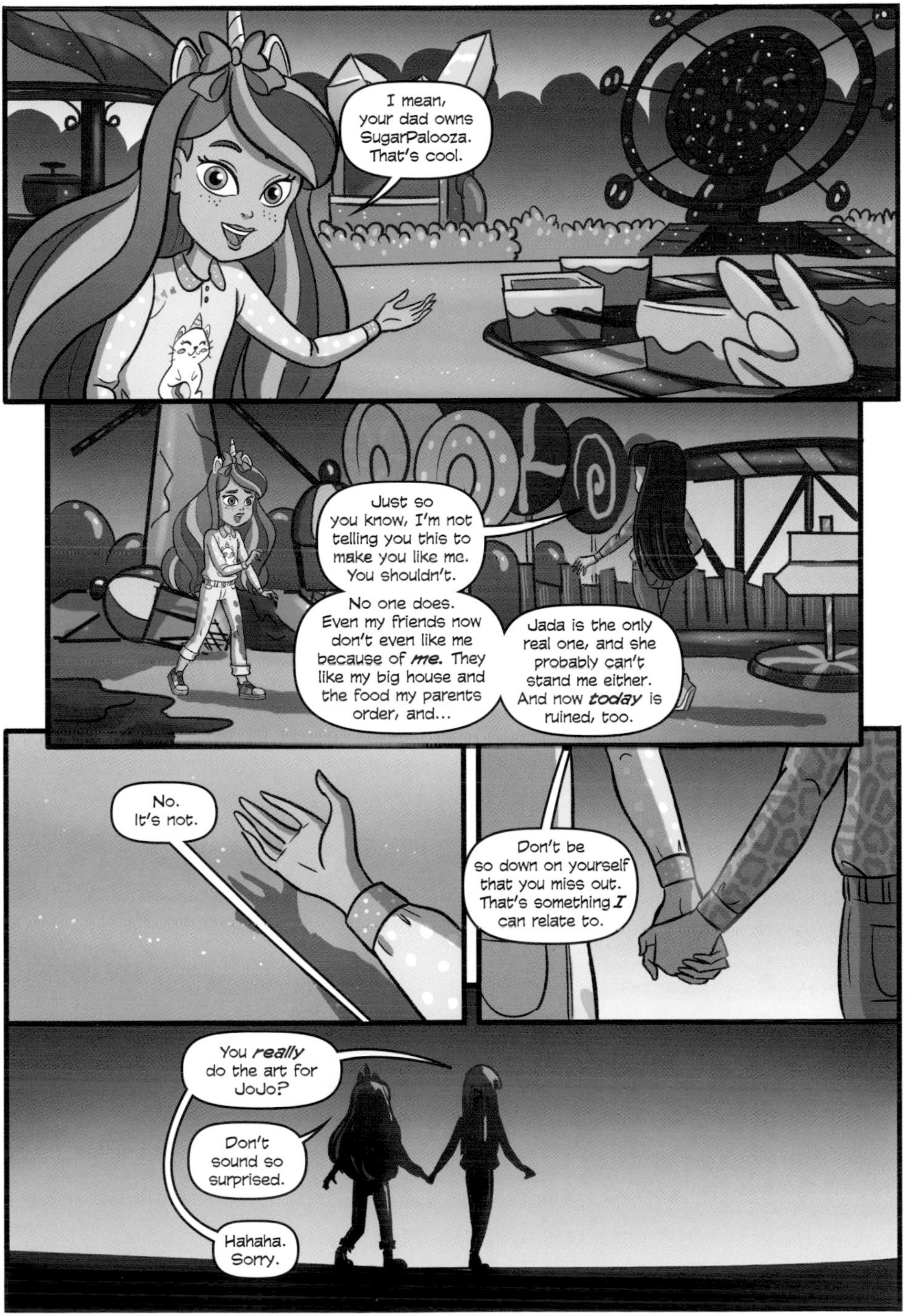
I mean, your dad owns SugarPalooza. That's cool.
Just so you know, I'm not telling you this to make you like me. You shouldn't.
No one does. Even my friends now don't even like me because of *me.* They like my big house and the food my parents order, and...
Jada is the only real one, and she probably can't stand me either. And now *today* is ruined, too.
No. It's not.
Don't be so down on yourself that you miss out. That's something *I* can relate to.
You *really* do the art for JoJo?
Don't sound so surprised.
Hahaha. Sorry.

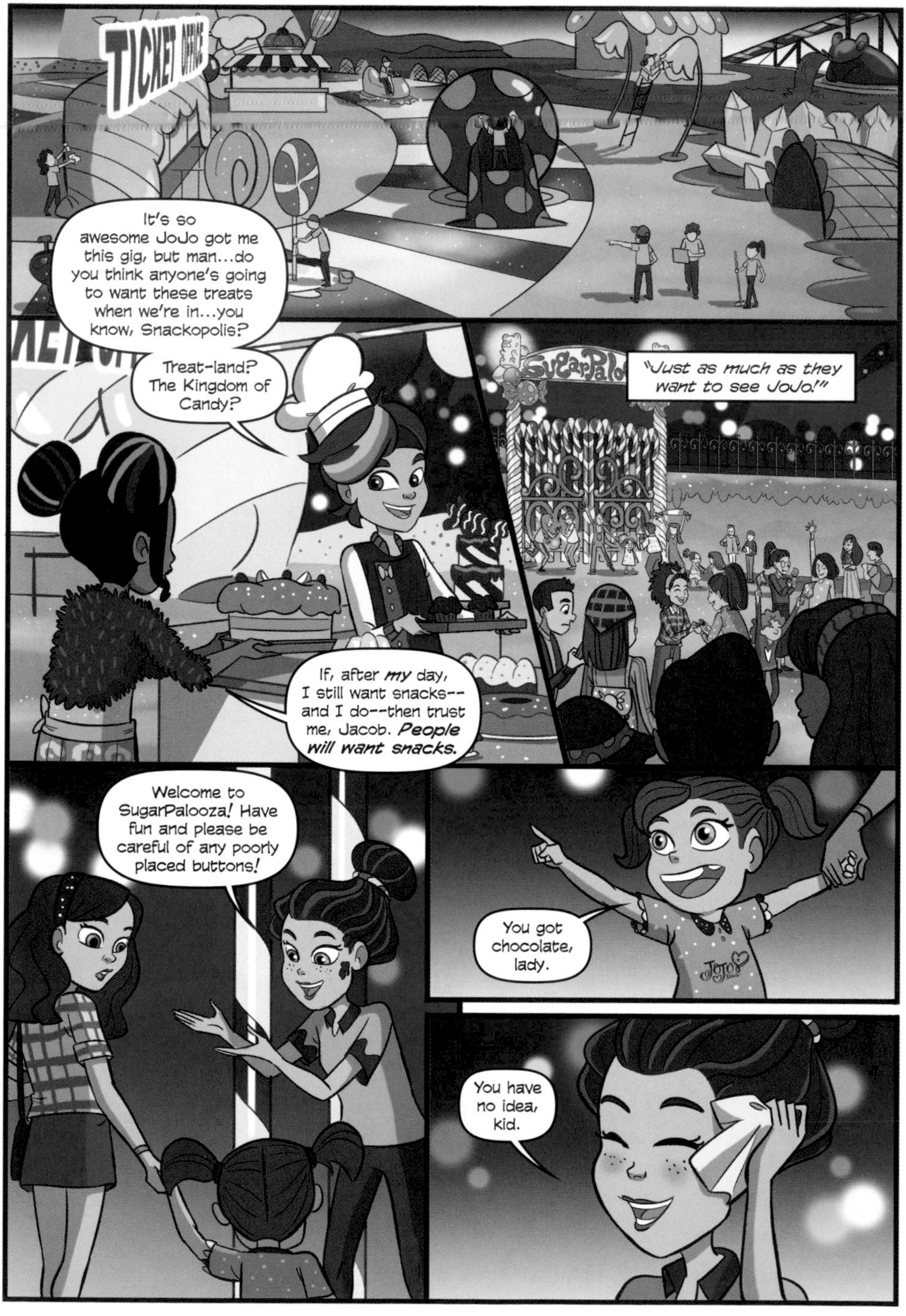
TICKET OFFICE
It's so awesome JoJo got me this gig, but man...do you think anyone's going to want these treats when we're in...you know, Snackopolis?
Treat-land? The Kingdom of Candy?
If, after *my* day, I still want snacks--and I do--then trust me, Jacob. ***People will want snacks.***
"*Just as much as they want to see JoJo!*"
Welcome to SugarPalooza! Have fun and please be careful of any poorly placed buttons!
You got chocolate, lady.
You have no idea, kid.

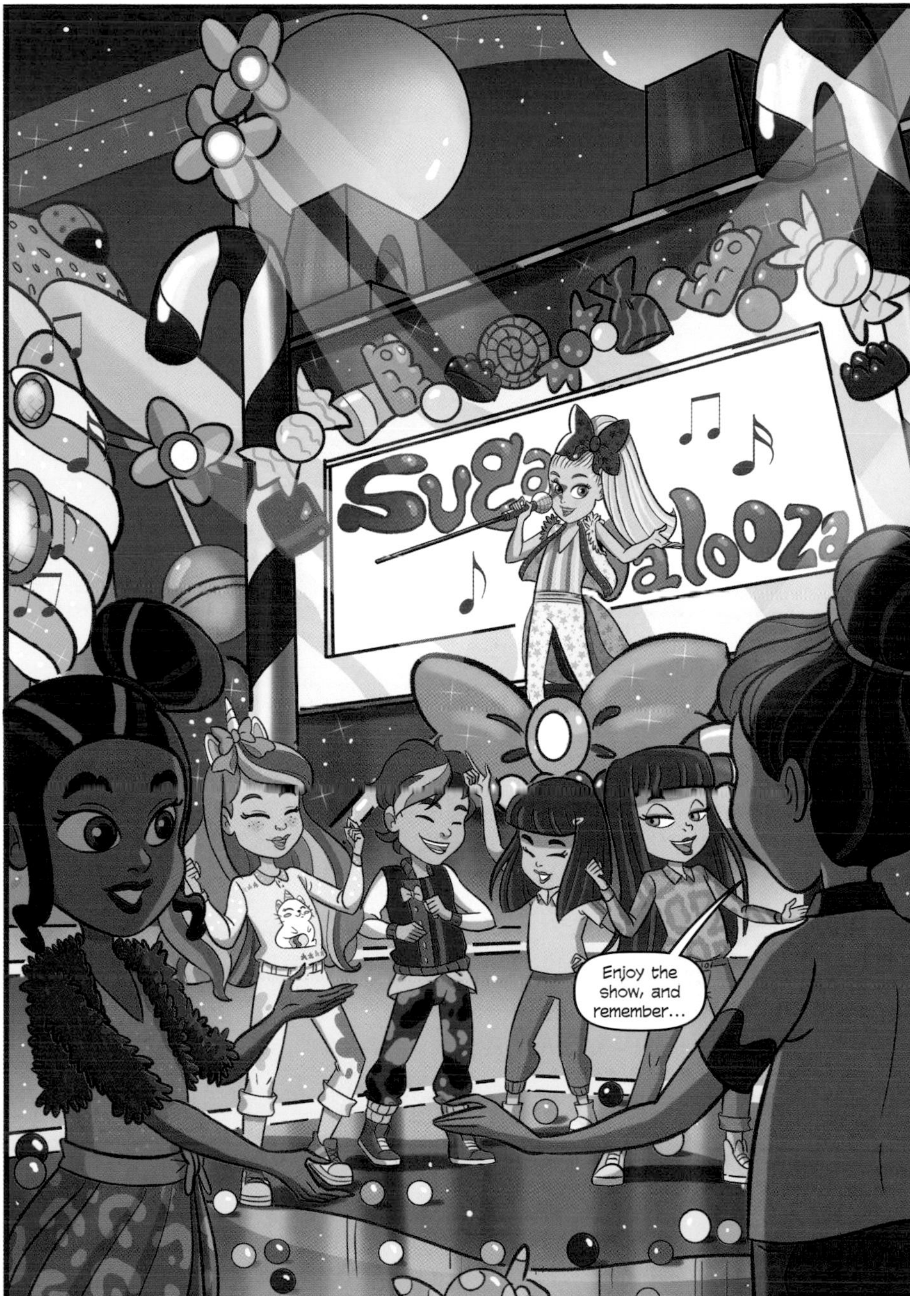
Sugarpalooza
Enjoy the show, and remember...

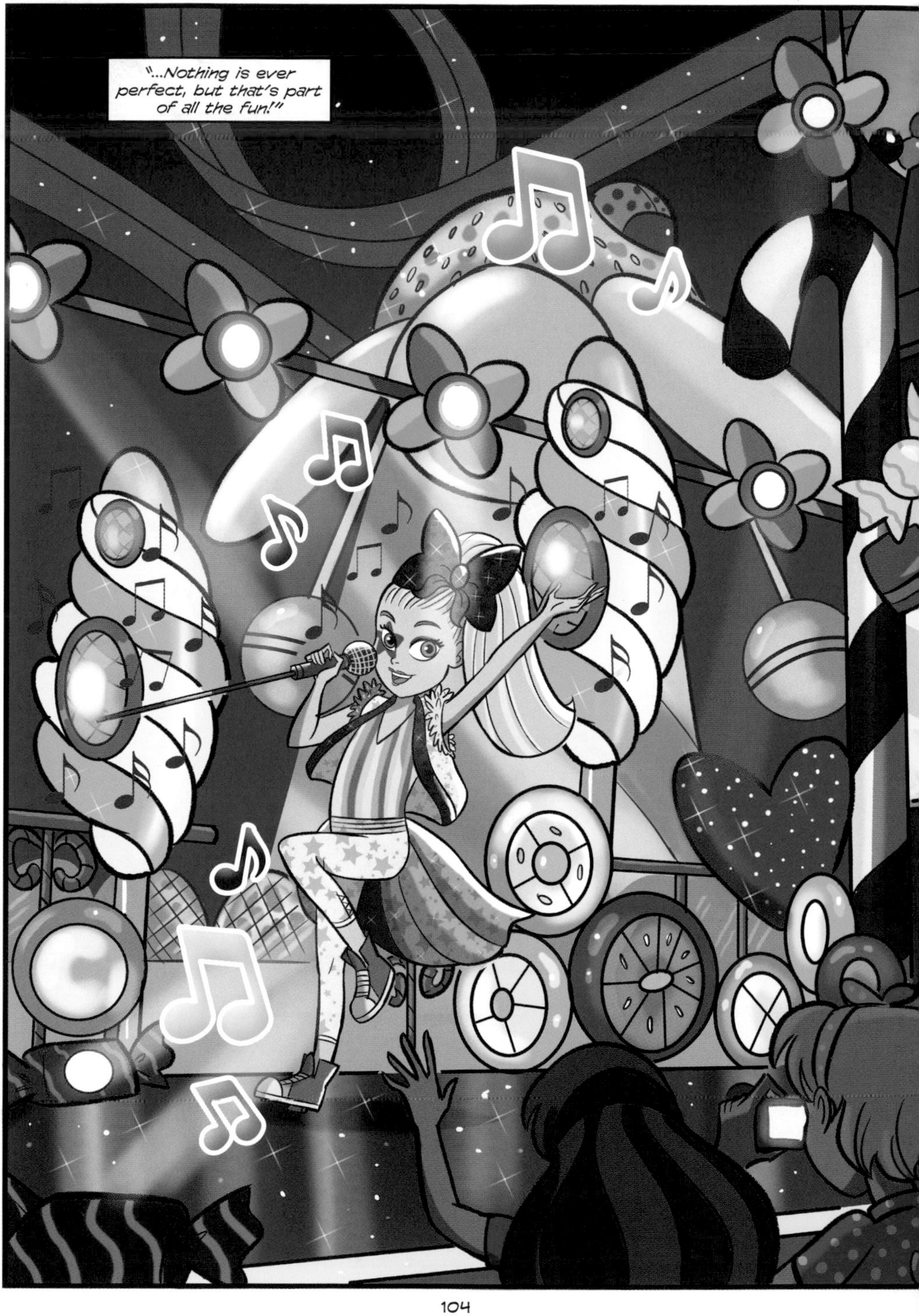
"...Nothing is ever perfect, but that's part of all the fun!"

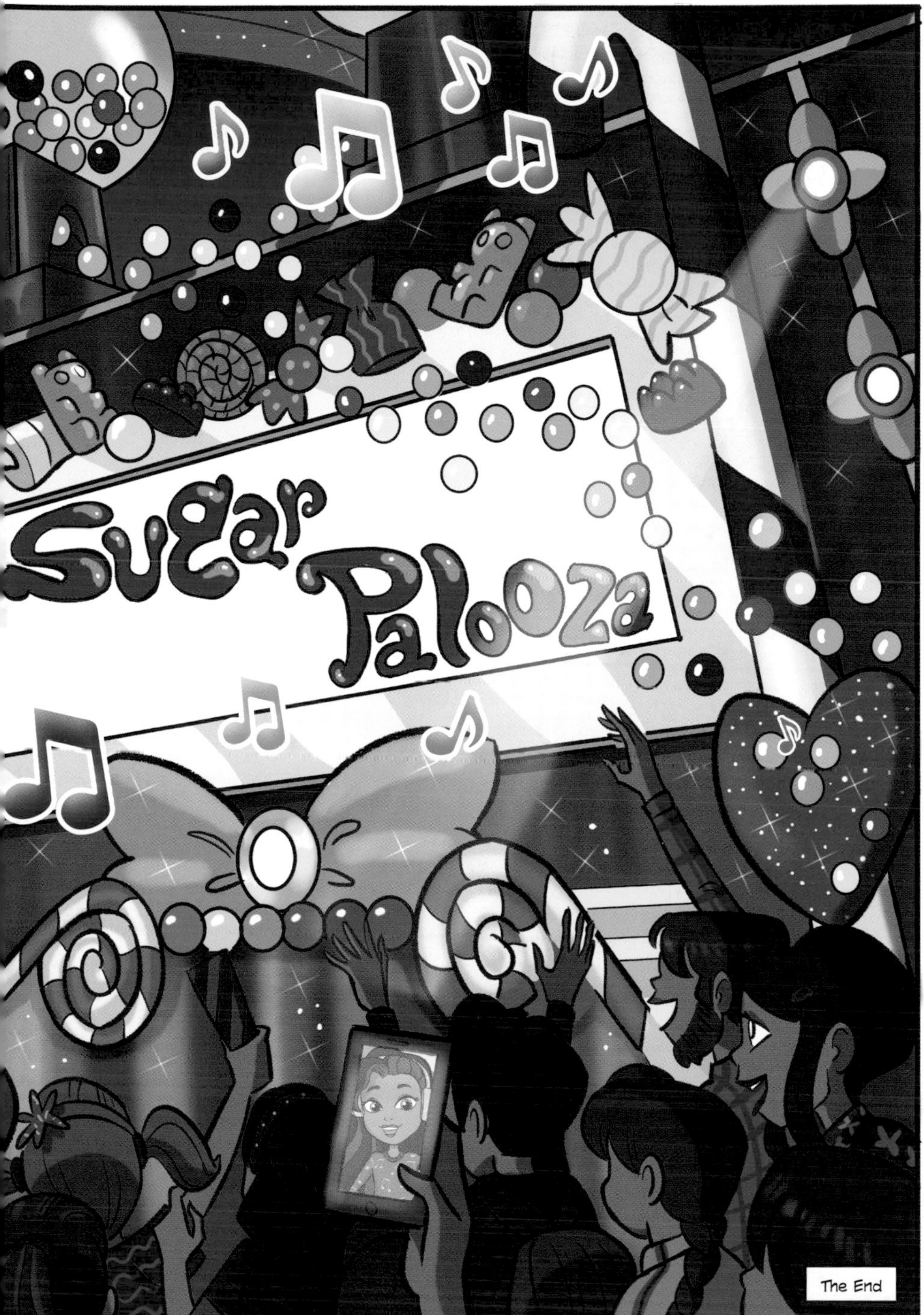
Sugar Palooza
The End

MORE BOOKS AVAILABLE . . .

JoJo's Guide to the Sweet Life
NEW YORK TIMES BESTSELLER
BY JOJO SIWA
#PEACEOUTHATERZ

nickelodeon
JoJo Siwa
THINGS I LOVE
A FILL-IN FRIENDSHIP JOURNAL

JoJo's Guide to Making Your Own Fun
BY JOJO SIWA
#DOITYOURSELF

JoJo Loves Bow Bow
A DAY IN THE LIFE OF THE WORLD'S CUTEST CANINE
BY JOJO SIWA
#BIGBOWLITTLEDOG

1
JoJo & Bow Bow
TAKE THE STAGE
BY JOJO SIWA
nickelodeon

2
JoJo & Bow Bow
CANDY KISSES
BY JOJO SIWA

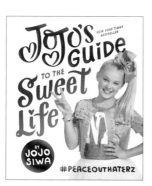

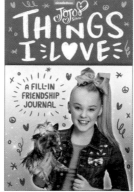

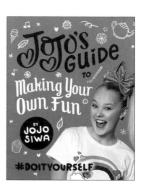

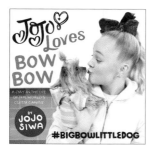

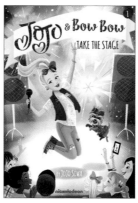

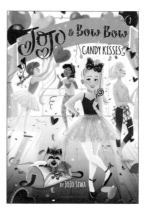